Finale

Joan Druett

Finale

Old Salt Press

Finale

AN OLD SALT PRESS BOOK, published by Old Salt Press, a
Limited Liability Company registered in New Jersey, U.S.A.
For more information about our titles, go to
www.oldsaltpress.com

© 2018 Joan Druett
ISBN 978-0-9941246-5-4 (eBook)
ISBN 978-0-9941246-6-1 (print edition)

Cover art (clipper under full sail) © 2018 Ron Druett

Introduction

Back in 1990, there was a peculiar rumor going around writing circles in New Zealand. A hotel that staged Murder Mystery weekends was looking for an author. The inducement was a free two-night stay, with food and a murder thrown in. The catch was that the hotel management wanted that author to write a novel set in that hotel. It was a rather different kind of publicity stunt, but I'd also heard that there was a publisher who was interested in taking part.

Odd as it may seem, the rumor proved to be true. One author after another went off to sample a Murder Mystery Weekend, to come back with a reminiscent smile, but a definite shake of the head. An impending deadline was the usual excuse. Or so I remember.

It took quite a while for the invitation to come my way, so I must have been well down on the list of possible murder-weekend novelists. Though I'd had a couple of non-fiction books published in New Zealand, my romantic sagas were published in New York and London, so I didn't really qualify. In due course, however, the telephone rang, the invitation was issued, and a date was arranged. And so my husband and I made the journey to Thames, which is on the eastern coast of the North Island of New Zealand.

It was all rather quaint. The gold-mining town had once boomed, but, with the usual transience of a goldrush, it had quietened considerably since 1867, when that rush had begun. It was now a pretty village, dependent on a small tourist trade, local farmers, and a surprising number of artistic communities for custom. The hotel was equally quaint, being definitely colonial. For a start, the bedrooms did not have en suite bathrooms. One had to put on a dressing gown and scurry down an echoing passage to do normally private things. There was a balcony that ran outside the whole of the second floor, and the floors were made of ancient wooden planks that creaked. We were also warned that there was a resident ghost.

The first evening, the proprietor welcomed the dozen or so guests to the Murder Mystery Weekend, gave out door keys, showed everyone the location of the bar (drinks were definitely not on the house), and issued the weekend's agenda, along with a light supper. We were to get up at an unearthly hour, and then, after a hasty breakfast, clamber into a coach for an educational tour. And that, more or less, is what happened. We did look at a goldmine, which turned out to be a hole in the ground that was overgrown with ferns, and then the skeletal remains of a stamping mill, where the gold-bearing quartz was once ground into dust, but the rest of the tour was more scenic than historic. White-water rafting was included for the brave, and there was a great kettle of mussels steaming at a lunch stop at the beach. But, while we were told to look for clues, the "murder" was very much in the background.

We arrived back in the middle of the afternoon, to be told to take our pick from the proprietor's wardrobe of fancy dress. I have no memory at all of what we chose, but it did lead to a comic moment. We went up the street to a wine store, to buy a bottle (cheaper than glasses at the bar), and found that the owner and his wife had only just taken over the establishment.

"You're staying at the Murder Hotel?" she demanded.

"Yes," we admitted.

"Oh dear," she said. "Very *strange* things happen there."

"They do?"

"Last Saturday, without a word of a lie, a *priest* came in and bought a bottle of wine. And, it was certainly not his first bottle of the day. When he hauled up his *cassock* to get at his wallet, he *wobbled*. Without a word of a lie, I had to hold him *up*."

I was tempted to ask if he was accompanied by a nun, but had too much trouble keeping my face straight.

So, we showered and dressed in whatever, had a glass or two of wine, went down the stairs to the dining room, ate a meal, and then waited around for the murder. When it happened, there was a fire alarm, a body at the bottom of the staircase, a local policeman pontificating, and some of the local volunteer fire brigade rushing around. It was then that I realized why the other writers had all had convenient deadlines. Strange things certainly happened at the murder hotel, and some of the strangest were the murder scenarios. It was impossible to turn any of them into a book.

But, when I got home, and the phone went again, and I was asked to write the novel, I said yes.

Why?

Why on earth?

There was a surprisingly good reason. I had just published a Californian goldrush novel, called *A Promise of Gold*, and I was still engaged with the characters. Captain Jake Dexter, a flamboyant nineteenth century pirate, and his mistress, the actress Harriet Gray, were still very much with me. I had left them on the verge of sailing somewhere else, having made an unexpected fortune in Sacramento in 1849, and I rather wished I knew what was happening to them after that. And this was my chance.

The Thames goldrush did not happen until 1867, which left me 18 years to fill. But a very convenient Australian goldrush intervened. I had to set the story in the hotel, but that was easily turned into a theatre. And the fates of the much more mature Harriet and Jake and Harriet's actor-brother, Royal Gray, had to be developed as well. My mind was working frantically and enjoy-ably, filling in all the gaps. It was fun — and I was being commissioned to do it!

But I had forgotten something. When I signed the contract, I was suddenly part of the Murder Mystery Weekend. I was supposed to act — sometimes as the murderer, and occasionally as the victim. And my husband was supposed to do that, too. And there was always the job of escorting the party on the day trip ... and if either of us was left behind, there was something to do in the hotel. I even presided behind the bar!

But that is another story.

So the novel got written — as a sequel to *A Promise of Gold*. To my immense satisfaction, I saw Captain Jake Dexter and Harriet

Gray through the final, astonishing, decades of their scandalous lives. But then something totally unexpected happened.

The hotel went bankrupt.

The bank foreclosed, and the Murder Mystery Weekends lurched to a stop.

Publication stopped, and what had been printed was pulped.

And so I was left with a virtually unpublished novel. But, once *A Promise of Gold* had been reproduced by Old Salt Press, it seemed to me to be a very good idea to haul out the manuscript and have a look, with the view of giving it a new lease of life.

Twenty-six years later, I could see big flaws. Family sagas, no matter how stirring, and no matter how authentically historical, are not supposed to be murder mysteries. There were blanks in important pieces of evidence, and the audience was not given enough clues. And there were no red herrings. Because of the fate of the original hotel, it had to be given a new name. And, of course, the characters had become rather old for traditional romance. But, withal, the book was well worth reworking — for the very good reason that, as the publisher said at the time, it's a bloody good story.

And here it is, afresh.

1

This cross-continental journey had proved very pleasant, particularly considering that he was dead.

Or so Timothy ironically mused.

For here he was in the year 1905, technically dead for thirty-eight years and yet gliding across America in a train — a train, what's more, that was luxuriously replete with every modern convenience. The lighting was electric, and the heating came from steam. Timothy sat in a lushly upholstered wickerwork chair in a Pullman car, surrounded by mahogany paneling, brass fittings and velvet drapery. Each morning, fresh flowers were placed in the sconces on either side of his wash-stand. A deferential attendant responded promptly to the slightest tug on a bell-rope. There was a table reserved in the dining car, baths, valet service, every requisite for Timothy's comfort. Confound it, Timothy brooded, even at this space in time it was mortifying to think that the old bastard's judgment had been so spot-on.

Back in the New Year of 1867, as a youngster, Timothy had been involved, though only peripherally, in the building of this railway. The crafty old merchant had sent him from Salem, Massachusetts, to Denver, Colorado, with a satchel full of dollars tucked fatly under his arm, on a mission to buy up the franchise of an obscure little company called the Kansas Pacific Railroad. Now, moodily, Timothy remembered how it had been. He had carried cash and travelled in anonymity, because the key to the plan was secrecy, meaning that his youth and obvious callowness was an asset. Once he'd made the purchase, his orders had been to return to Salem, where the old schemer who had fathered him would make himself a fortune by staging a private auction. The only bidders invited would be the moguls of the Union Pacific and the

Central Pacific Railroads. But that, the old man had reckoned, was all that was needed to fetch a most gratifying little pile.

At least, that had been the plan.

Back then, Timothy had realized that the old man had been gambling that the railway financiers would accomplish what they had set out to do, which was to span the North American continent with steel tracks, and that they would need the Kansas Pacific franchise to link Denver to the line. However, he had also been gambling on Timothy's honesty, and at that time, placing money on Timothy's sense of family loyalty had been a very poor bet. What the old man hadn't realized was that Timothy was uncommonly pleased to have a good excuse to get out of Salem, leaving a number of embarrassingly large debts in his wake, along with problems with a couple of girls.

So young Timothy had arrived in Denver as per instructions, but had made no attempt to buy up that Kansas Pacific franchise. Instead, he'd bought a ticket on a mail coach and had kept on a-going, heading off into unknown territory with that well-packed satchel gripped firmly in his hand. Along with farm boys from New England, city slickers from New York, and tall Mississippi men, Timothy had jounced about in Concord stages and Celerity coaches, and had chugged along the mighty Sacramento on a dirty little steamboat. All of it had been on his route to San Francisco, where — or so he believed — the streets were paved with gold. It had taken just days to learn better, and then he'd kept on a-running, shipping before the mast on a ship quaintly called the *Rolling Moses*, on the way to Auckland, the gateway to the gold-fields of New Zealand.

Timothy hadn't felt guilty about abusing the old man's trust. Back then, he'd believed he was doing the old skunk a favor. With blithe facility he had reasoned that spending money on this railway project was a sheer waste of good resources. Like most of the people he spoke to then, Timothy had believed that the railway scheme was doomed.

There had been plenty of evidence to back up that belief. At the western end of the railway countless thousands of wretched Chinese laborers were trapped by immense snowdrifts at Donner

Pass, while far to the east, in Nebraska, hapless engineers were being scalped alive. Or so people said. And, in between the Sierras and Nebraska, there lay a barely charted immensity of hostile wilderness — a region of wild beasts, shifting sands and bitter springs, almost impossible for men to cross, let alone build a railway.

Well, Timothy thought now, staring at huge snow-covered mountains that bobbed past his fleeting window, he had been proved extremely wrong, and the old bastard had been proven right. Within just two years of the escape from Salem, the railway had been completed. The American continent was spanned by iron from sea to shining sea, and the merchant had missed out on a fortune. Timothy didn't have the slightest doubt that the old dog had been most righteous in his fury when he found out what had happened to his money. It was perfectly in character that he should have declared his only son and heir dead, and put up a gravestone to prove it.

Finding that grave had been a hell of a shock, though. It might have been funny, in a ghoulish sort of way, if the old merchant had died penniless. However, he nasty truth of the matter was that Timothy should have been a multi-millionaire right now, but he couldn't lay claim to his rightful inheritance because in the eyes of the law he was dead. But, as he emphatically thought, that was a state of affairs that was about to change, and very much for the better. The next time he travelled on this railway he would be heading back east, having accomplished a small but crucial quest in New Zealand, and, once back in Salem with a certain document, the old man's millions, rightfully his all along, would be his in lawful reality.

Timothy grinned complacently to himself as he stubbed out a fine cigar. He was a man who enjoyed his comforts, usually funded by other people's money, and so, in the meantime, dead or alive, he had managed to enjoy this journey to the full. A bell rang discreetly for dinner, and Timothy responded with alacrity, stepping with an eager stride from one carriage to the next.

Over the last four days, dining on this train had proved a most rewarding experience. Apart from the spectacular vistas that fled outside the windows, and the sense of motion, the dining saloon could have been a top-rated New York restaurant. Timothy sat down at a table that was covered with a snowy linen cloth, and consulted an elaborate menu while a deferential waiter hovered attentively at his side.

As with all his other meals on board this train, he sat alone. He preferred it that way. A youngish English matron and her daughter were seated at the table behind him, and he could hear their light upper-class voices discussing their steamship crossing from London to New York, but most of the chatter flowed past him unheard. He preferred to give his whole attention to his food.

Today, after a bowl of delicious onion soup with hot buttered rolls, he was offered a choice of European pheasant or Californian quail, antelope cutlets or a New York steak, and — because they were passing through the Sierras — fresh brook trout cooked four succulently different ways. Timothy took a long, deliberate time to choose, finally selecting Flamed Trout Arcadian, gently grilled and then coated with fresh rosemary, fennel, parsley and thyme, soaked in hot cognac and ignited by a benignly approving waiter at his table. A Greek salad, with crisp lettuce, feta cheese and black olives, was the perfect accompaniment. To wash it down, he ordered a whole bottle of the best French chardonnay on the extensive wine list, its crisp crab-apple bite the perfect foil to the delicacy of the fish.

He ate slowly, savoring every last flake, making the most of this last dinner on the train. The flavor of the trout was subtle, both exotic and refined. The serving was generous, too, so that the dessert menu that was propped in front of him as his empty dishes were taken away seemed almost superfluous.

Almost. Profiteroles were featured there, and Timothy had a distinct weakness for tiny choux pastry puffs filled with sweet brandied cream and swirled with chocolate ... and superb they were, too, eaten one by one, along with sips of strong, well-sugared coffee and Benedictine liqueur. At last, replete and regretful that the memorable dining experience was over, Timothy pushed back his chair. He was only vaguely aware that the two English females at the other table were collecting their reticules and standing, too.

Then, when he was only halfway out of his seat, the wine bottle caught Timothy's eye. It was the chardonnay — that superb chardonnay. The waiter had not removed it after the main course, and in that glimpse Timothy saw why it had been left. There was almost a glassful still inside it. Without the slightest hesitation Timothy turned back, took his glass, and emptied the bottle into it. Then, still half-standing, Timothy lifted the glass to his lips.

One of the Englishwomen bumped into him. The wine went flying. An icy-cold stream shot down Timothy's shirt. He bit back a startled profanity, and one of the light voices said, "Oh, dear!"

Timothy turned. The two females stood in the aisle, blocking his exit, hovering about in dismay. The mother was quite pretty, plump but dainty, in impeccable black silk. The daughter towered over her, as gawky as a boy, fair curly hair allowed to fall freely over the shoulders of her white Russian-style blouse, almost as far as her waist. She looked only about fifteen, but in that first impression Timothy thought he saw what she would be like if no man ever married her, and she became a fidgety old maid.

The girl was the one who had bumped into him. However, it was her mother who said, "We are so very *sorry*!"

Timothy didn't want gushing apologies. All he wanted was to disappear into his Pullman compartment and change his sodden shirt. Exasperated at this clumsy end to the sumptuous meal, he said briefly, "My fault entirely, ma'am."

"No, no, I must ... Your wine, you've lost your *wine*. I really must insist that we make amends..." The woman fluttered, her small hands waving meaninglessly. "Another bottle of wine, to make up for ...."

Timothy had drunk and eaten more than enough. Nevertheless, he wavered, for that chardonnay had been magnificent. And expensive.

Then he looked at the table, where the remains of his cream and chocolate pudding smeared his plate and spoon. The napkin was crumpled, and the tablecloth had suffered almost as badly as his shirt when the wine had been spilled.

Without bothering to hide his chagrin, he said, "Thank you, ma'am, but no."

The woman blushed, going nearly as scarlet as her awkward daughter. For a moment Timothy thought his brusqueness had embarrassed her, but instead she fumbled in her reticule and produced a visiting card. It was the impropriety of offering a strange man a bottle of wine that bothered her, he saw. The *carte de visite* was to make up for the lack of a proper introduction.

Timothy took the card she thrust towards him, and glanced down at it with little interest. The matron's name was Miller, Mrs. Clara Miller. An American woman would have put her husband's name in front of the surname, he thought, and assumed that this was the English fashion. Then he glanced at her black gown again, and thought that she might be a widow.

The address was a cozy-sounding village in Devon. "The address is our English one," she said. "It's our address at *home*. We're on tour."

That, thought Timothy, was glaringly obvious. He reluctantly lifted his hand towards his inside breast pocket. The daughter was staring at him, her large grey eyes unexpectedly intelligent.

"To *New Zealand*," her mother added.

Timothy's hand dropped back to his side. Alarm bells were ringing in his head. His whole manner altered.

He said heartily, "Well, that surely is a coincidence, ma'am, for I'm on the way to New Zealand, too."

"You *are*?"

"I don't have a card with me, so allow me to introduce myself. Dexter — Timothy Dexter."

They shook hands, all around. The mother's plump smooth hand fluttered, but the daughter's was surprisingly strong.

"But you must excuse me," he said, and made an apologetic gesture towards his wet shirt, by now clinging clammily to his chest. He waited, but neither of them moved.

"My compliments, ma'am, Miss Miller," he said firmly, and executed a small formal bow, moving a deliberate step forward at the same time.

The ploy worked. Both Mrs. Miller and her daughter stepped back, giving him room. Timothy seized the advantage, thankfully escaping to his compartment and clean dry clothes.

2

When the shirt was changed, Timothy sat back in the wicker-work chair, unwrapping a cigar with fingers that trembled. He rang the bell, and when the attendant came he ordered a large brandy. Those goddamned English females, he thought. They'd utterly destroyed his pleasant mood.

Had he panicked unnecessarily? He hated the risk of intro-ducing himself by the name of "Dexter." Perhaps he should have brazened it out, he thought. It was as dangerous here to be known as "Dexter" as it was by his real name in New Zealand. He'd gone under his proper name ever since he'd returned to the States, and had bought his ticket in that name, too. So, why hadn't he given the woman his business card? He had lived through so much frustration in the last few weeks in Salem that he was too easily spooked.

He'd grown so heartily tired of dancing attendance on an obstinate old woman who had refused to admit that she was his aunt, the old bastard's only sister, for God's sake! The old harridan had giggled with senile hysteria when he persisted in trying to make her see sense, and had cackled that his motives were obvious. If he didn't stop his wicked attempt at fortune-stealing, she threatened, she would have him horse-whipped as a charlatan. She would leave her money to her nearest *legal* heir, and how could an heir be legal there was a memorial stone set up in the graveyard to prove him dead and gone, huh?

He could imagine, wincingly, the screeching hilarity in Salem if the old hag ever found out that he had introduced himself to these strangers as "Timothy Dexter," when he had spent so many frus-trating hours trying to persuade her that his name was the one on the gravestone. But then, he thought, who could possibly tell her?

The thought should have been bracing. Nevertheless, when the brandy arrived Timothy took a fast gulp.

The gravestone was the very devil, he brooded. Any man would have felt somewhat underwhelmed to see his own name on a memorial stone, complete with a death date that read "1867." But even that confounded stone was not a fatal impediment, if only the old woman had agreed to cooperate. Timothy chewed at his cigar, shooting it from one side of his mouth to the other, thinking how typically nasty the old woman had been, and how the whole rotten interlude had brought back unpleasant memories of his childhood in Salem. Aunt Hetty had done a great deal to make life miserable for the young woman who lived in adultery with her brother, and had been sneakily cruel to the son that young woman had borne — Timothy himself. He had told her enough stories of his childhood to convince any sane person that he was, indeed, her brother's son, but the terrible old harridan had simply snickered. Then, when he had finally lost his temper, and revealed in an infuriated shout that there was a letter in New Zealand that proved without doubt that he told the truth and she was a lying bitch, she'd called for the gardeners, and had him — her own nephew! — thrown out of her house.

Her house? *His home*, Timothy thought savagely. He felt amazed that the presumptuous old harridan had allowed him to stay in his childhood home at all, or that he'd taken so long to lose control of his temper. Somehow, he'd endured three weeks in the place. He truly believed that Aunt Hetty had allowed him to hang about so long only because she'd had so much fun watching him writhing with frustration. Though she had also got a lot of nasty amusement out of watching Essie putting on airs for this self-described prodigal nephew.

Essie was Aunt Hetty's companion, a tall, thin spinster of about thirty-five, who looked after the old woman and the household affairs with silent efficiency. Timothy had regarded her with contempt at first, for she was so meekly obedient, unresponsive even when insulted. Then he had been puzzled, for Aunt Hetty referred to her as "Cousin." She wasn't a relation, or so Timothy thought. Or, if she was, the relationship was very remote, for she didn't feature in his childhood memories, not even as a topic of conversation.

So the old harridan had probably been calling Essie "Cousin" to mock him, he thought. The wonder was that Essie had stuck it out for the time she'd been looking after the old bitch. Aunt Hetty treated her as badly as she did everyone else, poking spiteful fun at "Cousin" Essie's prim demeanor, and criticizing her painstakingly trimmed and mended dresses. The outmoded old shrew would have laughed on the other side of her face, he thought with a grin, if she'd known that "Cousin" Essie slipped into his bed most nights, to perform in a manner that wasn't old-maidish in the slightest.

He'd nearly had a heart attack the first time it had happened. The furtive scrape as his bedroom door opened had woken him, and then he had lain there utterly still, his heart thumping as he listened to the rustle of garments being shed. Wild thoughts had raced through Timothy's head at that moment, for he'd even imagined with utter horror that it might be the old harridan herself. The smooth naked body that finally undulated between his sheets had been a mighty relief. The experience had been a pleasurable one as well. Essie had proved to own a surprisingly full-breasted and enticing form, and to be as efficient in bed as she was at Aunt Hetty's desk, where she did the accounts.

But then he'd been slung out of the house, and Essie had shown another side to her nature. She had called at Timothy's hotel and discreetly informed him that those weeks of trying to sweet-talk the old woman into seeing sense had been a waste of time. He shouldn't have bothered, for it didn't matter whether Aunt Hetty recognized him as her nephew or not. The family wealth was locked into a trust, and Aunt Hetty merely had the use of the income while she was still here. Aunt Hetty, in fact, had no way of bequeathing it to anyone. Once she was dead, it would all go automatically to her late brother's nearest relative.

And that nearest relative, obviously, was Timothy. But, as Essie had stressed, the authorities had to be satisfied that the claim was legal. She herself was willing to believe that Timothy was truly the old merchant's son, for she had listened to his stories, and, unlike

Aunt Hetty, she had found them convincing. However, Essie's opinion didn't mean a thing, as she modestly pointed out. Timothy couldn't claim a cent, not until he produced the letter — the letter that, or so he had said, proved without doubt that the tombstone stood over an empty grave.

As she also pointed out, that letter — if it existed — was crucial. Understandably, his parents had neglected to register his birth with the local church. After all, they had been living in adultery, his mother's legal husband being away at sea at the time. According to what Essie remembered, Timothy had been almost six years old before his mother was free to marry the man who had fathered him, and no doubt she had felt a trifle too embarrassed to have the fact written down in the parish records. Indeed, the thought had probably never crossed her mind. And then, not long after that, she had died — or so Essie had learned.

Also, obviously, Timothy's priority was to get to New Zealand to retrieve that letter. A lawyer should be found and consulted first, though, and then, while he was making the long journey to the other side of the Pacific, Essie was willing to delve about in the family papers in the hope that something indiscreet the old man had written about becoming a father would turn up. It might take months of quiet digging about in old papers, but surely that would happen — the old man must have been overjoyed to have a son at last, and must have noted it in a journal, if not in a letter to some intimate friend.

Timothy had become quite enlivened by the idea. Not only was it plausible, but evidence like that would back up the letter — once he had it in his possession — and make his case a cast-iron one. But then Essie let him know that she would do all this, and take the risk of losing her position, only at a price. And that price, as she made very clear, was marriage.

Timothy had been forced to revise his opinion of Essie, who had always seemed so humble out of bed. Obviously, she had not wasted all those hours at Aunt Hetty's desk in merely paying bills and totting up accounts. However, he had smiled and murmured agreeably, and next day, he had packed up and journeyed to Boston, to spend a quiet and thoughtful couple of weeks consulting books and making plans, while Essie returned to work. Also as agreed, he had consulted a lawyer, who had been increasingly interested as the true story was revealed, and positively enlivened when Timothy had described the old letter that would prove his true heritage, which was held by Captain Jake Dexter, of the Golden Goose Hotel, Thames, New Zealand.

And, meantime, if Essie was successful in finding more evidence in the family papers... On hearing these details, the lawyer had felt no qualms at all about loaning Timothy the wherewithal to buy a ticket on this transcontinental railway and passage from San Francisco to New Zealand.

Until that letter was safely in his possession, however, Timothy couldn't afford to take the slightest risk that Jake or any of that goddamned Gray family associated with him might learn even a hint of the value of that document. Everyone who toured New Zealand visited the Thames goldfields, for the Thames was the current tourist Mecca, and so that garrulous Englishwoman and her clumsy daughter were almost sure to go there . . . and if they did, they would almost certainly stop at the famous Golden Goose Hotel, even if just for a cup of tea.

And, if that intrusive and talkative female took a look at the family photographs that covered the walls in the public lounge, and just happened to cry, "But *surely* isn't that Mr. ...?"

He'd done the right thing by giving them the Dexter name, he decided, and rang for another glass of brandy.

3

"Do you remember the gentleman on the train — the one who said he was going to New Zealand?" Mrs. Miller asked.

The Englishwoman and her daughter were in their hotel room in San Francisco, *such* a nice hotel, so reassuringly *English*, as Mrs. Miller had several times declared. She often declared, too, that she must write to the Thomas Cook people in London, complimenting their choice. The hotel was called the Royal George, and was not too large, though centrally placed near Union Square. There was a gilded cage of a lift, and hunting prints on the walls.

The manager and his wife were most approachable, very anxious that their English guests should feel at home here. In fact, they had struck up quite a friendship. There was even an English-style afternoon tea made available — tea in *proper* teapots with muffins and crumpets and tiny sandwiches, served on the balcony that overlooked the foyer — and Mrs. Miller and her daughter had several times shared a table with the hotel manager and his wife, enjoying a convivial chat.

Clara Miller and her daughter were off to indulge in yet another tea, this being their last chance, for their ship to New Zealand sailed next day. They had just come in from a sightseeing jaunt that included a scenic ride on the famous cable cars, and were changing from their sensible walking costumes, because this tea, quite apart from being their last, was to be a special occasion. As they left their room Mrs. Miller was wearing a neat afternoon gown in watered silk. Her daughter wore a "Gibson girl" costume, with a plain ankle-length skirt matched with a very pretty high-necked, full-sleeved, white muslin waist, and she was carrying a flat packet that held sheet music.

"*Such* a fine-looking gentleman," Mrs. Miller mused aloud. "Mr. Dexter, I mean. Don't you agree, dear?"

~ 17 ~

She had already said several times that she approved of Mr. Dexter's kind of looks. His complexion was rather weathered, perhaps, but all fair-skinned men became florid in middle age, or so Mrs. Miller had observed; and he had been so handsomely outfitted too, perfectly up to fashion, his lounge suit in the latest mode and just right for dinner on an American express. So well *groomed*, freshly shaved so that she had been able to smell his toilet lotion, his moustache nicely trimmed and still quite *dark* in color, his eyebrows black though his hair was grey, and such urbanely polite brown eyes.

"Americans have such wonderful *manners*."

"Yes, Mama," said her daughter, who was nicknamed Cissy. Privately, however, she thought that Mr. Dexter's manner had been somewhat brusque. Almost rude — and then, suddenly, it had changed.

Miss Cissy Miller liked to watch her fellow humans, and that alteration in manner had interested her. She also wondered why Mr. Dexter had been carrying a gun. She had felt it when she'd lurched against him and made him spill his wine. It was a small gun, she thought, but its shape had been unmistakable.

It had all been rather exciting, especially when Mr. Dexter had lifted his hand towards the inside of his jacket. For a wild moment she had fancied he was going to produce the pistol and threaten them with it. Cissy had been an avid reader of detective books for about as long as she'd been reading novels, and because of that knew beyond doubt that Americans were very keen on guns and self-protection. However, she had never expected to come across the evidence in real life.

Anyway, he had dropped his hand. Whatever he was reaching for, he had changed his mind about it. Almost as if the name "New Zealand" had been a kind of trigger. But why? It was an absorbing little puzzle — so absorbing that she forgot to reflect on the other thought-provoking aspect of Mr. Dexter's behavior.

Instead, she said to her mother, "What brought him to mind, Mama?"

"I feel almost certain he's staying in this very hotel, dear. I'm sure I glimpsed him at the desk this morning, talking to the clerk.

He didn't see me, and I didn't like to *interrupt*, but — good gracious, there he is. What a coincidence."

They had arrived on the balcony, and there, indubitably, was Mr. Dexter, as impeccably groomed as he had been that last evening on the rain — before the glass of wine had been spilled, that is. His tweed suit was cut in the style that King Edward VII had just made fashionable, with tapered trousers and a double-breasted waistcoat where the bottom button was deliberately left undone.

Cissy thought his expression was anything but pleased when he turned and saw who hailed him, but to her embarrassment her mother insisted on buying him afternoon tea. "It will quite *salve* my conscience," she said, while Cissy squirmed internally. "And you can tell us about New Zealand."

There was a bustle as a table was found and Mrs. Miller and Cissy were seated. There was quite a crowd on the balcony, and heads turned to watch them. Mr. Dexter's manners were certainly polished, Cissy thought, shooting little glances sideways at him. His jacket, cut with a seam and a vent at the back, had broad shoulders and deep-cut armholes, so that it was impossible to tell if he still carried a gun.

He said to her mother, "Are you staying here much longer, ma'am?"

"Oh no, we sail tomorrow afternoon. And *that* is quite a coincidence too," Mrs. Miller confided, and poured tea from the big silver pot.

"Coincidence?"

"Yes! The ship we are sailing on is called the *Royal George*, the same name as this hotel. When the people at Thomas Cook in London gave me the itinerary, I felt certain that they had made a mistake. But no, they said. Then I wondered if they chose the steamer simply because it has the same name as the hotel. However, they said they had other reasons entirely. The line has a name for *reliability* and for being most terribly up to date. The ship, they say, has electric lighting throughout! The Thomas Cook people always recommend travelling by steam, of course, and the *Royal George* gets to Auckland more quickly than even its fastest rival. Well, that's what they *claimed*, though a person like yourself who travels the route frequently..."

And at that she paused, in the delicate way that she had. Her inquisitive and imaginative daughter often wished she had inherited the talent, as Cissy admired the ploy greatly, it being a splendid means of satisfying curiosity without being seen to be curious. That discreetly questioning pause often tricked the unwary into dropping their guard, or so she had noticed.

Mr. Dexter was no exception. "I'm certain the Thomas Cook people are right, Mrs. Miller," he genially agreed. "Steam is fast and reliable, to be sure. When you voyage by steam you know what day you leave and what day you will arrive. You can plan ahead and make an itinerary. That isn't possible with sail, of course, because everything depends on the variable winds. For businessmen and tourists, steam is a blessing. The Thomas Cook choice is a wise one, Mrs. Miller.

"I'm an old sea-dog, however," he confided then, with a rueful grin. "A sea-dog with sentimental memories. Sail has had its day, undoubtedly, but it's hard to beat the sheer romance of skimming along under canvas."

Apparently, as part of an adventurous youth, he had shipped before the mast on an old bark called the *Rolling Moses*, for a voyage from San Francisco to Auckland, New Zealand. It certainly sounded a most romantic way of getting to that place, as Cissy's mother exclaimed, and Mr. Dexter benignly agreed.

Cissy silently wondered how he had coped, because despite the slightly weathered appearance of his face, Mr. Dexter didn't look like an outdoorsman at all, and from what he told them after that, it seemed that he'd had quite a cosseted childhood in New England. However, according to his account, his mother's family had been keen on the sea, and he'd done a good bit of sailing and sword-fishing off Cape Cod in his youth, which no doubt had helped.

Mrs. Miller then set to asking him what Auckland had been like, back then when he had first arrived. "After all," she explained demurely, "we expect to be touring the city ourselves, and it's so *useful* to have a little prior knowledge."

Mr. Dexter laughed heartily at that, and promised that the sights that awaited Mrs. Miller and Cissy were entirely different from the poor place he had found in that month of June, 1867, almost exactly thirty-eight years ago. In fact, he became quite loquacious about it.

Auckland had looked amusing in the beginning, he allowed. He had landed with all kinds of high hopes, fully expecting to make a gratifying little fortune, to repair fortunes that apparently had failed. Disillusionment had swiftly set in, however. Up to the moment the *Rolling Moses* had dropped anchor in the port, he had pictured Auckland as the capital of the colony, with plenty of business going on, but he had been rapidly proved wrong.

If he had arrived in 1863, just four years earlier, Mr. Dexter would have been right — or so he had been told, in a dozen or more taverns. Auckland must have been a very fine city then, he gathered, because people had prized the place enough to fight for it. Mr. Dexter had heard over and over how thirty thousand Maori warriors had advanced in force on the town, intent on wiping Auckland off the face of the globe. But instead of running away, the male settlers had taken up arms — or so they proudly related.

According to the tavern gossip, the town had been saved by some kind of miracle, along with the outstanding bravery of a few colonial troops. In that year of 1867, however, those days were well gone. No one would give a tinker's cuss — "Excuse me, ma'am, Miss Miller" — if providence had never intervened and the Maoris had turned Auckland into a smouldering heap. Auckland as a town had died, without the warriors' help.

The British troops stationed in the Albert barracks to fight the land wars had just about all of them gone, taking their business along with them; the seat of government had shifted south to Wellington, and Auckland was in the grip of an economic depression.

Cissy, listening with interest, decided that Mr. Dexter had a strong and evocative talent for description. The streets that he pictured had been about empty, and most of the shops closed for lack of trade. Women in crinolines had clattered up and down the wooden sidewalks in their wooden shoes, making a lot of noise but with little cash to spend. Drays had rattled through mud and rubble, only half loaded. Indeed, Cissy gained the strong impression that Auckland in that faroff year had looked like a Californian ghost town, without there ever having been the excitement of a goldrush to make up for it. In fact, Cissy gathered, a goldrush was exactly what Auckland had needed, to perk up the port and get dull energies brightened.

And a goldrush was exactly what had happened, just a few weeks after Mr. Dexter had arrived. At the start of August, the Thames goldfields were opened and a town called Shortland was established in a hurry. And of course all the supplies came from Auckland. The Thames goldfields had saved Auckland from depression and extinction — and had saved Mr. Dexter, too. He had joined the goldrush to make his fortune, and had stayed to settle down.

"So now you know why I choose to sail under canvas, ma'am, but I'm sure you didn't reckon on such a flood of boring reminiscence!"

Really, Cissy thought as she listened to her mother laughingly deny this, it had turned out to be quite a pleasant little interlude, after all. Then they were interrupted, as the manager's wife arrived, to remind Cissy about the promise her mother had made for her, that she would entertain the guests by singing at her last afternoon tea. Cissy, feeling rather hot, got to her feet and went over to a piano where a fat lady had been tinkling.

She and the accompanist and the manager's wife held a long consultation over choice of songs. It went on so long that Cissy glanced rather nervously over at her mother, expecting a reproving frown. Mrs. Miller was obliviously enjoying herself, however, chattering vivaciously to Mr. Dexter, while he listened with an extremely attentive expression. Then, after a short embarrassing announcement by the manager's wife, and a brief round of applause from the people at the tables, the fat lady struck up again, and Cissy began to sing. She was quite proud of her voice, knowing it was sweet and pure, not very strong but perfectly tuneful, and as soon as she was well launched into the first lyric she forgot to be shy. She sang "Love is Ours" and

"Home, Sweet Home," and received such encouraging applause that she gave several encores.

At last the little concert was over. Cissy arrived back at the table, feeling diffident again, wondering if her mother and Mr. Dexter had heard a single note. "Don't apologize, please Miss Miller," Mr. Dexter said, but his smile seemed forced, and his eyes didn't quite meet hers. "Your voice is really quite pretty."

"I'm so glad to hear you say so," exclaimed Clara Miller, and, most despairingly, Cissy knew that her mother was going to embarrass her yet again. Being manipulated into singing in public was bad enough, but this was going to be worse. She frantically searched her mind for words to forestall the threatening confidences, but inspiration failed her.

"We were hoping for a musical career for her," her mother said in lowered tones.

"What — in singing?"

"She plays the piano quite exquisitely, but..."

She was halted. Cissy, miraculously, had found her voice. She said loudly, "I saw a poster this afternoon that would interest you greatly, Mama."

"Poster, dear?"

"Up outside the opera house, advertising Miss Minnie Gray in Franz Lehar's latest operetta."

Mr. Dexter interrupted sharply. "Minnie Gray? In San Francisco? You can't be right."

"Of course I am," said Cissy, rather pert in her relief at having changed the subject. "I read the poster particularly."

Mrs. Miller didn't appear to hear either of them. "*Miss Minne Gray?*" she cried. "In *The Merry Widow*? Oh, heavens! Cissy, why didn't you tell me this earlier?"

She was flushed with excitement. Clara Miller had thrilled to the Minnie Gray story for years. She owned all the dramatic songstress's recordings, which she played on their Victrola gramophone, and she read everything about Minnie Gray that she could. Minnie Gray had the kind of glamour that penetrated even to quiet Devonshire villages. In her agitation Mrs. Miller didn't even seem to notice that the waitress was standing beside her with the chit for the afternoon tea. It was on a tray, ready for her to sign, but she ignored it.

"Cissy," she declared, "we must get tickets, and I don't care how much it costs. One of my *dearest* ambitions has been to see Minnie Gray on stage," she explained — rather unnecessarily, Cissy thought — to Mr. Dexter. "And perhaps even meet her afterwards, backstage...."

Oddly, Cissy fancied she glimpsed a sudden wariness in Mr. Dexter's expression. Then the uneasy look fled, replaced by a blandness that veiled his eyes. "Is that possible?" he murmured.

"I *believe* that is the custom here, just as it is in England. Admirers often send their cards backstage after the show. There is not impropriety in that now, not in these enlightened times. Particularly when the star has the perfectly *unblemished* reputation of Miss Minnie Gray."

"I see," said Mr. Dexter. He looked at the waitress, who had been standing in a relaxed kind of way, listening quite openly, and cleared his throat, drawing Mrs. Miller's attention in that direction.

"Oh!" said Clara Miller, and signed the chit rapidly, her mind patently not on what she was doing, but on the prospect of seeing her stage idol instead. The waitress picked up the tray with the signed paper and carried it off. "Perhaps you've seen Minnie Gray yourself, Mr. Dexter," she said after the girl had gone. "I know she is from New Zealand, too."

"Seen her?" he echoed, and chuckled condescendingly. "I should say I have. I'm connected with her family. Mind you, everyone in New Zealand calls her 'our Minnie'."

"Family?" Cissy stared, wondering whether to believe him. Her mother didn't seem to have the same trouble, though, gazing at Mr. Dexter raptly instead.

She said dreamily, "How amazing it must feel, to see someone so close to you being applauded by so many."

"Indeed, Mrs. Miller."

"I'm certain you go to every concert you can manage."

"Of course."

"So you'll be going tonight — now that you know that she is here. How lucky you are!"

Then Mrs. Miller sighed, "I *must* buy tickets to the show tonight."

Mr. Dexter said, "It'll be difficult."

"I *know* that, Mr. Dexter."

"The theatre will have been booked out weeks ago. Now that she's past her first youth everyone is very aware that the magnificent voice won't last much longer. Her manager has been coaching her to go on to purely dramatic roles, but in the meantime people flock to enjoy the last of her singing career."

"I know," repeated Mrs. Miller sorrowfully.

Mr. Dexter let the pause go on, gazing reflectively in the middle distance. Then he smiled.

"I'll tell you what, I'll try to get tickets for you. I make no promises, mind, and it will take all afternoon. You will have to be patient. At such late notice, it will not be easy. But I will try!"

And he nodded in the most reassuring manner possible.

4

It was, indeed, a dream came true. Outside the great theatre, crowds were being turned away, for there wasn't even standing room left, while the carriages of the more fortunate rattled up to the grand entrance. Silk-suited footmen jumped down from boxes and opened doors with a flourish, while fashionable women were assisted down by their frock-coated escorts. The gaily chattering women were as brilliant as peacocks, their silk gowns tightly boned to display décolletage to the best advantage, the swelling bodices embroidered and appliquéd with jet beads and glittering jewels. Billowing sleeves flounced and frilled, waists were cinched in to incredible slenderness, and voluminous overskirts were trimmed with lace, often trailing along the ground behind. French perfume gusting out with each flourish of massed yards of expensive fabric. But, as Clara Miller kept on saying to Cissy, she had expected nothing less.

As she also kept on marveling, it was a miracle that they had been able to be part of this glittering occasion — a miracle, Cissy mediated, that had *not* been wrought by Mr. Dexter. Cissy and her mother had waited all afternoon to hear what success he'd had in organizing tickets, but had heard nothing at all. If they had relied on Mr. Dexter, they would have missed out. But here they were — thanks to the waitress who had served them at afternoon tea and who had so frankly listened to their table conversation. The young woman had called at their hotel room just one hour before the show began, offering to sell them two passes. The waitress had made a good profit, said Mrs. Miller, looking worldly wise. But the money didn't matter. The *important* thing was that they were here, and with good places too, having been ushered into front row seats in the grand dress circle.

The Merry Widow was the newest composition by the brilliant young Hungarian, Franz Lehar, and though it had been disdained by many serious critics, the music was already a hit across Europe and throughout North and South America. The Merry Widow waltz was played at every popular occasion and the Merry Widow hat was the *beau monde* rage. This was its first stage production outside Vienna, and the costumes were correspondingly lavish. The set was as breathtaking as the reports from Europe had boasted, created by the world-famed designer Will Williams — but the first appearance of the star left no doubt of why the house was booked out. Miss Minnie Gray, being short and rather dumpy of figure, had no kind of impressive appearance, but the audience adored her. Her presence flowed across the footlights, and the wholehearted love of the crowd flowed back.

Perhaps the sweet ringing voice that had first captured the hearts of her listeners had lost some strength, but the applause at the end was unstintingly rapturous. Dignified gentlemen jumped to their feet, crying out over and over again, "Brava, brava!" and "Diva, diva!" Sophisticated women unpinned expensive corsages and tossed them down to Minnie Gray's feet. In the common galleries men stamped and both men and women shouted themselves hoarse. For long moments the star could not make herself heard, but the orchestra struck up, loudly at first, and then softly as the audience quietened in response.

Then she said, in a voice that was low and caressing, but which reached every corner of the great auditorium, "This song is dedicated to the memory of a wonderful man — my uncle, Captain Jahaziel Dexter." And with a massed sigh like the ebbing tide on the beach, the huge crowd silenced, to listen to the lyric that epitomized the great Minnie Gray for people all over the world.

> *I found an old letter, long-lost, today*
> *The ink has faded, the words are few,*
> *But they speak to my soul, and softly say*
> *Remember the heart that was deep and true.*

In remembrance his hand is clasped in mine
And the bustling hours of the day are done
Together we watch clematis twine
In the last golden glow of a dying sun.

I fold the letter, the sweet dream flies
Away through the mists of memory lane
He sleeps alone 'neath southern skies
Alone ... till we meet together again.

At the end Minnie Gray stood very still, her arms uplifted to the enraptured audience. Such was the spell she'd wrought, the utter silence continued for a long breath-held moment, while women wiped their eyes with lace-edged handkerchiefs. Then the great theatre echoed and re-echoed with thunderous waves of renewed applause.

Ten minutes later, as they moved through the packed foyer, Mrs. Miller grasped Cissy's arm and hissed in her ear, "She said *Dexter*."

"Excuse me, Mama?"

"I suspected Mr. Dexter of exaggerating, dear, but Minnie Gray dedicated her encore to a Captain *Dexter*."

Without waiting for whatever kind of reply Cissy might produce, Clara Miller turned impetuously and beckoned over an usher. Then she wrote on the back of one of her visiting cards. The attendant looked doubtful, but she tipped him lavishly, and Cissy watched him approach the house manager, a formidable figure in full formal fig.

That impressive personage pursed his lips, but then Cissy saw him scan the back of the card and nod. The usher went off with the card in his hand, and was away a long time, while Mrs. Miller quivered with suspense. Then at last he came back, nodded gravely, and led the way.

To Cissy's surprise, they weren't ushered to the back of the stage, but to the champagne bar of the dress circle instead. This was where the sophisticated part of the audience had bought crystal flukes of sparkling wine during the intermissions, and many of those people were still present. It was all extremely intimidating. Everyone else looked at home there, evidently because they were friends of the management or some of the cast. They all seemed to be having a first-rate time, chattering and laughing loudly, as gorgeous as peacocks and as noisy as rooks. Cissy had never even imagined a place like this, let expected to find herself inside one. What would she do if anyone wanted to shake her hand, and what would she say if anyone spoke? She was mortified at the very thought of the awful social blunders she could so easily make.

Then Miss Minnie Gray arrived, and Cissy felt even worse.

The star was escorted by a plain stalwart middle-aged gentleman with a bushy moustache. The vivacious throng hushed instantly, but for a moment Minnie Gray seemed unaware of them all, still deeply involved in her conversation with this man. Then she turned and smiled, embracing them with her famous radiance, and commenced to move about shaking hands with some and then almost immediately moving on, stopping to converse with others.

A maid wheeled in a trolley laden with dishes of savories and another presided over a huge coffee pot. Cissy took a cup and then wished most fervently that she hadn't, agonizing about what to do if Miss Gray wished to shake hands. There were no tables or benches nearby. Her awkward fingers fumbled as she furtively tried to free her right hand. Then, just as the star arrived, coffee sloshed into the saucer and splashed on the carpet, right at Minnie Gray's feet.

The great star leapt back with unexpected agility. Up to that awful moment, her gown had been spotless, without a crease or unseemly wrinkle. "Mercy!" she exclaimed, in the world-famous voice.

Mercy, poor speechlessly scarlet-faced Cissy thought, was what she should have been beseeching for herself. "Oh *dear*," she heard her mother say. "Cissy, that really was *too* clumsy of you, and when it was so *kind* of Miss Gray to let us meet her, too."

Then Minnie Gray turned Cissy into her admirer for life by lifting the black lashes about her famously dark-blue eyes, and smiling right into her face, as she waved away apologies with a small plump hand. "You have come so far — and you are travelling to my homeland. How could I refuse?" She had Mrs. Miller's card in her other hand, and she looked at it and said casually, "You say here that you are acquainted with a Mr. Dexter?"

To Cissy's secret pleasure, her mother had the grace to blush. Mrs. Miller said, "I must confess that we're not really *acquainted* with him, but have met him a couple of times. We got into conversation because he is travelling to New Zealand, too. Mr. Timothy Dexter claims, in fact, that..."

And she trailed off into one of her pauses — into utter, dead silence. Cissy felt a totally unexpected chill, shocked by the sudden violence in the actress's eyes.

Miss Gray said in a low voice that trembled with ferocity, "Did you say *Timothy* Dexter?"

Mrs. Miller nodded, looking as alarmed as Cissy felt. Then Minnie Gray glanced quickly all about the room.

There was no one nearby. Most of the guests had gone, accompanied by the man who had come in with the actress. Minnie Gray turned back and said in that low tense voice, "And he's on the way to New Zealand?"

"Yes, to *Thames*."

"The Thames? With no warning that he is on the way? *Oh dear God*, I'll have to let them know."

"I beg your..."

Cissy, fascinated, saw the actress's face go smooth. It was as if she'd been caught off-guard, but had managed to take control of herself. Minnie Gray smiled warmly again, and her voice was perfectly polite and normal as she said, "Mrs. Miller, may I ask where you met him?"

Cissy's mother blinked, looking cautious. "In our hotel. But we met him first on the train."

"The railroad? From where?"

"We embarked in New York and changed trains at Omaha. My late husband was an American, with business interests in New York and it was necessary for me to see his lawyers..."

"But Timothy Dexter? Where did he catch the train?"

Mrs. Miller shook her head.

Cissy said, "We don't know."

The lambent eyes focused on her face. "Your name is Cissy?"

Cissy hesitated, but said, "Yes."

"So, Cissy, why don't *you* tell me about meeting him?"

The actress listened with deep attention. "Wine?" she said, the smile widening. "Down his shirt?"

Cissy nodded and blushed.

Miss Gray looked extremely amused. Eyebrows arched high, she teased, "You are taking a glass of wine, my dear?"

Mrs. Miller looked scandalized. "Certainly not! *Mr. Dexter* was drinking the wine when the accident happened, Miss Gray."

"A chardonnay," said Cissy. She remembered the label on the bottle.

"You know wines?"

"My dear husband was a connoisseur," Mrs. Miller explained hastily. "He kept a cellar. Even a *child* couldn't help but be aware of his interest in the vintages."

"It was a very good wine, I believe," said Cissy. "I think Mr. Dexter must be a connoisseur too." She had overheard him discussing the wine list with the waiter.

"And yet," the actress said slowly, "he finished off the bottle as he was getting up to leave. You did say that he'd finished his dinner?"

"Yes," said Cissy. She was definite about it, because that was the other odd thing about Mr. Dexter that she had noticed. She listed exactly what Mr. Dexter had eaten.

"And does that seem like a connoisseur to you, Cissy?"

"I thought the wine must have tasted very strange after eating so much sweet stuff," Cissy confessed. Then she reddened, thinking that she'd sounded improperly knowledgeable again. "Or so my father would have said, I am sure."

"And what else did you think?"

"I thought that..." Cissy stopped, remembering that Mr. Dexter had claimed to be related in some way to Miss Gray, and what she was about to say was unpardonably rude.

"Yes?"

Cissy met the compelling gaze and blurted out, despite herself, "I thought he must be very greedy, to spoil the after-taste of the lovely meal for the sake of a glassful of wine."

Her mother gasped, "Cissy!"

Miss Gray ignored her. Cissy saw the lovely dark-blue eyes shut and then open to stare thoughtfully into her face again. "Yes," said Miss Gray softly. "My first impression was right. You are very perceptive, my dear."

Then she waited, as if she expected more of the story, and so Cissy described the second meeting, that day in the hotel. Minnie Gray listened with the same perfect attention, he face unreadable. When Cissy finally stumbled to a stop, the silence went on so long that her mother filled it by saying anxiously, "Perhaps we should not have tried to take advantage of his relationship..."

"Relationship" Minnie Gray smiled again, but rather thinly, Cissy thought.

"He did say that ... he was *connected* with your family."

"Mrs. Miller, up to the age of five I didn't even know that Timothy Dexter existed," Minnie Gray said, so bluntly that the effect was rude. However, her tone was warm as she said to Cissy, "I find you very interesting, Miss Miller. You're a very acute observer, for one so young. I even wonder if you've told me everything you noted about this man."

Cissy shifted uncomfortably, thinking about the gun. She avoided the implied question, saying, "You are too kind, Miss Gray."

"Am I?" the actress echoed dryly. "I think I make a statement, not a compliment. To act convincingly one has to watch people, all the time. It becomes second nature. And I think you watch people too. You have a watching face, and thinking eyes. Life's drama intrigues you. And — who knows? — one day you'll become very famous, simply because you enjoy the study of human nature so much."

Then, as if Cissy had been dismissed from her mind, Minnie Gray turned to her mother and said briskly, "And tell me, Mrs. Miller, what do you intend to do when you arrived in New Zealand? You're touring the Thames goldfields, of course."

"We hadn't really..."

"But you must! The stamping mills are famous, and the cruise up the river enchanting. The thermal springs at Te Aroha, a town not far from the Thames goldfields, must not be missed. And you must stop at the Golden Goose Hotel in the Thames. My family owns and manages the hotel, and organizes the Golden Goose Murder Experience. Surely you have heard of it?"

"*Murder?*"

"Acted, of course," Minnie Gray said airily. "The Golden Goose Murder Experience is unique, you see, and becoming very famous, known worldwide as an ingenious blend of touristic attraction and melodrama. A group gathers together for a weekend in the hotel, and a murder is staged, with everyone in the troupe encouraged to take part in the unfolding mystery. Mrs. Miller, tell I am right, that you enjoy amateur theatricals?"

"Well," said Mrs. Miller, fluttering, "I must admit I have never aspired, but my daughter..."

Cissy tensed. But before Mrs. Miller could go on to describe Cissy's mortifyingly unsuccessful attempt at a stage career, Minnie Gray exclaimed, "Then, as an affectionate mother — as I know you are — you really must give your daughter the chance to take part in a murder weekend! Tell me, what dates do you expect to be in New Zealand? So soon? Marvelous! But wait, don't tell me more, come with me now, and I shall write a letter and not only that, I will lend your daughter one of my own costumes. You should wear masquerade dress on the murder night even if you don't have a part in the melodrama — did I tell you that? Never mind," she said without waiting, and turned, setting off at a brisk pace across the room, which had emptied in the meantime. When Cissy and her mother hesitated the actress called out impatiently, "Come — come. Quickly, follow me."

And so, obediently, they followed her out of the bar and down the stairs. The empty curving flights echoed despite the rich carpets. Then they were back in the theatre.

The house lights were off, so the immensity of the auditorium was veiled in vast shadows. Lines of tipped-up seats serried off into the distant dark. The walls soared up and up to a barely seen roof. The great curved tiers of boxes seemed to Cissy like gunports in the hull of some fabulous gilded galleon, and plaster cherubim peeped out from cornices like watching imps. The wide tongue of the forestage, still lit, thrust out towards them, speckled with the faint smouldering of footlights. The drop curtain was three-quarters raised, and behind it, things were awry. Long ropes dangled like snakes in ambush, a ladder was propped against a cardboard balustrade that belonged to some formal garden. Cissy heard echoes, and clattering in the distance. There was a smell of gas and dusty leather, and an all-pervading sense of waiting.

Miss Minnie Gray hurried on, down the aisles and alongside the railing that fenced off the orchestra pit. When she opened a door below the wings a rectangle of bright hot gaslight shot into the gloom. Then all three were in a rough corridor. Doors stood open along its length. Cissy glimpsed a carpenter's workshop, the scene-painter's domain with its huge palette, a store with racks of great rolls of canvas, rope lockers, a sulphur-smelling place where the theatre gasman contrived his lighting effects. Narrow stairways ran steeply up to the fly galleries. Then, at last, Minnie Gray opened a door and ushered them into her dressing room.

This room, by contrast to the other places that Cissy had glimpsed, was extremely clean and neat. Great wickerwork hampers stood about the walls, all with big fabric labels. The dressing table where the actress made up was covered with a cloth that was as starched and frilled as a petticoat. There were fresh red roses in the sconces on either side of the looking-glass, but the perfume of the flowers was lost in the overriding scent of warm grease and orris-root.

Here, in her backstage domain, Miss Minnie seemed more intense than ever. When a snappish looking elderly woman turned from laying out gorgeous costumes on a table, she spoke to her swiftly. This, Cissy deduced, must be Miss Gray's dresser. The woman turned, looked Cissy up and down, nodded curtly, opened a hamper, and produced a costume of motley-colored silk.

Cissy didn't want to accept it. Accepting the costume seemed too significant, for taking it committed her to going to the Golden Goose. To a Murder Experience. It made her feel shivery.

She stammered, "I can't take this."

"Of course you can." Miss Gray's tone was brisk. "It's not a gift, but just a loan. Give it to my sister Gladys when you leave the Golden Goose, and she'll get it back to me."

Her hands thrust it at Cissy. The fabric felt soft and luxurious, cool despite the close warmth of the room. Cissy held it so loosely that it fell out to its full length, and she could see it was made up of tunic and trousers, the silk a bright patchwork of colors that shimmered in the gaslight.

"Do you not recognize the costume?" Minnie Gray asked. Her voice was casual, deceptively so, Cissy thought, for she could sense the actress's tension again. "You will have seen him in pantomime, perhaps even at the circus, for he's an enduring fellow, popular since all the way back to sixteenth century Italy. He's the classical Arlecchino — nowadays Harlequin. See — you have a black velvet eye-mask to wear with it. No one will recognize you, for Harlequin is anonymous, a catalyst rather than a character. Have you heard of a catalyst?"

Cissy thought she knew Harlequin well, for Harlequin had featured in all the Christmas pantomimes that she had viewed as a child. Catalyst sounded terribly scientific, but she thought she knew what the actress meant. Sometimes Harlequin was a clown, sometimes that treacherous, conniving servant, sometimes even an enigmatic kind of hero. Even without taking part in the story, he made things happen. He changed the former way of things. However, too embarrassed to try to put anything so formless into words, Cissy shook her head.

"You must try to understand." As in the bar upstairs, Minnie Gray's great eyes fixed on Cissy's face. "Harlequin is the observer, part of the drama and yet not part of it. He watches and he manipulates, but he reveals himself only at the end. And it is then, when Harlequin removes his mask, that the audience finds out who is the real hero, and who is the black-hearted villain."

"The ... murderer?"

"Yes. The conniver and killer." Minnie Gray nodded so emphatically that Cissy thought she didn't have just the Murder Experience in mind.

Cissy paused. Finally, she said, "Why me?"

"Because you will be perfect," the actress declared, and smiled as vivaciously as if this was a perfectly normal conversation. "You are taller than I am, but much slimmer, so the suit will fit — as will the part you will play. How I wish I could be in the Thames with you! But I cannot, my schedule forbids it, and so you must stand in my place. All those dear people there, how I wish I could see them, too. Tell them to remember..."

She broke off, turning to Mrs. Miller and asking about their travel plans. Then, still brisk, Minnie Gray turned to the dressing table, opened a neat little writing desk, and scribbled busily. It didn't take long. While Cissy watched, Miss Gray folded the paper and inserted it into a yellow envelope.

However, she didn't seal the envelope at once. Instead, she drew a newspaper out of the desk drawer and spread it out, very neatly. Cissy could see the reflection of the actress's absorbed expression as she found the item she wanted. It was a three-paragraph story, illustrated in some way, but Cissy didn't have a chance to even read the headline. Taking scissors, Miss Minnie picked up the paper, snipped neatly around the item, and then slid the clipping into the envelope. Finally, the envelope was sealed and addressed with a flourish, in large flowing script.

Minnie Gray stared at Cissy then, with her characteristic wide-eyed intensity. She said, "You *must* make sure that this goes to the person named on the front — and not to anyone else, not even any other member of the family. Will you promise me that?"

Cissy hesitated. Her eyes dropped to the envelope that was thrust so imperiously out to her. She read the name, *Miss Harriet Gray*, and the address, *Golden Goose Hotel, Thames, New Zealand*."

She asked tentatively, "Is she perhaps your sister?"

Minnie Gray laughed. "No, no, she's my aunt, the actress Harriet Gray. She was the sister of my poor, dead father, Royal Gray, who was quite famous as an actor and dramatist."

"I see," said Cissy, wondering if she should murmur polite condolences on the loss of a father, though it sounded as if he had been dead quite a while. Then she forgot it, as her eyes moved to the mutilated newspaper, which was still spread out on top of the dressing table.

"Give her the envelope with my dearest love, and remember Arlecchino. I know you will play Harlequin to perfection."

Looking at the paper while she folded the costume into a square, Cissy said, "I'll do my best."

"Play the murder melodrama as if it were real life, and watch *everything*. And remember how much I love the dear family there. I can't begin to tell you how important this is. You must practice your part all the time, not just when you are in costume."

"I see," said Cissy. Her hand reached out and plucked up the newspaper to use as a wrapping for the Harlequin suit, and Minnie Gray said nothing to stop her.

Instead, when Cissy finally looked up after making her parcel and put out her hand to take the letter, the actress's eyes were bright with warm approval.

Half an hour later a cab deposited Cissy and her mother in front of the Royal George Hotel. It was very late, but one guest was still lingering in the foyer, sitting in one of the big leather settees, smoking a cigar in leisurely fashion, flicking the ash into a nearby aspidistra. With no sense of surprise whatsoever, Cissy recognized Mr. Timothy Dexter.

He hoisted himself to his feet when he saw them. "Late hours, ladies, late hours!" His voice was so hearty that Cissy wondered if he had been drinking.

Clara Miller said nothing, just smiling in a distracted way. All the excitement had given her a headache, and so she kept on going, intent on getting to bed. Cissy followed, and Mr. Dexter made no attempt to delay them.

He watched them narrowly, however. Cissy saw the sharp look on his face as he sank back into his chair, and he didn't look drunken at all.

5

Despite its fine reputation with the Thomas Cook people, the *Royal George* was not quite in the same class as the huge trans-Atlantic liner that had sailed from Southampton to New York, or so Cissy decided after her first tour of inspection of the decks and salons. It was understandable, she supposed, for the *Royal George* was primarily for the fast mail service, and carried only about fifty passengers. And, while the interior couldn't be considered grand, it was certainly comfortable. There was plenty of solid wooden paneling, and the carved balustrades on the stairway that wound about the three deck levels were impressive. Altogether, though the *Royal George* might have been small, she was a fine, fast, turbine-powered steamer with electric lighting throughout, and, in Cissy's estimation none of the passengers should be disappointed.

She hung over the balustrade halfway up the stairwell, observing people as they arrived. She could see the purser directly below, with an assistant purser beside him. This personage called out each name as it was given to him, as pompous as a butler, his voice roundly enunciating the syllables. Then the assistant checked it off with a list that he carried, and gave out a cabin number. At that, the lordly purser issued directions, and his assistant summoned a baggage boy for those who had not sent the luggage on ahead. It was as entertaining as a play.

Most passengers came on board in noisy groups, surrounded by well-wishers, exclaiming loudly and sending echoes up the stairs. It was only two in the afternoon, but several had been celebrating their departure in liquor already, judging by the commotion they made. Others arrived much more quietly, coming in pairs or alone, seeming to know exactly how much to tip the purser and that now was the right time to do it, at the same time glancing about in a knowledgeable kind of way. Cissy felt very impressed that one of these was a woman, a straight-backed figure with a marvelous ostrich-trimmed hat and a long feather boa to match, who introduced herself to the purser with superb hauteur.

A new lot of luggage arrived in the lobby with a crash, so Cissy did not hear the woman's name. A baggage boy arrived at a run and was given a stateroom number. Then, hoisting a trunk onto his back, he began to mount the stairs. The lady followed. Cissy straightened quickly, before she could be discovered eavesdropping, and the woman passed by, her mouth primly straight. Then, no sooner was she gone, than Cissy forgot all about her — because she heard the name of the next person to come on board and present himself to the purser.

"Mr. Timothy Dexter!"

Shocked, Cissy leaned precipitously over the rail. And the man, most certainly, was Mr. Timothy Dexter, as well-groomed as ever. Cissy distinctly remembered the conversation in the hotel tearoom, just about word for word. Mr. Dexter had most definitely said that he preferred the romance of sail. He had even told her mother a long entertaining yarn to account for his preference. Surely, she thought, if he had his passage booked on the *Royal George*, he would have said so, even if only to save himself from embarrassment when they encountered each other on board.

And so, logically, it seemed that he had altered his arrangements, to travel on the same ship as her mother and herself. But why? There were all kinds of plausible motives, she reasoned. An urgent summons might been wired from New Zealand. Perhaps his other booking had been cancelled. Or else, Cissy thought slowly, he had found out that they had not only got tickets to the theatre, but had spoken to Minnie Gray as well. Had he changed his plans just so they wouldn't have a chance to pass on any message that Miss Gray might have given them before he got there?

Surely not, she told herself, because there was no way he could know about the envelope she carried. But then, he had apparently made no attempt to get them those theatre tickets, despite his promise. It was as if it had been a deliberate deception, to forestall them from getting tickets themselves — and Cissy's mother had said that she would try to see Miss Gray backstage, or so Cissy remembered. It was nothing more than a wild guess, Cissy thought, but it made the envelope seem terribly important, and she watched him thoughtfully as he set off along a passage, heading forward for another set of stairs which led up to the cabins on the promenade deck.

He was soon lost to sight, for there was quite a queue waiting to be introduced to the purser, as more people came on board in a last-minute rush. It did cross her mind that a stalwart gentleman near the front looked a little familiar, but she was so involved in speculation that she paid little attention.

"Mr. William Williams!" enunciated the purser.

The name meant nothing, but Cissy still felt the little nudge of recognition, though she had certainly never met the fellow who was with him, a very much younger but equally solidly built man with straw-colored hair. This second man's name was very familiar indeed, however. "Mr. Clement Gray!" boomed the purser's voice, and Cissy jumped with surprise. Suddenly, too, she realized where she'd seen Mr. Williams before — at the theatre, with Miss Minnie Gray on his arm. He was the serious-faced man who had escorted the actress into the champagne bar.

Mr. Williams, like Mr. Dexter, was directed to the promenade deck, and waited while the purser summoned a baggage boy for his trunk. By contrast, the robust Mr. Clement Gray had only one valise, which he opted to carry himself. Cissy, impelled by curiosity, pursued him with no hesitation at all — but not on the same level. Instead, she whisked up the rest of the stairs and walked along a short passage to a door that led to the open deck. Cissy might have been only two hours on board, but two hours had been plenty to learn the layout of the ship.

Sunshine sprang out at her as she opened the door to the deck. Outside, it was a beautiful day for going to sea. A brisk little breeze pulled at her hair, smelling wonderfully of blown salt and seaweed. Out on San Francisco Bay ferries and tugboats hooted at each other, puffing plumes of smoke in the crystal air, churning up the sun-sparked water. A great four-master bent poetically to the outgoing wind. The whole harbor was bustling — and things were busy on the *Royal George*, too.

People popped out onto the promenade deck, had a look around, and then returned to their unpacking. Some of them hailed Cissy in a friendly way, even though they were perfect strangers, obviously exhilarated by the occasion. Cissy could hear animated chatter filtering through many of the portholes she passed. She kept on walking forward, wondering which of the cabins belonged to Mr. Dexter, Mr. Gray and Mr. Williams. Then she stepped round the corner of a deckhouse and saw Mr. Timothy Dexter himself, standing on the deserted foredeck, not three paces away.

He was turned away from her, and had his palm cupped to his face as he lit a cigar. Cissy stepped silently back. Then she glimpsed Mr. Gray coming, so she slipped behind a lifeboat. Safely hidden, she squirmed along the bulwarks, her head ducked down to avoid the davits. Then she was able to see again.

The blond-headed Mr. Gray stopped short when he saw Mr. Dexter. "My God, you really are determined to come back," he said, his voice low and furious. "I thought when Jake threw you out for the last time, he had made it plain that you were never to show your face in the Thames again."

Mr. Dexter betrayed no surprise at all. Instead, he flicked his spent Lucifer over the rail into the sea, and drawled, "Well, well, so it's young Clem himself. It must be more than a year."

"Until we checked at the shipping office, I didn't believe Minnie when she said you were headed back to New Zealand. I didn't think that even a man like you would have had the nerve. Are you determined to make trouble?"

"Trouble? I don't know what the hell you mean."

"If you think we're going to tamely sit by while you contest Jake's will—"

"Jake's *will*?" The blank amazement in Mr. Dexter's voice was unmistakable. "The old man is *dead*?"

"Don't pretend to be surprised."

"But I am!"

"And you're delighted."

~ *41* ~

Mr. Dexter laughed. "The old man wasn't such a saint, Clem. Nonetheless, I am his only son and legal heir — though I presume from what you say that his will fails to recognize that."

"Heir?" echoed the other furiously. "Don't even start to suppose that you're going to benefit from Jake's death! Why do you think Will and I dropped everything to get on board this ship? If you have any idea of taking over the Golden Goose, Timothy, then I advise you to concede defeat right here and now. We'll both make sure you get away with nothing whatsoever, even if someone dies in the attempt. I'm serious!" he shouted, when Mr. Dexter laughed. "If you want to save yourself a lot of pain and agony, Timothy, you should pack up your duds and get off this ship!"

"You're threatening me?" Mr. Dexter's snort was as derisive as his laughter. "After all these years, Clem, you still don't know me very well. If I contest that will it's a certain bet I will win, for I have the only legitimate claim. I assume *Miss* Harriet Gray thinks she's inherited — but she'll have to think again about that. Or did Jake's harlot expire, as well?"

Clem Gray whitened, but did not answer. Instead, he slammed his fist into Timothy Dexter's face. Cissy heard the thump and saw little sparks as the cigar in his mouth was smashed to shreds. Mr. Dexter cursed thickly, blood running freely from his mouth and nose. His hands came up and Cissy gasped, thinking he was going for his gun, but instead he clenched them into fists, and lunged.

The much younger man ducked easily out of range and then danced forward again. Before he could hit Timothy Dexter again, however, another man came running along the deck, shouting, "For God's sake, Clem, stop!"

It was Mr. Williams, the man from the champagne bar. When Clem swung again he gripped him from behind. "For God's sake, Clem," he shouted again. "The cad might deserve it, but do you really want to go down for murder?"

6

The shouts had drawn attention, Cissy realized then. She could hear running footsteps, and people asking what was happening, so she ducked down and wriggled backwards out of her hiding place.

She was back in the open just in time, for Clem and Mr. Williams passed her, walking quickly aft. When she peered around the deckhouse she saw Mr. Dexter going off, too, in the opposite direction, a large handkerchief held to his face. A few spots of blood on the planks was all that was left to show that the confrontation had ever occurred.

Slowly, head down, feeling very pensive indeed, Cissy walked back to the stateroom she and her mother shared. Mr. Clem Gray had forgotten to ask a very important question, she thought. If Mr. Timothy Dexter hadn't known that Jake Dexter was dead, *why* was he going back to the Thames? It was a mystery that made her wonder even more about Minnie Gray's agitation, and the message she had written for *Miss* Harriet Gray — her aunt, the once-famous actress. Timothy Dexter had called her *Jake's harlot*, and his tone had been so vicious. Shivers ran down her spine.

Mrs. Miller was in the cabin, bobbing about in front of the dressing table, watching herself in the looking glass as she tied on a big Leghorn hat.

"So *there* you are," she said. "You're looking a little pale, dear. I hope you are not seasick already."

"Of course I'm not," said Cissy with some hauteur. She hadn't been sick at all on the trans-Atlantic crossing. "Mama, you would never believe who else is on this ship."

"You know I don't play guessing games, dear."

"It's Mr. Timothy Dexter."

"What! Surely not, or he would have said. You must be mistaken. He certainly gave *me* the impression that he wasn't in any hurry *at all*."

Cissy had had that impression, too. She said curiously, "What were you two talking about, when I was over at the piano, trying to decide what to sing?"

"I would have thought you would have decided what to sing *before* afternoon tea, dear. I wasn't going to mention it, but now that you've brought it up, I can't help but observe that you did keep the audience waiting rather a long time. Not that I minded, but it's not *professional* to be so unprepared."

"I was perfectly well prepared," Cissy said, with a great deal of irritation. "It was that stupid piano player, who could scarcely play a thing. Did it matter? You looked as if you were enjoying yourself."

"And so I was, dear. Mr. Dexter and I were having quite a little chat about Boston."

"*Boston?*" echoed Cissy. "But why? You've never even been there."

"No, of course I haven't," Mrs. Miller agreed placidly, "but Mr. Dexter was telling me a little more about his childhood in Massachusetts."

On this enigmatic note, she left, for the ship was about to sail, and she was determined to go on deck and view the departure. Then she was gone, and Cissy opened the valise that was set on her berth.

The newspaper that had held the piece that Minnie Gray had cut out lay uppermost, neatly folded into its original creases. It was three weeks old, a Boston daily. Cissy had read every column last night, including the death notices and advertisements, and read it again this morning, but had found nothing that seemed significant. There was no hint at all of the nature of the item Miss Minnie had cut out.

The letter lay at the bottom of the valise, under all the clothes. Cissy fished it out and turned it over, looking at the name and address again.

Miss Harriet Gray, Golden Goose Hotel, Thames, New Zealand.

So this was the same Miss Harriet Gray who had been left the hotel in Jake Dexter's will. Cissy remembered Timothy Dexter's jibe, just before Clem Gray had hit him.

"Harlot," he'd said.

Cissy swallowed. It was a horrible word. She knew what it meant, but wondered if it had been an insult, rather than a statement of truth. After all, when Timothy Dexter reckoned he was going to contest the will it had been a mere taunt, because he had only just learned that Jake Dexter was dead. But then, she thought, if Timothy Dexter was Jake Dexter's legitimate son, he would have a case. He'd said he had a *legal* claim, which implied, by logic, that Miss Harriet Gray did not. So perhaps Miss Harriet Gray had been the dead man's...

Mistress.

It was a much nicer word that *harlot*, but Cissy doubted that even a mistress could inherit her lover's property, and certainly not if that lover had a wife and son in Massachusetts. And even if that wife in Massachusetts was dead, her son had the best claim. If Timothy Dexter did contest the will, Miss Harriet Gray would need a lot of documentation to support her case — which meant that whatever Minnie Gray had put in the envelope could be crucial.

Cissy wondered what relation Miss Harriet Gray was to Miss Minnie — and to Clem Gray, who could be Minnie's brother, though he looked a good ten years younger. Both of them hated Timothy Dexter. Mr. Williams had asked Clem Gray if he wanted to be arrested for murder — and murder, most surely, had been in Mr. Gray's expression.

And, seemingly, there were other people in the Thames goldfields who felt that way. Clem Gray had darkly suggested that he would have plenty of help. But if they were all on the side of Miss Harriet Gray, and violently opposed to Timothy Dexter, why was it so important that the letter should be delivered to Harriet Gray and nobody else?

Cissy's fingers touched the seal of the envelope. It could so easily be pried loose and then closed again...

A shadow fell across her lap. Cissy nearly shrieked.

It came out as a gasp, instead. Mr. Williams was standing in the doorway.

He said, "Do please excuse me. When I knocked the door came open."

Her mother must have left it ajar, Cissy thought. She could also feel a slight swaying as the *Royal George* left her moorings, which would have helped the door to swing. However, she most surely had heard no knock. Cissy said nothing, staring at him rigidly.

He said, "I believe you are Miss Miller?"

He spoke kindly, as if to a small girl, which didn't reassure her in the slightest. Behind him, the passageway was deserted. Everyone was out on deck, she thought, watching the ship's departure. No one would hear if she screamed.

Somehow she summoned her dignity, saying, "I am she."

"I know we haven't been introduced, but I think you might remember me. My name is Williams. I'm Minnie Gray's brother."

"*Brother?*"

"Half-brother," he amended. "We had the same mother. Most people call me Will." He put out his hand as if to shake hers, and Cissy half-stood before remembering the letter, still safely unopened in her lap. She subsided, noting nervously that his stare had focused on the yellow envelope.

Mr. Williams said, "Ah."

"Yes?"

"That is what I am after, I think. My sister gave you an envelope to deliver to her family in the Thames."

Cissy wanted to deny it, but the address was uppermost and he was looking right at it. She said very carefully, "This is a letter that Miss Minnie Gray entrusted to me, yes."

And she was right to trust you, I'm certain. But when she gave it to you, she didn't know that I'd decided to head home. It was a spur of the moment decision. And so we don't need to trespass on your good nature any more. I can deliver the letter myself."

Cissy hesitated. Then she remembered Minnie Gray's explicit instructions and shook her head. "I'm afraid I can't give it to you."

He began to look exasperated. "But that's ridiculous."

"I'm sorry, but no."

He paused, frowning, obviously surprised by her determination, studying her and evidently revising his opinion, for he said then, slowly, "You're quite right, of course, not to believe what I say without some kind of reassurance. Perhaps if I told you a little more about me and my family, it would help. Harriet Gray is my mother-in-law. Her daughter, Jess, is my wife. So you have no reason at all not to trust me."

Cissy studied him. Then she said, "Can I ask a question?"

"Of course."

"Is *Jake* a short form of *Jahaziel*?"

Mr. Williams frowned. "Why do you ask?"

"Miss Minnie Gray dedicated her encore to a Captain Jahaziel Dexter. I gather that he died quite recently?"

Mr. Williams paused a long time, and then he said gravely, "Yes, my father-in-law was known familiarly as Jake. He died just four months ago, and the world is a poorer place without him. Despite what people say, he was a very fine man. Exceptional."

"Despite...?"

Will Williams sighed. Then he looked about, put his hand on the back of the little chair that was placed in front of the dressing table mirror, and said, "Do you mind?"

Cissy hesitated, torn between curiosity and doubt. Then she nodded, for the door, after all, was open, and he turned the chair round and sat down.

"Perhaps," he said, "I had better tell you how I first met Captain Jake Dexter. And how he became my foster father, first, and then my father-in-law. It's a story that goes all the way back to when I was just three years old."

In the month of May, 1851, Harriet and her brother, Royal Gray, were managing the theatre Captain Jake Dexter had built in Honolulu, while Jake carried freight and passengers from island to island in the northwest Pacific, with Oahu as his base. They had been there for over a year, were making good money, and seemed perfectly settled, but then fate intervened, in the form of the Australian goldrush.

Suddenly, Honolulu emptied out, as men rushed out of the port to take part in the new bonanza, and the theatre was playing to half-empty houses. It was time, Captain Jake reluctantly decided, to sell up and move on. So he sold the theatre, shipped a scratch crew for his brig *Gosling*, and took on a very profitable load of passengers for New South Wales. By the time the brig got to the southwest Pacific, however, events had moved so fast that even the port of destination had changed. Such huge deposits of the yellow stuff had been found in even more southern Victoria, that they steered for Port Melbourne, "the golden trap," which turned out to be a lasting nightmare.

When the brig dropped anchor at Sandridge Pier the colony of Victoria was in a frenzy, with more than three thousand people flooding in each week. The harbor was choked with deserted vessels, and one third of the houses in the settlement were empty, as everyone streamed inland to the diggings. Stores were closed, their entire stocks sold out, and bank vaults were emptied as if they'd been broomed. Men mortgaged themselves to buy passage to Geelong or Seymour, or made risky journeys on foot through the trackless bush. The scratch crew of the *Gosling* was no exception. Within two days the lot had jumped ship, and so Captain Jahaziel Dexter found himself stranded by the goldrush.

He was alone on the brig, except for Harriet and her brother, the actor Royal Gray, along with a most unusual cargo. Captain Jahaziel Dexter had no desire at all to fossick about in the dirt for a few problematical nuggets of gold. He had tried it in the past and it had brought nothing but disappointment and grief. So instead, he wanted to be more sure of a fortune, and so he was carrying the pre-cut frame and boarding to build another playhouse. But, before he could erect that theatre and get it going and start raking in the cash, he had to make the difficult decision of where to put it up. Inland, around Buninyong and Mount Alexander, men rushed from one strike to another. Whole towns built up in a day and then lay deserted a week later. It would have been crazy to invest in a place without making sure that it was reasonably permanent. While Harriet and her brother Royal stopped on board the brig as ship-keepers, Jake travelled about the diggings alone, spying out the territory, all the time trying to make up his mind which goldrush town might prove substantial. Ballarat seemed to hold the greatest promise, but he didn't know if he dared trust his own judgment and he worried constantly about how Harriet was copying back in Melbourne.

Countless miners were in a similar predicament. They had carried their families as far as the port, but hadn't bargained that the cost of getting inland to the diggings would be so extortionate. Puntmen were making ninety pounds a day ferrying folk across rivers, and wagon drivers charged eleven pounds a head to carry men to Buninyong, only about one hundred miles away. And so, like Harriet, the wives and children were left behind in the port until the menfolk had made enough money to come and fetch them — but most were not as fortunately placed as Jake's mistress, because most of those women existed in a town of tents that grew up alongside a dirt track called St Kilda road, a place that the miners called Little Adelaide.

Little Adelaide was unrelievedly wretched, made of calico and canvas, haunted with want and misery. Most of the inhabitants were penniless, many were sick, some were dying, all of them drenched with persistent spring rains. In Bendigo Jake Dexter saw men prying apart rocks to expose nuggets lying about in the dirt like grapes, while in Melbourne Harriet, going about with what food and wine she could spare, saw children starving to death. Lucky fortune-hunters were going mad in Ballarat, eating sandwiches made of five-pound notes set between slices of bread, tearing the buttons off their filthy shirts and sewing nuggets in their places, buying silks for harlots, tossing coins to dogs. Meanwhile, in Little Adelaide, their wives tried to sell Harriet pathetic household treasures that had been lugged all this way from God alone knew where, for money for food and medicine.

Many people died. As space ran out, corpses were interred standing up, or tied in a bundled sitting position. Whole families of women and children were wiped out, and strangers buried them, the emaciated corpses still clothed in the garments they had been wearing when they died.

In Little Adelaide, the great many depended on the charity of the few, and Harriet and her brother Royal were two of the very few. When Jake finally returned to the brig, weary and travel-worn and very much the poorer, the plot of land he'd finally bought in Ballarat having cost him five pounds *a square foot*, he found the brig not quite as empty as he'd left it. Two strangers had joined the company.

One was a petite, fragile woman named Constance Williams, whose husband had drowned while crossing a stream. When Harriet had found her she was wracked with fever, and looked set to follow her husband within hours. Harriet found her because a little chap with a freckled face and bewildered eyes, had led her to their tent. When Harriet first noticed him, he was carrying a pitcher that was half his own size, looking for water for his mother to drink. He'd led Harriet to where Constance shivered in the only blanket they still owned, lying on the damp, chill dirt.

And so, because of Will himself, Miss Harriet Gray had saved his mother's life. And, because of little Will, Minnie Gray and her brothers and sisters were born, for Harriet's brother Royal fell in love with Will's mother, Constance, and married her, giving Will a family and a future.

Cissy listened silently, feeling the steamship take on a rocking motion as Will Williams talked. By the time he had run to a conclusion she could hear people in the corridors, returning to their cabins now that the *Royal George* was headed for the Golden Gate and the open sea.

"So now can you understand why you can trust me with the letter?" he demanded. "I would never, ever, do anything that could bring harm to Harriet, or anyone she loved."

Cissy hesitated. She had been moved, but who wouldn't have been touched by such a sad and sentimental yarn?

She said, "Miss Minnie was absolutely insistent that I give the letter to Miss Harriet Gray and nobody else. I don't suppose you have a story to explain that, too?"

He shook his head, looking angry.

"Then I have to keep my promise."

He snapped, "But can you keep your promise if the letter is stolen?"

"*Stolen?*"

"There is a man on board this ship who would stop at nothing — *nothing!* — to get it."

And that man was Timothy Dexter, thought Cissy. She said calmly, "Then all I can suggest that you and I go to the purser's office, and ask him to lock it in his safe."

Mr. Williams stared at her, his eyes narrow and his anger hidden, and she noticed how he brushed his thick moustache with one finger as he thought.

Then he said slowly, "You are a very shrewd young woman, Miss Miller, and I see that I have gravely underestimated you. And it is an excellent solution. Please allow me to accompany you to the office, to give me the satisfaction of seeing Minnie's letter safely deposited."

7

"My daughter is musical, you know," confided Clara Miller to Miss Fleet. "A *real* musician, a star pupil," she elaborated, while Cissy squirmed internally. "And we made sure she had *excellent* teachers. We were hoping for a career, you see..."

Her voice trailed off as she blinked at her companion. Miss Fleet was the woman Cissy had watched embark three days ago, and had admired for the businesslike way she had dealt with the purser. Now, Miss Fleet was just as elegant, garbed in an elaborately trimmed purple day dress with a high boned neck and narrow sleeves, but her manner was a great deal less unbending.

"On the stage?" she prompted obligingly.

"Yes, as a concert pianist."

Cissy squeezed her eyes half-shut, lifting her book higher and pretending to read it, trying to close out her mother's voice.

She and her mother and Miss Fleet were sitting in three of the deck chairs that had been set out in a long row on the sunny side of the promenade deck. Most of the passengers had succumbed to seasickness the moment the *Royal George* had passed through the Golden Gate, and even now, the third day out, fewer than half the chairs were occupied. Miss Fleet and Mrs. Miller were two of the few with iron digestions, and because of this had set up quite a cozy little friendship.

"And she has such a lovely singing voice, though I say it myself," Cissy's mother sighed. "We really must persuade her to sing at the ship's concert, as I see that one is scheduled for next week. She gave a *lovely* little recital at the hotel tearoom in San Francisco, which was well received by quite a little crowd. Fortunately enough, she is not shy when she sings, for without a word of a lie she truly has the voice of an angel."

There was a masquerade ball scheduled as well, Cissy remembered. Quite soon. Tomorrow night, in fact. She thought about it, trying to distract her mind from this embarrassing series of family confidences. However, she heard Miss Fleet murmur, "But at the piano...?"

"The poor girl is *excessively* shy on the public platform, or so the pianist who examined her said. *Far* too shy for a career on the stage. Or so he determined. And her voice, though sweet, is not strong enough for an operatic career. Or so he decided. *Very* disappointing. I feared a nervous collapse. So, when I found that I had to travel to New York — on matters to do with my late husband and his affairs there, you understand — I determined to take her along, and when I approached the Thomas Cook people, they said, why not continue all the way around the world? A real bargain, they said, and it was surprisingly cheap, I thought. Six hundred and fifty dollars American from New York all the way westward around the globe to London, including the trans-continental railway fare and all necessary expenses ashore and aboard."

"It certainly does seem a bargain."

"There are extra costs, of course, quite *substantial* ones, for the basic fare allows for a tour of 110 days only, while we, of course, wish to make stops now and then, particularly in New Zealand. We had thought just Auckland, but now we are quite determined to devote at least a week to the goldfields of Thames."

"Thames?" the other echoed. She seemed quite bewildered. "Goldfields?"

"They're world-famous — or so Miss Minnie Gray informed me. Did I tell you that we met the famous actress? It was quite a coincidence that we did, for I wouldn't have even known she was playing in San Francisco when we were there, if it had not been for meeting a Mr. Dexter, who was staying at the same hotel. We also met him on the train. He's *related* to the famous star. She even gave us a letter to carry to her family in New Zealand — along with a cutting from a newspaper, which may seem strange, but is such a *compliment* that she should place such trust in two strangers. And — oh look, here comes yet another of her relatives, Mr. Will

Williams. They say he'd the greatest set designer in the world. He designs for Miss Minnie Gray exclusively, and is *particularly* lauded in London, where the critics were quite breathless about his sets for *The Belle of New York*."

Cissy looked up. Mr. Williams bowed gravely and lifted his hat, just as he had the two or three other times she had seen him, but did not stop to talk, even though her mother called out a hello.

He hadn't stopped to talk the other times, either. The envelope was safely stowed in the purser's office, and so, apparently, there was no need to converse any more. She had seen Mr. Clem Gray on her strolls about the ship, but hadn't said anything to him, either, for of course he did not know who she was. Mr. Timothy Dexter had not been out at all, whatever meals he had eaten having been taken to his room. The reason given out was that he was about the most seasick person on board the ship, but Cissy thought he was really lying low until his broken nose had healed.

"...and so, of course, we shall take great delight in signing up for one of the Golden Goose Murder Experiences," her mother meandered on. "But doesn't it seem strange that we should make the acquaintance of such a highly rated theatrical family, considering the *reason* we're making this tour?" — This with a significant glance in Cissy's direction. Mrs. Miller's voice lowered as she said, "Miss Minnie Gray was quite firmly of the opinion that my daughter will be world-famous one day..."

Cissy, unable to bear it any more, escaped by walking off along the promenade deck with her book in her hand. She had the kindest of mothers, she knew. During her childhood she had gone in for the usual feminine pursuits of embroidery and needlework, drawing and painting and playing the piano, along with all kinds of domestic work, but her mother was a liberated woman who had encouraged her to take up any kind of sport she wanted to, even if it involved wearing boy's clothes. Cissy had been allowed to swim, walk, bicycle, play golf and skate, tramp the moors and go boating. No expense had been begrudged in developing her musical talent. Clara Miller had been as devastated as her daughter when the examiner made his cruel decision. But, Cissy thought emphatically, at times Mama was a little too much.

Out of habit, her step slowed as she passed the window that she knew belonged to Timothy Dexter's cabin, but, as always, it was silent. There was nothing to show there was anyone in there.

Cissy walked a couple of steps further to the next exit, and went inside, stepping over the high door sill, and then proceeded down one flight of stairs to the reading salon. There was no one there except for the ship's librarian, a bald-headed man who took great pride in his little domain. The books sat neatly in their shelves with their spines towards her, and the netting that held them in place when the ship pitched was rolled up tidily and secured with strings, for the sea outside was very calm.

Cissy went into her favorite corner, where a slant of sunlight fell through a porthole onto the seat of a big wing chair, and absorbed herself in her mystery novel. So engaged in the plot was she, that she didn't notice for quite a while that someone else had come into the room. Then she roused with a jerk at the sound of a woman raising her voice.

The American voice was familiar. The woman was Miss Fleet. Miss Fleet snapped in reply to whatever the ship's librarian had said, "My good man, do you call me a liar?"

"Begging your pardon, ma'am," said the bald-headed man, not bothering to hide the fact that he resented being called *my good man*, "but I keep records, and I know they are good ones. I know who borrowed that newspaper, and I know it was you. Whatever happened afterwards is none of my business. All I know is that you did not return it. If you cannot produce the paper *or* the man you reckon stole it, then the responsibility is yours, and the fine will be added to your ship's account."

"Petty larceny!" the American woman snapped. "I've never heard of such an insult. I've told you what happened, but you prefer not to believe me. Please be assured that I will be carrying a complaint to the purser, and will inform the captain himself, *unless* an apology is offered before the day is out."

Tossing her head, she went off down the passage. Cissy, feeling much intrigued, watched her from behind her book. Miss Fleet lifted her skirts as she stepped, so that Cissy could see the ruffles of a multitude of petticoats. Then the American woman was gone. Cissy turned and eyed the reading room attendant hopefully.

The attendant was muttering crossly to himself as he checked off columns in the book where he recorded borrowings and returns, and Cissy thought for a while he'd forgotten that she was there. Then he said, "I don't care if she does go to the purser. I know my rights, and I know when I am right, as well. No haughty passenger is going to put me in my place, not with the records I keep. She borrowed it and she did not return it, and that is all that concerns me."

"The newspaper?" ventured Cissy.

"The newspaper, miss, the newspaper!"

"I didn't know you had newspapers."

"Of course we do, of course." And the attendant stood up and yanked open a wooden case. And there inside, sure enough, were newspapers, as neatly laid out as a plate of sandwiches, each with a large label pasted across the end. "See," he said. "We have papers from all over, London, Paris, New York, San Francisco of course, and none more than a month old on the day of sailing."

"And Boston?" Cissy was holding her breath.

"Boston's the very one that's gone missing!" He slapped his hand to his head in a renewed fit of temper. "She borrowed it, but did not return it. She swears she brought it back and a man took it off of her while I was out of here. Walked out without bothering to sign the book. But I will only start believing her when that so-called gentleman brings that Boston paper back. What's that, miss?"

However, the word Cissy had muttered under her breath was not ladylike at all, and she didn't care to repeat it. Instead, she asked the date of the missing paper, and knew, hollowly, which one it would be even before he said it.

Next morning, after a night that had been made restless with speculations, Cissy called at the reading salon early, and was pleased to find the ship's librarian alone. When she politely asked him if the Boston paper had turned up, he frowned and snapped, "No, it has not. The person who borrowed it has not returned it — and she hasn't complained about me, either."

This last was said with a righteous sniff, as if Miss Fleet's failure to complain was a confession of guilt.

Cissy said hopefully, "I don't suppose you read it? Before it was loaned out, I mean?"

"Read it?"echoed the librarian. He seemed extremely affronted at the very idea. "What a suggestion! I don't have time to read, miss. What would the passengers say if they saw me wasting my time in reading? I've got a library to run!"

Cissy sighed, and bought some stationery items from his little store. Then she went up to deck, her spirits so depressed that the luncheon bell seemed a more than usually cheerful interruption. When they were in the dining saloon, she said thoughtfully to her mother, "Mama, do you know where Miss Fleet belongs?"

"Belongs, dear?" said her mother vaguely. She was deeply immersed in the menu. Dining on the *Royal George* was not as flamboyantly grand as on the trans-Atlantic liner, where the first class passengers had been able to cast lines for live fish in large tanks on the awning deck, and then place an order with the chef, stipulating how they wanted their catch cooked. Nevertheless, the choice of dishes was imposing.

Cissy said patiently, "Where does she come from?"

"Who?"

"Oh, Mama, please do listen. I'm talking about Miss Fleet, your American friend with the beautiful clothes."

"They're not her own, you know."

"I beg your pardon?"

"He clothes, dear. I noticed it right from the first time I saw her. Her suits and gowns are of very good material, but the colors are dark, chosen by a much older person, and the styles are *quite* out of fashion. Those ostrich-feather boas are perfectly *outré*. And the bodices have been let out at the bust and taken in at the waist, you can tell by the seams. If you look, the next time you meet her — discreetly, of course — you will see what I mean. And her petticoats *rustle*, my dear. Petticoats haven't rustled for *years*. In my opinion," Clara Miller said wisely, "her clothes have been given to her. They are excellent quality, and must have been very expensive when new. But they have been definitely altered, though by a very good needle-woman. And I must admit that she wears them with *flair*, possibly much better than their original owner."

"Good heavens," said Cissy, amazed by this flood of deduction.

"She comes, I believe, from Boston. Definitely from somewhere in Massachusetts. From the hints she lets drop, her address is in one of the *rich districts*, and she is connected with a wealthy merchant family, but I suspect she is not of much substance herself. Perhaps she lived with some wealthy relative, as a kind of *companion*. It's quite common, you know. And there she is," said Mrs. Miller, without the slightest change in her tone.

When Cissy looked up, sure enough, Miss Fleet was walking towards them. The Bostonian woman exchanged a few amities with Mrs. Miller, who invited her to take a seat at their table, and all the while Cissy studied her garb with intrigued attention.

Miss Fleet's day dress was as splendid as usual. It was fashioned from a fine dark red wool, with a tight basque that dropped in points below the front of the cinched-in waist. Her draped overskirt was made of rich velvet in the same color, an elegant addition that was caught up with a silk ribbon bouillonnée on one side. Cissy thought she looked tremendously well, but, now that her mother had pointed it out, it was rather noticeable that the style was ten or even twenty years out of date.

Despite the small bustle that pushed out her skirt at the back, Miss Fleet sat beautifully, her mouth pursed primly in a little bow, her long graceful fingers holding a stemmed glass of iced water. While she was indubitably an old maid, Cissy thought, she was definitely a spinster with style. "And what a coincidence, dear Miss Fleet," Mrs. Miller exclaimed, interrupting her own flow of conversation, "for there he is — Mr. Dexter, over there, just coming in to the room."

Coincidence? Cissy blinked bemusedly, wondering what was coincidental about it, and Miss Fleet probably thought the same, because she looked puzzled as she turned to look at the man her mother was indicating. Then Cissy jerked back in shock, for Miss Fleet had knocked over her glass.

"Oh dear!" said Miss Fleet. Her lips were tight and white. The red velvet overskirt had suffered with the drenching, but not nearly as badly as Cissy's Gibson girl's outfit, which had absorbed just about all of the glassful.

"That's all right," said Cissy, who had perfect sympathy with anyone who had the bad luck to splash liquids around. She mopped absentmindedly with her napkin, much more interested in taking note of Mr. Dexter's appearance.

Timothy Dexter's nose still looked a little red and shapeless, and he had dark rings about his eyes, but no one would have noticed unless they were actually looking for the signs of battle. He was dressed in the same natty suit that he'd been wearing when they had met him the second time, in the hotel, and it was equally impossible to tell whether he was still carrying a gun.

What was interestingly obvious, though, was that he had a black crepe band about his upper left sleeve. Presumably it was to indicate that he was in mourning for Captain Jake Dexter, which seemed highly hypocritical, considering what Cissy had over-heard. He hadn't seen them yet, for he was engaged in conversation with the head waiter, probably because this was his first meal in the dining saloon, and he hadn't yet been allotted a table.

"What name did you say?" Miss Fleet inquired of Mrs. Miller. Her lips were still compressed and white, or so Cissy noticed.

"Dexter, Mr. Timothy Dexter," said Mrs. Miller gaily, not noticing a thing. "He's the man I was telling you about yesterday, the man who is connected to Miss Minnie Gray. Oh look, he's coming over."

Timothy Dexter, in fact, was following the head waiter, having been allocated a table beyond theirs. He bowed when Cissy's mother finally caught his attention, but didn't smile. Then, when he was introduced to Miss Fleet, his eyes narrowed, his face so expressionless that it looked like a rock. Like a poker player, thought Cissy, and glanced at Miss Fleet's equally stony expression. *They know each other*, she thought, *but Miss Fleet didn't recognize his name.*

Mrs. Miller, still oblivious, said teasingly, "But I thought your preference was for a sailing ship..."

He shrugged, as brusque as he had been when Cissy splashed his wine in the railway coach, his eyes glinting with what looked a lot like dislike. "A matter of some urgency came up, Mrs. Miller," he said shortly. With an abrupt nod, he passed on by, while Cissy watched him very thoughtfully indeed. Then she heard Miss Fleet say to her mother, "What did you mean?"

"I beg your pardon?"

"You mentioned a coincidence."

Mrs. Miller waved her hand and said lightly, "You and Mr. Dexter are both from Massachusetts, that's all."

"But I thought you said he's from New Zealand."

"Well, so I did." Mrs. Miller laughed, but the sound was nervous. "Boston sounds a fine place," she said, adroitly changing the subject. "There's some very rich folk to be found in Massachusetts, or so they tell me. Merchants, ship-owners..."

Miss Fleet paused. Then she said neutrally, "There are some very rich people in Boston, certainly, but isn't that general all over the world?"

Cissy stopped listening. Unable to stop the question, she said, "Miss Fleet, that newspaper you borrowed..."

Miss Fleet's eyebrows arched. Her expression had become glacial.

"What newspaper?"

Cissy swallowed. Suddenly, Miss Fleet looked more like a stern schoolmistress than an elegant woman of the world. Her voice was subdued as she said, "The Boston newspaper. I wondered if you had read it, before..."

"No," said Miss Fleet, through thin lips. "I did not."

8

The atmosphere on the *Royal George* was unusually animated that afternoon, because of the masquerade party that night. It was the first grand occasion of what the passengers called "the passage" and what the crew of the ship insisted on calling "the cruise." For many it was a celebration of getting over seasickness, while everyone joined in the spirit of the fun. Most people, unlike Cissy, had come unprepared for fantasy dress, so the animated hours were passed thinking up ideas and making up costumes. By the time darkness neared the general noise was very vivacious indeed, as people buzzed in and out of friends' cabins, shrieking with laughter or exclaiming in admiration, toasting each others' efforts in champagne.

After some dithering, Mrs. Miller decided that this was an appropriate occasion to abandon mourning and go into something frivolous, so she took one of her prettiest muslin dresses, gathered the skirt into flounces, tied her floppy straw Leghorn hat over her curls with a veil, and went off happily as a milkmaid. When she had gone Cissy fetched out the Harlequin costume, shed her clothes and put it on. When she sat down on the stool before the mirror, she saw the ghostlike reflection of a stranger, a fantastical figure from a stained glass pane.

The cabin was dim, for she'd not switched on the lights. The last of the golden sun fell in the open porthole, setting the motley colors dancing. Cissy, who usually felt rueful about having to pad out her bodices so that her blouses were filled according to fashion, for once was glad that her figure was so slim, for the brilliant silk skimmed closely, yet flowed with eye-deceiving suppleness. It was impossible to believe that plump little Minnie Gray had ever worn this costume ... which, somehow, made the loan seem still more ominous. Gazing uneasily at her reflection,

Cissy braided her waist-long hair into a single plait, which she wound about her head. When she pulled on the floppy cap, she thought she looked more sexless than ever. The black velvet eye-mask hid her identity, though, which gave her the courage to leave the cabin.

The ship's personnel had been busy, for the salons and saloons had been transformed with plants and flowers and decorations into a series of bowers. An orchestra scraped merrily in one corner of the biggest salon, and carpets were rolled back for dancing. Cissy wandered from room to room, feeling disconcertingly naked without her skirt and petticoats. A milkmaid fluttered by, crying, "Darling, you look *beautiful*, but be sure not to stop up past midnight!" Cissy, hovering uneasily about a potted palm, felt unsure that she was going to stop up another hour, even. Then she jumped as someone coughed politely behind her.

When she turned she saw a waiter with his tray. "A drink, sir?" he said. "Champagne, perhaps?"

Sir? Instead of being insulted, Cissy felt her awkwardness drop away. The Harlequin costume all at once felt marvelously comfortable and carefree. "Wine?" she said, throwing caution to the winds. "A glass of chardonnay would be most acceptable."

The chardonnay, when it came, proved rather too dry for her unaccustomed palate, so after drinking it down quickly she didn't order another. The wine wasn't necessary. Cissy found herself either the belle or the beau of the ball, for she was in great demand as a partner, by both girls and boys.

There were all kinds of young people. There were two American sisters called Patience and Harmony, who were quite mature, about twenty-one o twenty-two, but who refused to act their age. Dressed as Gypsies in flowing scarves and boots, they linked arms with Cissy and sang their way through the saloons. And no one recognized Cissy. The mask and the free boyish way she moved in the silken costume seemed to protect her identity — though she thought often about what Minnie Gray had said, Harlequin was the catalyst, who changed things without becoming altered himself, who could be hero or conniver, shrewd manipulator or acute observer — just about any role he decided to adopt. Here at this ball in the middle of the sea, Harlequin was the perfect partner. Or so she romantically decided. The presence of Harlequin made pretence seem real, and gave normal folk the license to lose themselves in a fairytale, even if just for a few hours. Harlequin, who had been instructed to disappear at the stroke of midnight like Cinderella's coach, made even the most farfetched seem reasonable.

And so, at midnight, Cissy ran out alone onto the promenade deck, to take the air and look at the stars before obediently heading off to bed. Her black velvet slippers were silent on the deck planks, and the moonlight bleached the colors of her costume, turning them to white and grey, so that instead of powerful Harlequin, she looked like clownish Pierrot. Cissy found a bench in the shadows, where she dreamily curled up.

It was odd, she thought, that much of the time only the swaying of the planks under her feet and a sense of being apart from the rest of the world told her that she was at sea, but now, alone on the shadowed decks, her ears were full of the steady swish of the waves. Then, like a little shock to bring her back to reality, she heard a familiar voice.

It was Mr. Williams. His voice came from the window behind her — the window to Mr. Dexter's cabin. He said, "Don't — please do *not* come to the Thames."

"And why not?" Mr. Dexter's voice was derisive, taunting.

"You'll only make trouble — upset people. There could be a confrontation that none of us want and that you won't expect — and for so little gain."

"Little gain?" Timothy Dexter laughed, an unpleasant sound in the dark. "The Golden Goose is worth a small fortune."

"Only as a going concern — and it certainly won't be going if you take it over."

"Are you threatening me?"

"Believe me, we certainly won't burn it down! But the day you take over the hotel, the Grays will all move out, and you know that as well as I do. It's the Murder Experience that makes the Golden Goose a tourist attraction, and without the Grays to orchestrate the melodrama, there can be no Murder Experience."

Silence. Cissy heard the scrape of a Lucifer as Mr. Dexter lit a cigar, and could easily picture his contemptuous expression. Then Mr. Williams said, "The vineyard, on the other hand, will turn a profit even if *you* own it. I'm willing to sell it to you — for half a crown, or some other kind of peppercorn sum. On the condition, of course, that you don't come to the Golden Goose, and that you don't try to contest Jake's will."

Timothy's voice became even more scathing. "You're trying to buy me off with a worthless vineyard? For God's sake, Will, you know me well enough not to take me for a fool."

"I know, oh yes indeed, how I know you," Will Williams said bitterly — but then Cissy lost attention, for she had suddenly become aware that someone else was eavesdropping. A woman. She could smell perfume, and had heard the faintest swish of skirts. There was a shadow by the corner of the deckhouse that hadn't been there before.

Cissy held her breath, utterly unmoving, straining her eyes to decipher the shape. But even if she glimpsed the listener's face, she suddenly realized, it would not be much use. Most of the passengers were wearing masks for the ball.

Then Mr. Williams spoke again, muttering, "I should have thought that a man who prized himself as a great connoisseur would have seen the profit."

"Profit? In a few acres of Albany Surprise? There is a great deal more at stake than that!"

"You have no reason to hate us — me —so much."

"Hate?"Timothy Dexter echoed. "My God, Will," he said, his tone so tormented that shivers ran up Cissy's neck. "I have more reason to hate you, Will, than anyone else in the world."

Why? She thought. *Why? What had Mr. Williams done that merited such bitterness?*

But there were no more words, just a faint rustle from the other listener. When a door opened nearby, her pulse jerked with fright. Then she saw a man's shadow step over the high sill. Mr. Williams. He had left Mr. Dexter's cabin very quietly, she thought, and watched his shape disappear along the deck forward. So he had merely shrugged — because that last accusation had defeated him? His shape certainly looked defeated as he disappeared around a corner, head down and feet tired. But Cissy didn't move. Aware of the other listener, she didn't dare.

Tense moments passed. The sea hissed and swished, and she could feel the slow thud of the ship's engines in her bones. The woman was so still that Cissy wondered if she was gone too, in the interval between one swishing wave and the next. Then, just as Cissy was about to shake herself out of her trance and take herself off to bed, the other woman moved.

She moved with quick stealth, rustling very quietly as she passed to the door. Something white fell out of her skirts as she moved, dropping to the planks without a sound. Cissy, trying to make herself smaller, sensed the woman look around. If that woman moved and looked sideways she couldn't fail to see her crouched up on her bench...

Instead, the door handle clunked down, the door swung open, and the skirted shadow passed over the threshold. Cissy heard the tap on Timothy Dexter's door.

It opened. His voice rasped, "You! What the hell are you doing *here?*"

"Ah, but why be *there*, when I can enjoy your company *here*," she murmured, and softly laughed. "After all, when we are married..."

"Was it *you* who broke that goddamned story?"

The woman laughed again, this time more loudly. "The editor liked it, I can tell you that. Lots of human interest there — and at a slow time of the year, too."

"And why the *hell* have you taken passage on this ship — to *the Thames*, for God's sake?"

A faint rustle, as if the woman had shrugged. "I was as surprised to see you as you were to see me. Perhaps I was planning to greet you ... with a present."

"You don't know what you're doing," he exclaimed, his voice tense and furious. "Keep out of this, for both our sakes."

"I know exactly what I am doing, my dear..."

More rustling, louder and more emphatic, as if clothes were being shed. Timothy started to say something, but his voice was abruptly muffled, as if someone had closed his mouth.

Cissy waited tensely, but instead of words she heard enigmatic sounds from the other side of the window, the sliding of cloth and harsh breathing, a loud gasp and then another, a sucking, pressing sound, a creaking of furniture that was much more emphatic than the regular creaking of the ship on the sea.

Cissy had heard plenty of schoolgirl whispers, but it took several puzzled moments before it crossed her mind what was going on. Then she leapt out of her seat and ran off as if stung, dipping briefly to snatch up the fragment of material the woman had dropped, stumbling at first because her limbs were cramped, but then running freely.

She arrived in the empty cabin in a rush and sat with a thump on the dressing table chair, staring into the looking glass while her breathing settled down. The reflection was as flushed as she felt, but was still the image of a stranger. Harlequin, she thought, her pulse still thumping. The observer. The listener. Then she looked down at the piece of fabric in her hand.

A perfumed handkerchief, beautifully trimmed with lace, a very expensive and fine piece of cambric. There was an initial embroidered in one corner.

It was the letter "H". A clue, Cissy thought, with a feeling of unreality. The woman ... who was doing ... *that* with Timothy Dexter had a Christian name starting with H. Harriet started with H, and so did Harmony. And so did a lot of other names. And it seemed that this woman was a journalist, which was definitely unusual, though Cissy had thought her accent was American, and in America women had more freedom to take up eccentric careers. Or that was what she had heard...

But what other clues did she have?

Minnie Gray had insisted that she should study human nature. And, Cissy realized that, through observation, she already knew Timothy Dexter quite well. He had revealed himself as a man who was a connoisseur, but nonetheless greedy. Not a gourmet, but a grasper.

He had also shown himself as a devious man. If her mother had relied on him for tickets to Minnie Gray's show they would have missed out, and would have had no chance to meet the star. So had he deliberately misled them? Cissy thought so. Her mother had meditated aloud about the chance of meeting Miss Gray backstage, and he had been determined to foil her.

And tonight he had revealed himself as a man who was wildly jealous of Will Williams. Why? Though they looked the same age, the two men were so different, one urbane and good-looking, the other plain and stalwart, so it seemed impossible, but yet it was the case.

And there was the mysterious item in a Boston newspaper — and a family feud, with the age-old motive of inheritance to fuel the fires of hatred. Men who were prepared to fight and bribe to prevent Timothy Dexter from getting what he wanted.

It was simple, on the surface. Timothy Dexter simply wanted to make sure he wasn't going to miss out on his rightful inheritance. Which was normal, if rather nasty. But then, there was the strange fact that Timothy Dexter's motive in heading for the Thames could not have been to contest Captain Jake Dexter's will, because when he boarded this ship he hadn't known that Jake Dexter was dead.

And, even more oddly, there was a paramour on board who had expected to get to his destination before him. An American paramour whose initial was H. And who had hinted that she would be waiting with a present. A gift? Of what?

Cissy's thoughts stopped there for the moment. She felt rather pleased with herself, though so much that was mysterious was unsolved. She particularly liked the word "paramour," and imagined that the woman writer must be very resourceful and devious indeed.

So, who was she? Cissy frowned, because something was nudging at her mind, as if the answer should be obvious...

The door opened. Clara Miller came in. "Oh, *there* you are, darling," she said. "Did you have a good time?"

"Wonderful," said Cissy. Then she said, "Mama, do you know Miss Fleet's Christian name?"

"*What*? What strange questions you ask, my dear. Why do you want to know?"

"So you don't know her name?"

"Of course I do. Elspeth Grace Fleet."

Elspeth, thought Cissy. So that was that. It had been a ridiculous idea, anyway, because it was impossible to picture the reserved and elegant Miss Fleet as anybody's paramour.

She took off her Harlequin mask, turning her mind to other matters. In the next few days, she resolved, she must settle down with pen and paper. She had a letter to write before they made the port of Auckland, and an envelope to buy, of a particular size and color, before she reclaimed the envelope that Miss Minnie Gray had entrusted to her.

9

The *Royal George* took on the Auckland pilot at dawn, at the beginning of the most picturesque day Cissy could ever have imagined.

It was June and, incredibly enough, mid-winter, but the sun was bright and quite warm. Light glinted along the slow heave of the sea as the steamer forged steadily along the green and granite coast of New Zealand. Waves dashed among the rocks on the beaches, making a noble froth and setting up a dance of little rainbows, throwing up sprays of seabirds that cried out a raucous challenge as they circled the tall funnels of the steamer. The entrance to the port was hidden until they were nearly there, with a curtain of hills and mountains that marched boldly down to the sea. Then the ship rounded a wide outcrop of land, which Cissy's map called North Head, and the Waitemata Harbour burst into view.

The harbor was set in a great circle of peaks and rolling downs, the iridescent shine of the water reflecting little islands. Far ahead, on the far side of this most lovely haven, a pretty little city sprawled over and about the slopes and gullies of the fringing hills. Distant towers and spires rose into the glistening air, and factory chimneys plumed tall with prosperous smoke.

There was every evidence of prosperity on the water, too. The *Royal George*, engines throttled back to a muted throb, threaded slowly through the bustling anchorage towards the city docks. Large sailing ships lay all around, many of them three- or four-masters with canvas loose and drying on their yards. Cissy poetically imagined the exotic cargoes these modern day galleons carried to this distant market — pepper from Batavia, machinery from Calcutta, rubber from Singapore, lacquer screens from Japan. Smaller but even more romantic brigs, ketches and schooners lay at anchor too, discharging their cargoes as busily as their larger sisters. Island traders, Cissy guessed, loaded with sugarcane, coffee and tropical fruits. Little steamers plied back and forth between this side of the harbor and the southern one where the city lay, their funnels bright red, puffing out gusts of grey smoke.

She was so immersed in this lovely scene that when a deep male voice sounded out heartily from behind them, bidding them good morning, Cissy jumped a foot in fright.

"So there you are, Mr. Williams," said her mother, not surprised at all. "And pleased to get home to New Zealand, I'm sure — and on *such* a lovely day."

Will Williams nodded and smiled, definitely looking gratified to be back in his homeland. He was much less formal that Cissy had ever seen him before, in a Norfolk jacket with breeches and gaiters and a deer-stalker hat. The country attire suited his stalwart figure, she thought, without taking away the dignity of his bushy moustache.

Clara Miller chattered vivaciously, also quite enlivened at the prospect of leaving the ship, and Cissy was more than content to let her mother run on. She thought she knew why Will Williams had accosted them, and waited for him to enquire about the letter. It was now back in her possession, for she had called at the purser's office the moment it was open, before Mr. Williams could get there first or forestall her in some way. She was still determined to follow Minnie Gray's explicit instructions, and deliver her message to no one other than Miss Harriet Gray. Oddly, however, Will Williams seemed to have forgotten about it, for he began to point out the most outstanding features of the view. Cissy, feeling curious, secretly studied his plain face and sturdy form. All the times she had seen him about the ship, he had been formal, grave and withdrawn, politely acknowledging her existence if he saw her, but with no attempt whatsoever to engage her in conversation.

This genial, smiling man seemed a different person, as if he was so pleased to be back home that he'd forgotten everything else in his delight. As the *Royal George* eased through a positive regatta of small boats towards her mooring, he proudly pointed out streets, fine churches, and impressive buildings. The *Royal George* finally thumped to a stop, with a loud clatter of reversing engines. The broad dock lay beneath the rail, packed with bags and bales, a great roofed shed at the end, men loading a scow on the other side. As the turbine engines quietened to a background hum, Cissy abruptly became aware that the air was full of activity.

Horses clopped back and forth and men sang out, while drays and handcarts rumbled over great squared timbers. The city side of the dock area was packed with people, and Cissy could hear shouts and whistles. Beyond the crowd, traps and carriages rattled back and forth, setting up echoes among squat brick and stone buildings that proclaimed odd things in signs that were blazoned on their roofs and high walls — ICY-COL, WESTFIELD CHEMIST'S, FAMILY GROCER and ROLLER FLOUR STORES. Electric tramcars rattled and clanged their way — up Queen Street, Mr. Williams said, along pairs of tracks that ran up and down, winding about a corner to disappear in a conglomeration of walls, buildings, spires, towers, chimneys, roofs where tiles and slates and rust-red tin vied with grandly greened copper. The arms of a windmill clacked on a rise — Partington's Mill, said Mr. Williams.

The decks of the *Royal George* were emptying fast. The gangway was run out immediately below Cissy's vantage point, and people were disembarking already. One of them was a trim gent in an Ulster and shiny top hat. She recognized Timothy Dexter and cast a quick glance at Will Williams to see if he had seen him too, and had been reminded about the letter.

It was impossible to tell. Will Williams' countenance remained genial. Timothy Dexter had often been seen about the ship after the night of the masquerade ball, but he was brusque and unfriendly to everybody. No one, Cissy noticed, was saying goodbye to *him*.

Then Cissy heard her mother say brightly, "Mr. Williams has very kindly offered to escort us to the Thames goldfields, Cissy. So instead of looking for a hotel in Auckland, we're going there with him today."

"Today?" Cissy echoed in surprise. While she had no objecttion, it seemed such a sudden idea.

"Mr. Williams has a very good reason for wanting to get there *post-haste*, my dear," Clara Miller said archly. "He tells me he hasn't seen his good wife for two months. And it's *so* much better than trying to find our own way."

"Very true, mama," Cissy agreed, a little ironically. Being apart from his wife for so long made Mr. Williams' hurry perfectly understandable, but it was also obvious that Mr. Williams had been to the purser and had learned that she's uplifted the envelope.

And, because of that, he was determined not to let her out of his sight until that letter had left her possession.

They arrived by sea, as the trip across the Hauraki Gulf on the Northern Steamship Company's crack paddle-steamer, *Wakatere*, was by far the fastest way to get from Auckland to the Thames. The *Wakatere* was billed as the Queen of the Hauraki Gulf, and though Will guessed she appeared rather startlingly small to his guests after the luxurious *Royal George*, she was still a fine-looking vessel, a side-wheeler with a promenade deck running from stem to stern, and a large single funnel forward of the paddle-boxes. There were no complaints to be made, either, about the passage. The sea was smooth, the views were marvelous, and the trip took only four hours, so that the sun was still above the horizon when they arrived.

The scene was breathtaking. Will's fingers itched for a paint-brush and canvas. Flat sheets of light lay on the calm expanse of the firth, in all the muted colors of mother-of-pearl. The pewter-colored sea was ruffled only by their wake and the scudding marks made by seabirds as they dipped and soared over the surface of the water.

Every time Will arrived home like this, he couldn't help but compare each arrival with all the others, and now he thought that Mrs. Miller and her daughter were extremely fortunate, for this was the prettiest arrival he remembered. Out of how many? My God, he thought with a kind of wonder, what a wildly mixed bag of memories he had of this place.

The first arrival was the most memorable. When the Thames goldfield had been declared open, at the beginning of August in 1867, Will had not taken much notice. After all, he was only nineteen, and still busy finding his way in the world. Even when the brig *Gosling* had called at Auckland briefly, and Will had arrived home from work to find Jake at home, with the news that he'd sold the theatre in Ballarat and intended to build another, Will had not listened properly. Jake had then amazed them all even further, by announcing that he was off to the new goldfield to size up the prospects there, but still Will had not paid attention. There had been far too much else on his mind, at the time. Within a few hours the brig had sailed for the Firth of Thames, but Will took no notice of that, either.

Then, halfway through the month, Will received a summons from Jake to pack up his tools and come to the new town that had sprung up, called Shortland, to assist with erecting the pre-cut building that Jake was unloading from the brig. Obedient as always, Will took leave from work, picked up his kit and complied, though still preoccupied in mind. Down on the Auckland wharf, however, he had been jolted out of his inattention, as he had discovered a teeming mass of men fighting and jostling to get passage on the steamboat to the diggings. Never for one moment had he expected to be embroiled in such a scene of hysteria. Judging by the wild commotion, men had responded to the new call of gold by the many thousands. Over-excited settlers' sons elbowed gaunt-faced men who had been victims of the depression in Auckland. Hard-bitten veterans of the Californian and Australian rushes were there as well, along with weather-beaten New Zealand miners come north from Otago and Westland.

These seasoned miners were instantly recognizable. One and all, whatever their origin, those men who'd journeyed from other diggings wore woolen shirts as chequered as their general reputation, and buckskin trousers tied with cords below the knee. The Blucher boots on their feet were battered with hard use, and the swags on their backs were stained and scarred with years of wear and weather. If there was one thing that this seasoned lot had learned from their past experience, it was that those who were first on the diggings were the ones who profited the most, for Will observed that they fought with grim passion for places on the boats, while the greenhorns stood about and gawped.

My God, Will had thought, it was California and Colorado all over again, all Captain Jake's colorful recountings personified — Bathurst and Ballarat reincarnated. Even the wild stories that had raced about the crowd were the same as the ones that had been told on those far-off fields. At Kuranui Creek in the Thames goldfields Clarkson had struck his gold as he idly swung a pick while crossing the top of a waterfall — or so they said — and there were stories, too, about rocks that were casually picked up by men who were gathering stones to make a bed for a camp-fire, and which on closer inspection had made those men a tidy sum. Some unnamed fellow who'd dug a posthole for a clothesline had struck a pretty vein of gold, and other anonymous folks had made a nice little pile by going over the stones of a public road. Even the gold-hunting slang was the same, directly descended from the Spanish borrowings of the forty-niners.

Luckily, considering the crowded state of the boat, back then, the passage to Shortland was just a few hours long, certainly not long enough for high spirits to be diminished, but long enough for Will to learn that the men in the Thames goldrush sang the same songs as the forty-niners, too, adapted only slightly for the great occasion —

> *Oh, Shortland be a damn fine town*
> *A very famous city*
> *Where all the streets be paved with gold*
> *And all the prospects pretty!*

For a long time, back then in August 1867, all Will had seen of their destination was a prominent range of hills running due north and south, with what appeared to be a swamp at their foot. Then, quite suddenly, they had arrived — or so Will, crammed at the back of the crowd on the deck, had deduced, for everyone had rushed to one side, and the little steamer heeled over with a wild clattering from paddles that were abruptly exposed to the air. Frightened cries and curses had risen up from those who were pressed to the downward rail. It was not until after the master of the ship hassled them back with a lot of panic-stricken hollering, that Will had his first glimpse of the future town of Thames.

That first look had been a huge disappointment — or so Will remembered. He had expect the firth to be as mighty as a cataract, certainly not a pond. But a wide flat pond was what he had found, a shallow sea. The wharf was nothing more than a long rickety plank stretched out across the mud, while scows and schooners jostled for anchorage out in the stream. The brig *Gosling* was much further out, anchored in deep water, and no boat was available, so Will stopped on board the *Enterprise* until a message could be sent. Meantime, he'd leaned on a rail, just as he did on this day so many years later, gazing at a township that was characterized then by mud and frenetic activity.

On shore men were surveying streets that were already lined with huts that were thatched with raupo reeds, sheds roofed with tin that apparently turned rust-red on the instant, and innumerable and varied tents. Canvas and calico shelters stood everywhere, crouched helter-skelter in the big spaces between the broad avenues that the planners were marking with sticks and string. Then he was jolted out of his reverie by the captain of the steamer, who had to get away again, and was ordering loiterers to shake themselves up into going ashore. And so Will had heaved his toolkit up onto his shoulder, and headed along the rickety plank, though there had been no message from the *Gosling*.

Being on shore had not been much improvement to being on board. As Will remembered now, darkness had begun to fall, and lamps popped into brilliance in the tents all around, rendering canvas and calico transparent. Inside them, distinct shadows of men moved about, picking up and putting down, laying out bed-rolls, hunching down at their books and their suppers. Up on the hills above the town more and more tents became apparent, dotting black slopes with little bells of light. The men inside were so patently unaware that the whole world outside could see what they were doing that the effect was oddly lonely. Will had started to feel like a disembodied spirit, wandering about. It had been a mighty relief to see Jake Dexter striding up to him, carrying a lantern.

"Come and see the lot I've bought," Jake had said, without bothering with preliminaries. "Best site in town, and I got it for six shillings a foot — six bob, think of that. Jehovah, when I think of what I paid for the land in Ballarat, all those years ago! There won't be many more bargains like that. This time next year it'll be worth eight pounds a foot, minimum. Come along — it's a bit of a walk, but worth it."

And then he'd turned, without waiting for Will to speak — which had been lucky, Will remembered, for hadn't yet formed the difficult words in his head. He hadn't worked out how to tell Jake the heartbreaking news.

Instead, when they arrived at a corner in a long, broad street made of strings, Will had stood silent beside his foster father, contemplating the section of land in the shadows. It was amazing what Jake, in his enthusiasm, had accomplished already. The framing for all four walls was up, like a skeleton in the shadows, and boards were stacked neatly all around.

"You've come just in time," Jake observed. "My crew hung around to help me with this, but today they took off for the hills."

"But you think Shortland Town will do?"

"It'll do, it surely will," Jake assured him. Will remembered how his foster father's face had creased up as he tipped back his old leather hat and looked all about, measuring what he saw.

"It's different from the other goldfields, though," he said, in his Yankee drawl. "Like my crew, the men who've headed for the hills have made a big mistake. It's quartz, not float gold, so the poor fools who think they can stake a claim by a creek and wash out a fortune with a pan and a cradle will be out of here by fall. But there'll be law and order here, for there is an excellent government agent in charge. No one can stake a claim without buying a miner's right. And the fact that quartz-mining is an expensive business has advantages, for there will be companies formed to find the finance and manage the mines. They'll employ men and pay regular wages. The gold is most surely there, but it's down in the bed-rock, right under our feet, and it will need gangs to dig it up. All that is needed is the machinery — stamping mills to crush that quartz so the gold can be extracted."

And Jake had been right. The old-time prospectors with their gold-washing pans and cradles had gone, but the machinery had most certainly arrived. Within five years mining companies with exotic names like "Black Angel," "Sons of Freedom," and "All Nations" were turning the bedrock beneath the town into a tunneled warren, and men like Jake were making good money out of the mines by buying scrip in whichever companies took their fancy. And men who did not make fortunes did make a living out of the town, by getting regular wages, for the amazing, world-famed place that Will contemplated in this year of 1905 had arisen.

This place was Grahamstown, the mining and processing part of the Thames. Today, Will leaned on the rail of the *Wakatere* as the paddle-steamer swished towards the long passenger wharf, and listened to the astonished comments of the tourists. Grahamstown stretched out before them, an extraordinary conglomeration of stores and machine-shops and roistering taverns, industries, businesses, miners' dwellings and mine head-frames, a bewildering maze of poppet heads and stamper batteries and tramways and huge heaps of tailings which were shoved by their own sheer weight hundreds of yards out to sea. The mining and grinding of the quartz had given Grahamstown its birth, and also its world-famous School of Mines. Here, in Grahamstown, mining and grinding the quartz was the prime occupation. It kept the Thames alive, and it employed a lot of machinery. And, because of all the machinery, it produced a horrible din.

As the paddle-steamer brought its load of tourists to the wharf, everything — absolutely everything — was dominated by the ear-battering thump of the stamper batteries. The stamps of Grahamstown gave out a commotion that rolled out across the water and echoed back and forth in the hills. It was a thump and a crashing that went on and on and on without cease, hammering the air without mercy, a mechanical thunder that was made by more than one hundred stampers, each of them weighing more than half a ton, crashing down in staggered series, crushing the quartz so that the gold could be extracted from the dust.

Will could see his guests wincing. "But how can people *sleep* through that noise?" Mrs. Miller plaintively asked.

Will smiled and brushed his moustache, wondering how she would have reacted in the great bonanza years of the seventies and eighties, when more than *six* hundred stamps had been in constant operation.

"One gets accustomed to it," he said. "It's like the sound of the engines on the *Royal George*. At first you wonder if you will ever get used to it, but then after a few nights you would wake with a terrible sense that something had gone wrong if the engines ever stopped. That is exactly what happens here. The stamping mills are turned off for the twenty-four hours of the Sabbath. That's the time when the tourists get a bit of rest. But the locals complain that they wake up at precisely midnight on Saturday, and can't get back to sleep after that."

"And today is Friday," sighed Mrs. Miller. "We have more than *twenty-four hours* of that noise to bear."

Again, Will smiled. *That noise* was the sound of prosperity, a guarantee that hundreds of men would still have jobs next pay day, and that money still flowed in and out of the Thames. "*Oh, Shortland be a damn fine town*," the first miners had sung, and all the prospects had been pretty, and *that noise* was proof that the song had proved right, in the end. Many mines had failed as tunnels met the insurmountable obstacle of inward flowing water, and it had looked for a little while as if those prospects might fail. The previous season of 1904 had been very dull, but a sudden bonanza at an old mine called Waiotahi had livened up the famous city once more. All the prospects were pretty again — and all because of the stamping batteries.

It was rather odd, Will mused that the *famous city* had proved to be Grahamstown, not Shortland. It was little wonder that the two settlements had merged, to become the double town of Thames. In Shortland, a mile or so along the waterfront, fishing smacks were moored at the wharf. In Shortland, there was a bracing smell of seaweed, fish and salty mud. The wide straight avenues that Will had watched the surveyors lay out in 1867 were graced with fine trees. Shortland was more like a regular town, with grand shops and demure houses. In Shortland, serenity reigned, despite intrusive echoes from her noisy sister in the immediate north. It was Shortland that was the tourist destination, while Grahamstown was the workmen's place.

Even in the dark, the difference was remarkable. Just as on the first afternoon that Will had seen the embryonic goldrush town of Thames, night was beginning to fall, and in Grahamstown brilliant lights were popping on everywhere, for Grahamstown worked both day and night — except, of course, for the Sabbath. There were lights all along the waterfront, too, and Will could see the hackneys lined up, ready to take the tourists to their various lodgings and hotels. Once loaded, off they went — to Shortland, where the streets were dim and shadowy, the streetlights well spaced out and the lights from windows primly curtained. Shortland, in fact, was reminiscent of that first evening, in August 1867. Will remembered again how the tents had lit up along the string-marked streets, and the quiet sounds of men talking as they tended their cooking fires.

He remembered how Jake Dexter had looked, tall and rangy, superbly confident, unmistakably American in his leather Californian hat, and how they'd walked all over the lot Jake had bought, and discussed the task ahead. For a long while, Will had avoided telling him the awful news from Auckland. All those years ago, he'd had to brace himself to reveal what had happened — that Jake's fifteen-year-old, dearly beloved daughter, Jess, had run away. That Jess had abandoned them all in a fit of rage, hurt and jealousy.

Because of Timothy Dexter.

10

Cissy would never forget her first sight of the Golden Goose Hotel, for it was in the last golden rays of the setting sun.

Everything had been fascinating. Now, as their hackney jogged out of the deafening maze of Grahamstown towards the relative quietness of Shortland, she listened to her mother and Miss Fleet exclaiming about the novel scene. There were two cabs behind theirs, coming the same way, for an American family from Connecticut named Bradford — whose daughters were Patience and Harmony — had decided to try out the Golden Goose Murder Experience, too. They, like Miss Fleet, had asked Mr. Williams if they could join the group, much to Mrs. Miller's delight.

"It is so much more *fun* if you're with people you know," she said.

It was indeed rather fun to arrive in convivial company, Cissy thought, but then forgot it, for the famous hotel had bobbed into sight— and, despite all the talk, she hadn't expected it to be magnificent as well as famous.

The Golden Goose was painted glistening white and double-storied, with three tall chimneys reaching high to the evening stars, a lovingly embellished embodiment of the grandest and most elaborate architecture of the colonial age. Two wide verandas circled the street-front walls of the big wooden building, the upper one forming a roofed gallery, and the other a lovely promenade, both with intricately turned spindle balusters and failings that were carved to fit the resting hand.

As the hackneys rattled to a stop a beautiful woman ran out onto this balcony, and leaned far over the railing, crying, "It's Will, dear Will! I don't believe it, but Will is here already! Gladys, hurry!"

There was an intent expression on Will Williams' normally staid countenance as he hurriedly jumped down to the street. Before he could call out, the woman whirled and ran inside the building, to come dashing out the front door and down three steps, flushed and breathless and laughing. Then she went up to Will and took both his hands in hers, gazing up into his face with wide, dark, sparkling eyes.

She seemed so young at that moment that Cissy thought she must be Mr. Williams' daughter. She was very slight in figure, dressed in a prettily trimmed skirt and a muslin blouse with frothy sleeves, her thick, dark uncovered hair coiled at the back of her neck in the Spanish fashion. Then Cissy glimpsed the silver streaks in that hair, and realized that she must be Will's wife, Jess. The woman he had hurried to rejoin because they had been apart for such a long time.

Oddly, after Jess's first exuberance, they seemed awkward in each other's company, as if each one was waiting for the other to kiss and hug first. Oh, embrace her, you silly man, thought Cissy, but more people arrived out of the hotel entrance in rush, laughing and calling out his name. Will had no time to kiss his wife, being engulfed in a rowdily joyous welcome.

It was a heart-warming sight. Everyone was happy and everyone was so pleasant to look at, the men smart and handsome whatever their age, the females all vivacious and lovely. A flamboyantly dressed woman called Gladys, who looked so like Miss Minnie that she had to be her sister, had no reservations at all about giving her half-brother a great kiss, and a bevy of what seemed to be nieces wrapped affectionate arms about his legs, while young men may have been nephews clapped him heartily on the shoulder. Cissy, smiling at the happy scene, didn't notice for a moment that another vehicle had arrived.

Then, with a sense of foreboding, she saw the laughing faces go blank, and Jess reach out convulsively to grip Will's hand. The throng all stared in the same direction. She heard the dead silence.

Puzzled, Cissy turned. The vehicle that had arrived was a dray, driven by Clem, who had been left at the quay to look after the party's luggage. The bags and trunks were all safely on the tray, but Clem's expression was tight and grim.

And the granite-faced man beside him was Timothy Dexter.

Cissy blinked, utterly stunned, for she had had no idea that Timothy Dexter was on the paddle-steamer. Though the steamer might be known as the Queen of the Gulf, the *Wakatere* was very small, yet Cissy had seen nothing whatsoever of the American during the four-hour voyage.

Which meant he had deliberately kept out of sight.

Which was ominous.

She saw the family exchange dismayed glances, but no one said a word. Consternation hung unspoken in the air. Then the silence was abruptly broken. A door slammed like a gunshot inside the hotel, and brisk footsteps rattled along a ground floor corridor, coming closer. The people on the veranda shifted to let someone through.

And a woman stepped forward. A woman whose deep-set eyes glistened when she saw Timothy Dexter.

She was a tall, spare, grey-haired woman, big-boned, and grim-faced, as if she had never learned to smile. Cissy thought at first that this must be Miss Harriet Gray, but then changed her mind. This woman was too worn and gaunt, too *un*beautiful. She wore a plain black dress that had gone greenish with age, with a white two-stringed kitchen apron over it. The apron was clean but old as well, starched so stiffly the frayed places stood out. It was as if she was determined to show up the Gray family as frivolous.

She stopped on the top step, her eyes unblinking as she studied Timothy Dexter. She betrayed no surprise, and said not a word. Instead, she jerked her chin, and turned, going back into the hotel. Cissy saw him shrug, and then he jumped off the dray, hoisted his valise onto his shoulder, and followed her.

Then he was gone. With an audible sigh, a semblance of normality returned. Within moments everyone was bustling about busily, almost as if there had been no interruption. Will disappeared inside with his wife, and others followed him, straggling away until the only one left was Gladys, who ushered them into the reception lobby, where she registered them all on the guest list and gave out the keys to their rooms. The lobby was cozy, with easy chairs and plenty of small tables for books and papers, and a big sideboard with a great silver salver on it. The tourist party quite crowded it out with their ruckus and noise.

Cissy, by contrast, kept quiet, waiting for a chance to ask about meeting Miss Harriet Gray, studying Gladys in the meantime. Though her surname was different, because she was married, and several of the children were hers, it was still obvious that she was Minnie Gray's older sister, because they had the same dumpy figure, and compelling, lambent eyes. There was an intensity that reminded Cissy of the actress, too. Gladys was certainly showy enough to be an actress herself, dressed in a gown that was cheerfully striped in blue, red and white, with a blue wool kirtle about her hips, and a big red silk rose tucked into her bosom. Her black-lashed eyes were laughing and warm — up until the moment that Cissy asked if she could pay an urgent call on Miss Harriet Gray.

The only answer was a dismissive glance and a shake of the head, so abrupt that Cissy wondered if her question hadn't been properly heard. She didn't have a chance to repeat her request, however, because Gladys moved away briskly, leading the party up the stairs, betraying for the first time that she had a bad limp. It must have been long-standing, as she moved as if she had forgotten the handicap. As she hobbled from step to step, she chattered incessantly, throwing questions over her shoulder, asking the tourists about their journey. It was a privilege, she said, to entertain people who had come so far.

They were ushered to their rooms, all in a row on the same corridor, and Gladys disappeared. Clem brought up their trunks not long after that, but wasn't communicative in the slightest. When Cissy, starting to become very anxious indeed about her chances of meeting Miss Harriet Gray, asked him the same question, she got nothing more than an uninterested shrug. It seemed uncharacteristically rude, she thought with distress, as he had been amiable on the *Wakatere*.

Then he, too, disappeared. It was impossible to ignore the obvious conclusion, that the Grays and Will Williams, faced with a family crisis, were holding an urgent private conference, because the hotel became so ominously quiet.

There was gas lighting in all the rooms but large parts of the corridors were unlit, and when Cissy peeped out of the door the hotel seemed peopled only by the tourist party and shadows. She could hear Harmony and Patience exclaiming in the room three doors along, but otherwise the hotel echoed only to the creak of timbers contracting in the evening cold.

Even Cissy's mother seemed uneasy, though she did declare that the room was *lovely*. And very comfortable it was, too, with neat beds, a pretty wash-stand and a window that opened out onto the upper balcony, but Cissy noticed that her mother stopped often, as she did, to listen to the silence all about.

Then, not long after they had finished unpacking, a sharp tap sounded in the passage, and when Cissy opened the door she found Mrs. Jess Williams, holding a lighted lantern in one hand, and knocking on Miss Fleet's door with the other.

Will's wife was wearing a beautiful blue tea-gown with a pale green shawl, and looked lovelier than ever, like a dainty figurine. "Hello," she said brightly when she saw Cissy's questioning face. "The rest of the Murder Experience party won't be along for a while, as they are coming by train, so we thought that you'd enjoy a tour of the hotel."

That would indeed be nice — or so the Americans exclaimed — though Mrs. Miller whispered to Cissy that she would have rather liked a cup of tea. Cissy didn't reply, wondering instead if Jess Williams had been delegated to keep the guests occupied. When she seized her chance to ask about an interview with Miss Harriet Gray, she received nothing more than a bright, vague smile, which bolstered her suspicions.

Miss Harriet Gray, she thought, was chairing a family council of war.

The hotel was as commodious as the exterior had promised, and looked surprisingly modern, with new paper and paint, the latest gas chandeliers, and baths and other fittings in the bathrooms.

"This place is new?" enquired the girls' father, Mr. Bradford. His Christian name, he had told them, was Schuyler, and, what's more, he was Mr. Schuyler Bradford *the Third*.

"No, no, the frame of the building was put up in August 1867," Jess Williams corrected, and turned to lead the way down the stairs. "My father carried the pre-cut frame, roof and boarding here," she continued, when they'd all arrived in the lobby. "And my husband, Will, helped him complete it, even though he was only nineteen at the time. Amazingly, considering there was just the two of them, the hotel was conducting business in just three weeks. Quite a feat," she commented with evident pride. "Even though the Golden Goose wasn't half as big as it is now. In 1868, guest rooms were added, and the hotel became the same size as the place you see now."

"Three weeks!" Mr. Schuyler Bradford whistled in amazement.

"The moment the roof was on to keep out the rain, the cabin furniture was brought over from the brig, and my mother moved in. She was a famous actress — hailed as the Rage of the Season in Sydney, earlier that same year — but she put on an apron, hired local women, and baked pies all day, which she sold at one end of the tavern counter. Will and my father were hard at it in the evenings, selling the beer and brandy that the brig brought over from the breweries in Auckland. Yes, it was a nothing much more than a grog shop and cafeteria — but very profitable. The miners either wanted to celebrate their early finds or drown their sorrows while they still had some money to do it."

"You keep on mentioning a brig," said Mr. Bradford.

"My father's brig, the famous brig *Gosling*. He used her to trade all over the Pacific."

"Where is that brig now?"

Jess Williams' smile faded. "The brig blew up," she said.

"Oh *no*," said Mrs. Miller.

"It was a terrible tragedy. My father had given the command to my oldest cousin, Robert Gray, just the previous voyage, and he was bringing her in with a mixed cargo that included a few barrels of blasting powder. Timothy said afterwards that some men must have stowed away in the hold — which often happened when me were desperate to get to the diggings. When they lit a lamp, or a stove to cook their supper..."

She had to stop, to clear her throat. "Well, there was an explosion. Most of those on board survived, but..."

Clara Miller said, sounding surprised, "Mr. Dexter was there?"

Jess Williams' lips pressed together. Then she said tightly, "Timothy Dexter is my half-brother, my father's child by an early marriage. And, oh yes, he had worked on the brig, right from the first day my father sailed the *Gosling* to the Thames. He started out as a foremast hand, but by the time the brig was lost, he had risen to the position of first mate."

Then Jess repeated, as if it was important, "Timothy was the first mate. The second-in-charge. My father had made my cousin Robert captain for that voyage, while it was more usual to give the command to the mate. Perhaps that's why Robert stayed with the ship, running her aground to give everyone the best chance possible. Unfortunately, he stayed on board too long."

Cissy's mother said, "I *am* sorry."

"It was a long time ago."

"Your family has known a great deal of tragedy..."

"That's true." Mrs. Williams looked about, at the spotless wallpaper and shining paint. "This hotel was almost burned down, you know. It had to be completely restored. That's why it looks so new."

"The fire was only a little while ago?"

"Yes, about this time last year."

Jess paused as Mr. Bradford whistled in surprise, and then added, "Most men would have pocketed the insurance money and walked away, but my father wasn't one to admit defeat."

And, it seemed, the Gray tribe had been summoned to help Captain Jake Dexter rebuild the Golden Goose, Will Williams had done the planning and design, and all the men had worked with hammers, saws and chisels, while the women were in charge of wallpaper and paint. Within a miraculously short space of months the doors had been reopened and business had resumed. It was a testimony to Will's talent and Captain Dexter's determination.

But had Timothy Dexter been part of the team that had worked the miracle? Cissy strongly doubted it. He had been in America for most of the year, she remembered.

"Well," said Jess, with a sigh. "That's enough of reminiscences of my father. Come and see the man for yourself."

Cissy, greatly intrigued, was the first to follow Jess through a double doorway that led off the lobby into a big room, four times as long as it was broad, a room with something odd about is proportions.

It was in two parts, the smaller part, to the left-hand side as they entered, was raised, with two broad steps leading up to it, while the lower, much larger area, was furnished as an elegantly grand dining room. There were three great gas candelabra in the flat white plaster ceiling, which was embellished with intricate moldings. The tall windows that lined this dining area were draped with claret-colored velvet curtains, and the walls between the windows were graced with large paintings, many of them set designs from Minnie Gray's operettas. Tables and chairs were laid out in rows, each table covered with a starched white cloth and set with crystal and shining silver. The clatter of pots and dishes emanated from the far end of this lower room, and savory smells wafted when someone opened a door.

Cissy studied the raised part of the room, looked all about, and exclaimed, "It looks just like the stage in a theatre!"

"You are most observant," said Jess. "That is exactly what it used to be."

"A *theatre*?" echoed Cissy's mother.

"This part of the hotel is the original building, the part that my father brought over from Sydney in the brig, and which he and Will built within three weeks. It wasn't meant to be a hotel, at first. It was built as a tavern and playhouse. Here, where we are standing, was the orchestra pit, if we had an orchestra." Jess waved an arm at the array of tables, and said, "The dining room is the old auditorium, except that the theatre was even bigger than it seems, as it was originally double-storied."

She pointed at the ceiling. "The dress circle was up there, with standing galleries behind it. The fire started in this room, and so it took the worst of the blaze, and was almost totally destroyed. When we rebuilt my father decided against restoring the theatre. Moving pictures, which came to the Thames as far back as 1896, had flourished since, and the theatre had stopped making money. So he had the ceiling put in, and turned the upstairs area into family quarters."

Galleries? Cissy saw that Jess was smiling at the open disbelief in her visitors' faces. "He really packed them in," she said. "My mother told me that they sat so tightly on the benches that one broad gesture could precipitate a lusty bout of fisticuffs. For that reason, while there were oil footlights, the lights in the auditorium were left on throughout the whole performance.

"And this," she said, pointing to their left, "was the stage, just as Miss Miller guessed. It still looks rather like a stage, does it not? That is why the floor is a little higher than the rest. My father and Will thought of lowering it when the place was rebuilt, but decided to keep it as a sitting room — out of sentimentality, I think."

It was easy to believe that it had functioned as a stage, Cissy thought. Another door led out of it on the other side, and she pictured costumed actors coming and going — *entering* and *exiting*, she thought. Now, there was a piano, and a cavernous wing chair with a settee alongside it, and a little table loaded with books and papers and scripts. To either side, big old jars held peacock feathers and oriental umbrellas. It was very much like the set for some drawing-room drama, she thought . . . and then Cissy saw the two paintings.

They were hung on the back wall of the stage, almost life-sized, hanging side by side. She had missed them at first, for the light was so poor there, but now they gripped her attention.

Jess smiled, and turned up the gas lighting.

"Meet my parents," she said.

Cissy gazed raptly, barely conscious of the other guests gathering to look.

The portrait on the right was of a beautiful woman, about twenty-five years old. She was seated on a great thronelike marble chair, one elegant hand resting on the arm, the other making a slight, eloquent gesture. Her draperies were dark-blue velvet, quite unembellished, so that contrast drew the viewer's attention to her rounded arms and those beautiful hands. Most compelling, however, was the cameo-like face, framed by a mass of thickly disordered dark-gold hair.

She was looking away from the artist, attention-caught by something the viewer could not see, lips parted, eyebrows slanted, black-lashed, dark-blue eyes glowing and intent. It was as if she were gazing at the man in the other portrait — unless it was a trick of the way the paintings were hung.

"She looks as if she belongs to another age, does she not?" Jess murmured. "It was painted when I was a very small child," she went on. "And for years I refused to believe that this goddess was my mother. The artist portrayed her as the Muse of the Drama, Melpomene, daughter of Zeus. That's why the background is a vineyard, representing grapes and vine leaves — the symbols of Greek theatre."

"The artist was Greek?" said Patience.

"Oh, no. He was English, an itinerant artist. The Gray family was very famous in England, which is why the painting is a kind of homage. My grandfather was Sir Charles Gray, my grandmother Mary Kemble Gray. My mother's aunt — my grandmother's sister — was the famous Sarah Siddons. Some people say they were rather alike — had the same charisma, certainly."

Perhaps that was so, Cissy thought, but she could see no resemblance to Jess herself. Despite her fragility, it was very obvious that dark-haired, green-eyed Jess Williams took after the man in the second portrait. Her father, Captain Jahaziel Dexter, had been painted standing in a piratical kind of pose, booted legs planted firmly, one hand resting on a globe of the world, dark hair swept back from a lean, clean-shaven face that held a go-to-the-devil expression. Jake Dexter, obviously, had not felt the least cooperative about having his portrait painted. Despite all the artist's efforts, that weather-beaten face was lop-sided, eloquent creases all awry, one of the piercing eyes half-shut, one eyebrow arched. The artist had managed to convey the character of his subject, however — a man who commanded ships, who built theatres and managed them, a stubborn and indomitable man who had overcome disaster.

A man, thought Cissy, who had fathered Timothy Dexter, but had left that hotel to his mistress.

"An interesting looking chap," said Miss Fleet.

"He was American, from New England, like yourself." Then Jess said wistfully to Mrs. Miller, "Was Minnie enjoying America? It's over two months since we saw her last, and there's so much that letters don't convey. She wired that you were coming, but... Tell me, does she look well? Will says she works too hard and keeps late hours, but our dear little Minnie was always thus. But he says too that she's become *over-imaginative,* and that's not like Minnie at all. He said that she's become rather nervous and highly strung. I do hope he's mistaken."

"She was everything that was kind and amiable," said Mrs. Miller. She sounded a trifle shocked to hear her idol described as *dear* and *little.* "And looked very well indeed."

"Then I am so glad to hear it."

Cissy was frowning, as something nudged at her mind. She felt as if she'd seen something important, but couldn't pin it down. She said slowly, "May I ask a question, Mrs. Williams?"

"Of course."

"How old was Minnie when you came to Thames?"

Jess smiled gently. "Just five years old — ten years younger than I was."

11

Jess next led the way back through the lobby to a large and pleasant sitting room. Cissy, her mind busy with speculations, kept silent. Harmony Bradford, however, burst into a torrent of questions. Had the theatre been as rushed as the opening of the tavern; how had they found the actors, and what had they staged?

"It certainly was rushed," Jess laughed. "So rushed that in the beginning the family was the entire cast."

Miss Harriet Gray, her brother, Royal Gray — and their children, Cissy thought. Even including five-year-old Minnie, who could easily have been precocious. And Clem? No, Clem was a lot younger than Minnie, so could have been no more than a baby, if indeed he was born. Gladys, who looked five or six years older than Minnie, would surely have taken part. There was another brother, she remembered, called Oscar, or something like that. And Robert — the brother who was blown up with the brig? It seemed very likely that he took part, she thought, though he would have been very young.

"But surely it wasn't a disadvantage," Mrs. Miller murmured, who had evidently been calculating ages, too. "In England, *children* go on stage to recite and sing."

"Well, the first performance could scarcely be called a great success, though the miners had a first-rate time. When my cousin Oscar and his little flock of geese arrived on stage for scene one — for geese featured in the script my Uncle Royal had scribbled in a hurry, to explain the hotel's name, you see — the miners wouldn't allow the poor little fellow to say any of his lines. They had heard from some Aucklanders that he and Robert did a great minstrel act, and so they demanded that Robert should fetch his banjo and give them a song and dance.

"Then, when my Uncle Royal stepped out to remonstrate, there was quite an uproar, for they all wanted to know where he had bought his natty blue-striped trousers. And then, when the commotion was finally over, it was discovered that the geese were gone. A story had been going around that someone had discovered gold in a duck's gizzard, and so those poor geese didn't survive the theft for long at all. I don't know if gold was found in their innards or not, but the word that the goose that laid the golden egg was roosting at the Golden Goose ran round like wildfire, and houses were packed from then on, even though the goose-supply had run out."

As Harmony and Patience and their boisterous father laughed immoderately at the yarn, Cissy looked about the lounge. It was a large square room, filled with a cozy clutter of chairs and settees and plenty of small tables. On one, a tray with steaming teapot, milk jug, sugar bowl and cups and saucers rested, attracting Mrs. Miller's attention on the instant. Three small children were seated around one of the others, demolishing rows of battered lead soldiers with toy cannon, so preoccupied with the massacre that they didn't seem to notice the intrusion.

The rest of the room looked as if it was quite accustomed to accommodating all kinds of homely activity. A hearty fire blazed in a big hearth, and the broad mantel above it was cluttered with knickknacks and souvenirs, a mixed assortment of shell boxes, shell valentines, pictures made of colored sand and glittery paper, scrimshaw and crochet work, fat velvet hearts and eastern carvings. The big windows were snugly curtained, and the walls were covered with a whole history of photographs, spread out for the viewer in all shades of grey and brown.

"So the Show Went On," said Mrs. Miller playfully to their hostess, after her first luxurious sip from her teacup, and Jess Williams laughed, though a little ruefully, Cissy thought.

"That first show has gone down as a treasured family legend," she said. "But having to cobble shows together with my little cousins didn't last long — within a couple of days travelling entertainers were lining up at the door, for there were out-of-work players all over Australia and New Zealand. My father and my

Uncle Royal were happy to employ them, too, as otherwise the Grays would have got the reputation of being clannish. And what a variety they were!"

Cissy, moving around the parlor, listened with deep interest, because many of the acts were memorialized in the pictures on the walls. Along with a vast assortment of family pictures, showing the large Gray family in many different costumes, at different ages, she found a photograph of a group that called themselves *The Lancashire Bell-Ringers*, a bill that advertised a panorama called *The Grand Moving Tableaux of the Apocalypse*, and a picture of a troupe of enormous females dancers who billed themselves as *The British Belles*. The Belles, wearing the minimum to veil their massed bulk, were hugely popular — or so Jess revealed.

"The Golden Goose did stage Shakespeare," she added, when her guests had stopped laughing. "The great George Darrel played *As You Like It* in our theatre, and married his sweetheart and mentor, Mrs. Robert Heir, in the local Shortland church. But what the miners really wanted was melodrama, and so the Darrels played that, too. They held sole rights to a very popular entertainment called *Blow for Blow*. Melodrama was the bread and butter of any theatrical enterprise then, and the Golden Goose theatre was no exception — except that our audiences tended to join in. Like children at pantomimes, they hissed the villain and called out encouragement and warnings to the hero. I remember that one of my cousins came to the front of the stage to plead with the miners to give him a chance, for he was only *acting* the villain. And then...

"Then one night we had a very poor audience. There had been a real murder up in Grahamstown at the Wharf Hotel, and everyone had gone there to view the scene of the killing, and, incidentally, drink at the Wharf Hotel. Two fellows had got into a dispute over a claim, and one shot the other and then killed himself. It was sensational — much more sensational than any kind of murder on the stage, and was the talk of the town for months, partly because the chap who had been murdered didn't actually expire for quite a while. Everyone who came into town went to view the scene, even though was no mystery about who had done it, or why, and so we were playing to half-empty houses, night after night. Then my cousin Gladys had an inspiration. Why not stage a murder and let the audience find the villain and solve the mystery? And so, with some experiment and adaptation, the Golden Goose Murder Experience was born."

"So you stopped hiring actors?" Mrs. Bradford asked.

"Oh no, the troupers kept on coming. We couldn't have Murder Weekends every day of the week! And then there were the single acts," Jess added. "They had their chance to perform in here..."

She opened a door in the further wall of the parlor, revealing the tavern, a cavernous low-raftered room with a great circular bar. Mrs. Bradford and Miss Fleet and Mrs. Miller, enjoying their tea, did not move, but Mr. Bradford and his two energetic daughters bounded in with a rush, so Cissy went along, too.

There was no one behind the bar and scarcely anyone in the tavern itself, just three old-timers in caps, who sat in a booth and cuddled small foaming glasses in great knob-knuckled hands, under an array of old beer-colored photographs.

It was almost impossible to imagine this as a roistering goldrush bar, but Jess Williams certainly had her memories. "Occasionally a single act would arrive, a comic singer or a magician, perhaps, and there was no space on the theatre programme, so he or she would come to an arrangement with my father or my uncle to perform in the tavern, their only payment being the tips they received. My uncle and father were most cooperative — they even had the bar planked over to make a circular stage, at times, to give the performer a good chance to make money, and some did very well indeed.

"I remember Chang the Chinese Giant, who had a very tiny wife. Her name was Kin Foo, and they had a baby named Fireworks. They did no more than wander around the tavern shaking hands, but the miners loved it. And then there was a Swiss girl who came and played a barrel organ for a week. She received thirty-five offers of marriage!

"But my favorite was Charles Thatcher, the famous comic singer. He had this knack of arriving in a place, and finding out the local gossip. Then he would make up verses and put them to some popular tune. And so, of course, he sang about our missing geese—

We've heard of the goose who the golden eggs laid
It is but a fiction, I'm really afraid
But here is a fact now, for gold has been struck
In Shortland they've got an auriferous duck
Quack, quack, says ducky
Come along ducky,
Let's open your gizzard, come here and be killed.

The geese have been bought up in Shortland like fun
Captain Jake Dexter secures every one
To open their gizzards, and if down there you stay
You get duckling pie or roast goose every day
Quack, quack, says ducky
Come along ducky
Let's open your gizzard, come here and be killed.

The doctors of Shortland are in a right state
The slaughter of ducks has been so very great,
They're going to clear off, from what I understand
Fearing there won't be a quack left in the land.
Quack, quack, says ducky
Come along, ducky
Let's open your gizzard, home here and be killed.

And at that she finished, her arms spread wide in an exaggeratedly theatrical gesture.

One of the old men puffed a cloud of pipe-smoke. The other two merely sank their noses more deeply into their ale. Cissy herself was so amazed she forgot to applaud at all. The American girls and their father made up for all of them, cheering and demanding an encore, not satisfied until they had learned the words and could sing along themselves. Because of the noise, when the door abruptly opened they were all taken by surprise. Silencing, they turned to look at the woman who'd come in.

She was the tall, spare, raw-boned woman who didn't look as if she belonged with the Grays. She still wore the plain black dress and starched apron, and was carrying a tray that held a meal of some kind. The large plate on the tray was covered with a kind of copper hat, evidently to keep the dinner warm, for there was a little vent in the top, which issued a faint twirl of steam and the succulent smell of roast meat.

Cissy's stomach rumbled. It seemed a long time since her last meal. She wondered where this tray was headed, and envied the recipient. The woman set the tray down on the bar, and then opened a flap in the counter and went behind it. As they all watched, she selected a bottle from a wine rack, and uncorked it with a special tool. Her gaunt face was expressionless, her movements deliberate.

Jess said, sounding awkward, "Oh, Megs, this is Mr. Schuyler Bradford." Then she introduced the girls. The woman merely nodded, going on with what she was doing, taking up a wine glass, giving it a polish with a towel, and then setting it by the opened wine bottle on the tray. The wine, Cissy saw, was a burgundy, so she thought the meat might be a good English roast sirloin.

Then she heard Jess Williams say, "I've been telling our guests about her theatrical entertainments here. Do you remember those madcap early productions?"

"That, I do remember," the other said. Her thin lips set tightly, and her expression was more closed than ever.

"But," she said deliberately over her shoulder, as she turned away, "I do *not* remember that you were here, Jess."

12

Mr. Bradford and Patience and Harmony had enjoyed the tour about the ground floor of the hotel so very much that they demanded a tour of the upper floor, as well The layout was certainly confusing enough, Cissy mused, so it was probably a blessing that they should get some idea of what was where. At the top of the stairway, large corridors led off in two directions, both ultimately ending at a door that opened out onto the upstairs outside balcony.

Then the American girls revealed that what they *really* wanted was to go out onto the balcony, so they all went outside into the cold night air and looked about at the empty streets and the silent stars and listened to the insistent thumping of the stamper batteries. Harmony and Patience were not satisfied with that, though, hanging over the rail and crying out lines, "Romeo, Romeo, wherefore art thou, Romeo?" And, "Rapunzel, Rapunzel, let down your hair," while their fond father laughed uproariously. Then they gave the dark town of Shortland a spirited rendition of *Quack, quack, says ducky*, As on the *Royal George*, Cissy realized, Harmony and Patience were determined to have a first-rate time, even if they created a lot of tut-tutting in the process.

Throughout it all the echoes of the stamper batteries thudded about the invisible hills, muffling the strong young voices and making the frosty air ring. When Patience and Harmony were silent at last, the stampers thumped on, on. Cissy shivered. The wooden balustrade was cold and clammy under her hands, and the warm squares of light thrown out by windows along the balcony were reassuring.

Then Miss Fleet pointed at a French door that Cissy hadn't noticed before, and said, "What's inside there? Another lounge?"

Cissy saw Jess frown. When she lifted the lantern the light bounced back from the small glass panes of the single French door that Miss Fleet had indicated. There were no curtains drawn across the door, but there was no light on behind it, so it was impossible to see inside.

Instead of answering Miss Fleet's question, Jess Williams said, "I think it is locked."

Then she proved it, by going over and trying the handle unsuccessfully.

"Is it the door at the end of one of the corridors?" said Miss Fleet, though it was obvious that it was not. Her persistence had made the others interested, and they were gathering around, reluctant to leave despite the cold.

"No," said Jess. "It's a room we don't normally use."

That seemed very odd, Cissy thought, for surely a hotel used all the rooms available, full rooms meaning money.

She said, "Is it a bedroom?"

"Once, it was. Now, it's a parlor."

Odder than ever, Cissy thought.

Harmony Bradford said, "What about the inside door? The one that leads into the corridor?"

"Oh, I'm sure that's locked, as well." However, when Harmony persisted, Jess led the way back into the hotel, and then along to an unmarked door.

Apart from not having a number, the door looked like all the others, made of solid wooden panels. As they all stopped and watched, Jess Williams tried the handle. "See," she said. "It told you, it's locked."

"You don't have a key?" said Miss Fleet.

"Will might have one, and of course there is..."

Then she broke off. The woman called Megs had appeared at the end of the passage.

"Oh, Megs," said Jess. "Would you have a key to this room? Miss Fleet would like to see inside."

And so would everyone else, Cissy noted, for everyone looked at the housekeeper hopefully. Megs' gaze flickered over them all, her eyes deep-set, unblinking and suspicious.

Still without speaking, she rummaged in her apron pocket. A massive ring of keys was produced and given to Jess, who, after a few false tries, managed to find one that unlocked the door. The handle was stiff, as if it had not been turned for a very long time, and Jess had to shove hard before the door grudgingly scraped open. Then Jess stepped inside, holding her lamp high.

Cissy gasped with surprise. There was a smell of dust and old paper, but the overwhelming impression was of salt — of the ocean. It was like stepping into a seascape.

Ghostly vessels sailed along the walls with an uncanny illusion of motion, a painted fleet that was interrupted only by the fireplace, the French door, the inside door, and one window. The ships and brigs that some artist had painted on the plaster walls bent to an unfelt wind, dipping and heeling in a painted sea. The illusion of movement was disorienting, but then Cissy realized that it was caused by the flickering light of the lamp and the eerie effect of the moonlight falling in the French door, for when Jess turned a knob and lit the gas with a taper, the procession of ships stood still.

Cissy went around slowly. She was aware that the others were following her, but her attention was entirely held by the lovely painted vessels. They were complete to the very last detail, down to the figureheads and stern-boards, painted with knowledge as well as artistry. Then Mr. Bradford, behind her, said, "Look, they are all American."

He pointed at the nearest one, and Cissy saw that he was right. Every one of them flaunted the Stars and Stripes.

"And they have the same house flag, too."

"I beg your pardon?"

"The flag that advertises the company that owns the ship. See — the flag flying from the top of each mainmast. This is quite a fleet — and yet they are all owned by one firm."

Not the Grays, thought Cissy, intrigued. Captain Jake Dexter had owned only one ship, the brig *Gosling*. The rest of his money had been invested in theatres.

She said, "It must be a very rich firm, to own so many."

"Grace Brothers," said Mr. Bradford.

Cissy frowned, not just amazed at this sudden revelation of special knowledge, but also with a sudden sense that she had either read or heard the name quite recently. Then she smiled, remembering that it was Miss Fleet's middle name. Her mother had told her that the American woman's name was Elspeth Grace Fleet. And Grace was a common woman's name, she knew — actually a rather nice one.

She said, "Does the firm still exist?" The ships looked pretty old, she thought. All of them were sailing ships. There were no steamers.

"That's open to question," said Mr. Bradford, and she could smell the brandy he had drunk in the bar. "It's in the lap of the gods, as they say. There were originally three brothers, but only one got married, and so it was all inherited by his only son. That son ran the firm until he was very old — right until the day he died, in fact, which wasn't very long ago. He himself had an only son, but the young man died as a youth, very unfortunate. So it's up to lawyers, now. The firm will be sold, I'm sure, and I wouldn't mind making a little flutter in that market. Even a big one," he added, with a wide smile.

So Mr. Schuyler Bradford III was rich as well as knowledgeable, Cissy thought. No wonder he could afford to take his family around the world.

She said, "I suppose the artist who painted Mrs. Williams' parents' portraits did these, as well."

Jess was listening. She said, "Oh, no. It was my half-brother, Timothy, who painted these ships."

"Mr. *Dexter*?"

"Yes. This used to be his room."

Cissy frowned, wondering why Timothy Dexter had not been put in this room, wondering where he had been put instead. Perhaps the lack of warning hadn't given the family time to shift his bed in here ... but if that was so, Timothy Dexter had not been back in the Thames for a very long time, since the room smelled so very unused. He had mentioned that he had been back in America for a year, she remembered.

Jess said, "Timothy was always drawing and sketching, but it was just a nervous habit — doodling, I suppose, for he always threw the drawings away, and had no interest in helping Will with his stage sets. None of us knew why he decided to paint these murals, even though he requisitioned Will's paint-box to do it. He's never painted anything else so permanent. If the fire had started at this end of the building instead of the theatre, there would be no record of his talent at all."

So why had he painted these ships? Cissy stared around the walls again, frowning. It was as if he had been trying to make a statement... A whole fleet, owned by one man, while Captain Jake Dexter had only one little brig. Could it be some kind of taunt?

Another thought was forming in her mind, but was forgotten as Jess Williams spoke again. "Isn't life strange?" she was saying. "Timothy neglected his talent, because he wasn't interested. And then there is Will. He had been apprenticed to a cabinet maker in Auckland — he looked to have a good steady future, but nothing more than that. But instead he came here to help with the theatre, and now he's the greatest stage designer in the world, or so they say.

"And Minnie. We loved her, and enjoyed the way she pranced about the stage from the moment she could walk, but we never suspected her pretty voice would blossom so. Gladys was the natural actress and singer, living for nothing else but the stage from the time she could walk. She could sing and dance and was a stand-up comic, as well. And all I ever wanted to be was a famous actress, like my mother and my grandmother and my great-aunt ... and then Gladys had an accident, and I found out that I didn't have the stamina..."

Mrs. Miller echoed, "*Accident*?"

"Oh, she has a limp, didn't you notice?" Jess Williams' smile was as sweet as ever, but her eyes held a disturbing suspicion of tears. "It was such a silly thing, but it put a halt to her career, and just when people were starting to talk about a great future as a dancer and singer, too. She was always a wild horsewoman, and she and Timothy were racing each other when the accident happened."

Timothy Dexter again, thought Cissy. A shiver ruffled the back of her neck. As if a goose had walked over her grave, she thought wryly to herself.

"Well, now," said Jess brightly, locking the door behind them and giving Megs the key. Sounds of many people echoed up the stairway, and her manner became brisk. "Here's the rest of the murder party," she said. "And not before time, either."

The Murder Experience party gathered in the lounge, which was otherwise empty, the children having been sent to bed. The twenty or so tourists who had come on the train still wore their travelling dresses, being too tired and hungry to change, but were jovial enough, to all appearances looking forward to the fun. Men warmed the seats of their trousers at the fire, while womenfolk perched on settees, chattering merrily away. Megs and a maid wheeled in trolleys with a hot substantial supper, while a second maid provided cups of tea. Then, once everyone had settled with a plate and a cup, Gladys arrived, and proceeded to introduce them all to each other, rattling off names that Cissy promptly forgot.

There were people from Auckland and from further afar, from Wellington and Christchurch and Dunedin. Two of the party had come from as far as Australia. There were some English travelers, too, so that Cissy and Mrs. Miller were not vastly outnumbered, but no Americans, so that the Bradford family got a great deal of attention, as did Miss Fleet. But, Cissy noticed then, Timothy Dexter was not there. Obviously, whatever his motive for coming might be, it was not to join in the Murder Experience.

"Some people here are not what they seem," Gladys warned as they ate. "Some are actors, taking part in the melodrama — the participants in the murder that will happen tomorrow night. One will be the victim, and sitting here supping is the vile murderer. Only they — and their supporting actors — know who they are, and all of them have been telling you lies already. It is the task of the rest of you to watch and listen, and try to make out what is the truth, and what is not; who is a real tourist, and who is a devious player."

Cissy, like everyone else, was scanning the faces all about. Some looked elaborately casual, others very self-conscious. Some shifted uncomfortably, and there was a bit of nervous laughter. "Aha, me Horty," Schuyler Bradford III called out, "I always wondered if you truly loved me, and now I wonder if you lied."

Horty? Mrs. Bradford was giggling merrily. So her name was Hortense — which started with H. But surely she was exactly what she seemed? Everyone was laughing, including Gladys. The Bradford family, incurably droll, was set on being the life and soul of the party. Patience flapped her eyelashes, and Harmony pulled her pretty face into what perhaps she thought of as a hideously villainous expression.

Then Cissy heard Gladys announce, "You will have plenty of time to look for clues tomorrow, ladies and gentlemen. Breakfast is at six!"

Six? Gasps of horror. Gladys waited, smiling, and then went on, "We are booked to board the river steamer for Paeroa at seven-thirty, and if we are late they'll go without us, for they have to sail on the tide. Then, after disembarking at Junction Wharf, we catch a very special train to tour the Crown Mine stamper battery at Karangahake, on the Ohinemuri River. It's the experience of a lifetime, I assure you!

"And then, on to Te Aroha we will go. After a light lunch, the gardens of the Domain are just splendid for strolling, but those of you who wish to take the waters will find them efficacious in cases of gout, the rheumatics, dyspepsia, sciatica, and any derangement of the kidneys, liver or spleen. Then we will come back on the regular train. I expect you to return in splendid health, ladies and gentlemen, and also with an abundance of deductions and theories!"

More laughter, and then she said, "And I also expect you to return with a hearty appetite. You will have an hour or so to rest and change into masquerade, and the murder may happen at any instant from then on. In the meantime, while you wait for the dastardly deed to occur, there will be a banquet in the dining room. And then, once the murder is committed and the investigation is over and the criminal is apprehended, you can celebrate with a tasty late supper, served in here. Sleep well — your day will be a full one!"

Taking the hint, the crowd broke up. Cissy hung back until the room was empty, hoping to tackle Gladys again about seeing Miss Harriet Gray. Gladys went off with the last group, however. Cissy hung around, waiting and hoping, but found herself alone, instead. When she gave up and went to the lobby, it, too, was empty. The whole ground floor of the hotel seemed deserted.

She hesitated, listening to people slamming doors and calling out to each other upstairs, but still no one came in. Making up her mind, she went to the double doors that led to what had been the theatre, and tentatively pushed.

The doors swung open. She stepped up onto what had been the stage, and listened to the soft thud behind her as the doors swung shut again. The gas candelabra in the dining room ceiling were out, and the only light came from the kitchen door at the far end. Silver and crystal glimmered faintly on the ghostly paleness of white tablecloths.

By contrast, gas sconces on either side of the paintings had been lit, so that the two portraits dominated the shadowy stage. Cissy, attention caught, slowly approached. Something had nudged at her mind while she'd studied these paintings earlier, and she was hoping the sense would come back. But her only thought was how much larger than life the two subjects seemed.

An actress and an adventurer, she thought, too dashing and romantic to bother with anything as mundane as marriage. Or perhaps they hadn't been able to get legally wed, because Captain Dexter was married to someone in Massachusetts — Timothy Dexter's mother. Timothy Dexter had insisted to Will Williams that he, Timothy Dexter, was the only *legal* heir, which meant that Jess was not...

Because Jess Williams was illegitimate.

Cissy winced, thinking what a tangled web had been weaved by the adventurer and the actress.

Timothy Dexter had spun a romantic story about coming to New Zealand in 1867, she remembered. Undoubtedly, his priority when he arrived was to contact his birth father. It must have been rather a shock, she thought, to find that Captain Jake Dexter was romantically involved with an actress, who had a large, loyal family. And how had the Grays felt about it? Altogether, she thought, it must have been a fraught and unpleasant meeting. She remembered the awful silence when Timothy had arrived, this late afternoon. It was very likely, she thought, that back in 1867 the Grays had given him exactly the same reception.

Indeed, it seemed amazing that Timothy had been thick-skinned enough to stay in New Zealand. After all, according to what he'd told her and her mother, he had a family of his own, back in Massachusetts. Hadn't he declared that he had come to New Zealand to retrieve his fortunes, presumably before returning home?

The Golden Goose had been a smash hit, Cissy remembered. Miners had come in their hundreds to drink and be entertained. The Golden Goose had laid golden eggs ... and Timothy Dexter was greedy. So, he had stayed to make sure of his share of the profits. Cissy wondered how Jess had felt when she had learned she had a half-brother — a half-brother who, unlike her, was legitimate.

Cissy knew how she herself would feel if she suddenly found that her father had another family in America.

Bewildered. Hurt. Angry. Very, very jealous.

Timothy Dexter had arrived in New Zealand in June 1867, Cissy remembered. So, when the family had moved to the Thames goldfields in August, Timothy had been with them — but, according to the housekeeper, Megs, Jess had not been part of the family scene at the time ... for she had gone somewhere else, instead.

She had been desperate to be an actress, but had lacked the stamina. She had told them that, herself. Poor Jess, Cissy thought slowly, had been a lot like herself, talented enough to warrant an artistic career, but lacking the confidence to blossom on the stage. When had she found it out? And how? Cissy had been told the bad news by an examiner, but it seemed more likely that Jess had learned the hard way, through experience. By logic, she may have run off to join an acting troupe, impelled by anger and jealousy, and a great need to become as famous as her mother. But, in the end, the result had been nil. Jess had been forced to return to the family fold, defeated by her own weakness. Cissy wondered how she felt about Minnie Gray's success — and Gladys, too, who had been defeated by a cruel accident. While it would have been hidden, it would be impossible not to feel some jealousy. Cissy's older brother, Monty, didn't do much of anything except spend money, and her only sister, Madge, was busily married. While Madge had had some stories published, she had not met with any great success, but Cissy thought she could guess how Gladys and Jess had felt.

Jess didn't even look like her actress mother, and presumably didn't look like the famous Mrs. Siddons, either. Both Minnie and Gladys had inherited the compelling, lambent, dark-blue eyes of the woman in the portrait, along with the Grays' typically blonde hair, but green-eyed, dark-haired Jess took after her father. Which, Cissy suddenly thought, Timothy Dexter did not. If he himself hadn't claimed that Captain Jake Dexter was his birth father, no one would have guessed it.

Minnie Gray knew a lot more than she had revealed, Cissy thought. That had been the moment that uneasiness had touched her mind, she suddenly remembered. She had been looking at the paintings and Jess had been asking about Minnie. Somehow, the two were connected.

Cissy climbed up on a chair to study the portraits more closely.

The long-fingered hand that rested on the globe of the world in Captain Dexter's portrait hid most of the countries, so that only Australia was revealed. That was where the portrait had been painted, she remembered. The artist was English, but lots of Englishmen sought their fortunes in the South Pacific. She looked, but the portraits had not been signed. The painter's identity was only a tiny mystery, however.

She turned her attention to the backdrop behind Harriet Gray's throne. It showed a vineyard, with figures running through the vines. Originally she had thought they were nymphs, but now, close up, she saw that the figures were masked, and were not wearing Greek or Roman draperies. Instead they were people from commedia dell'arte — Columbine, skirts tossing as she fled from angry Pantalon, her hand clinging to her companion, Pierrot, the white clown. And there was Harlequin, Arlecchino, enigmatic in motley, riding a dusty moonbeam, his attention not on the other pantomime figures, but on the actress on her throne.

So this was the source of Minnie's "over-active imagination," Cissy mused. She sighed, the long day catching up with her all at once, and turned and left the room.

When she knocked on the bedroom door there was no answer, and no one came to open it, and she realized her mother was in the bathroom, along the hall. But it didn't matter, because she had a second key. In her weary state she fiddled with the key for quite a long time before she realized that the door was unlocked.

So her mother had left it unfastened, she thought. Then a piece of paper fell out of the catch, and she picked it up. It was the torn corner of some kind of list. She read, "Room 6 — Mr. and Mrs. Brad—" and realized it was the list carried by whoever turned the beds down.

The housekeeper, Megs, or one of the maids? The list must have caught when the house key was turned, and so it hadn't locked properly. A simple explanation, she thought.

Nonetheless, she checked the bottom of her trunk.

And the envelope she had hidden there was gone.

13

Cissy was fast asleep when her mother came back to the room, and when she woke in the night, it took several disoriented moments to remember where she was. It was dark, and a queer thudding went on and on outside in the night. Then she remembered that it was the noise of the stampers, which ceased only at midnight on Saturdays, to mark the Sabbath for twenty-four hours.

Cissy lay still then, on the verge of falling back to sleep, groggily wondering what had disturbed her. Not the stampers, or the soft breathing sounds of her mother in the next bed, but stealthy sounds in the hotel corridor, she thought. Then she heard the soft footsteps again, and the quiet closing of a door.

Someone else had arrived, she thought, though she was also reminded of the woman who had stolen into Timothy Dexter's cabin on the *Royal George* — the woman with the initial H, the one who might be a journalist, because she had broken a mysterious story. The woman who had told him she was headed to New Zealand to greet him with a gift.

Then, even more eerily, Cissy remembered how the Grays had been summoned to help rebuild when the hotel had been burned. They had come to assist in the family emergency ... and another family emergency had arisen, for Timothy Dexter was here. Cissy listened. The hotel was perfectly quiet. Not a word, not a step, not even a creak...

She fell back to sleep.

She woke again very early in the morning, knowing exactly where she was and what had happened. She got up at once, and washed and dressed quietly, trying not to disturb her mother, shivering a little, because there was no fire in the room. Then she stole along the corridors and out onto the balcony.

The thunder of the batteries greeted her, the echoes of the stampers clamoring in the hills where the nocturnal mists drifted up to the rising sun. The scene was otherworldly and fascinating, fully worth braving the noise and the cold. Cissy leaned on the rail, looking past the wood-fronted buildings with tin-roofed verandas towards the shine of the sea. There was a brief glimpse of a small steamer with a broad white streak about her hull, slowly churning across the flat silver of the sea — not the *Wakatere*, but another vessel, coming into a wharf at this end of the town. Perhaps, she thought, it was the steamer that would take the party up the river.

Despite the constant din of the stamping mills, she could hear a chugging locomotive, not too far away to the south, shifting freight cars up and down a distant line, the sounds as homely as England. Below her, an occasional dray rattled by with a hunched figure at the reins, but otherwise the street was deserted. Perhaps, later on, it would be filled with men trudging by with their lunch boxes, heading for a day down the mines. Or perhaps all the miners lived in Grahamstown. When she strolled slowly round the balcony to the other side of the hotel, it was to see skeleton-shapes of poppet-heads dotted in the distance.

She was the only guest up and about, she thought, for there was no sound or movement from any of the windows she passed. The square sash windows were spaced evenly all along the wooden white walls, tightly shut and snugly curtained to keep out the noise of the stamper batteries, the array interrupted only by the French door that led to the parlor with the painted ships.

Cissy stopped, puzzled. The curtain over the French door had been drawn. She cast her mind back, trying to remember if Jess had closed the curtain. Or, perhaps, Megs...

Someone was in there. Cissy heard a small scraping noise that was familiar, though she couldn't place it. She knocked, but there was no reply. Impulsively, she tried the handle, but the door was locked. Still moved by impulse, she ran back to the balcony door she'd used, to hurry down the passage to the unmarked door that led to the parlor with the painted ships.

The wooden door looked just the same as it had the night before, and was locked just as tightly. Cissy tried several times, remembering that the handle was stiff, but to no avail. In the end, she gave up and went downstairs.

The lobby was deserted, so she ventured into the dining room. The rows of tables were set for breakfast, but no one had arrived. Cissy peeped through the communicating door to the kitchen, but saw no one she recognized. She felt too shy to go and ask for Miss Harriet Gray. Everyone in there was so busy that they hadn't even noticed when she had pushed open the door.

The lounge and the tavern were equally deserted. Defeated again, Cissy went back to the lobby. It was as empty as before, though someone had been that way, she saw, for there was a fancy tray with a teapot, milk jug, sugar bowl and two cups and saucers left out on the big sideboard, a folded napkin set neatly by each cup. Then Cissy nearly jumped out of her skin as a thunderous hammering sounded at the outside door.

No one came to answer it. When the loud knocking started up again, she ran across the lobby and opened the door. A messenger boy stood there, in some kind of uniform, early morning mist dewing his shoulders, puffs coming out of his mouth. He scowled, and thrust a bundle of letters and a small package at her.

He said, "Post and delivery."

"Excuse me?"

"The label tore off, so I was told to say the package is for Mrs. Dexter."

Then he went on his way, whistling steamily. Cissy inspected the package, feeling extremely intrigued. It was little wonder that the wrapping was damaged, as the package had come a long way. The postmark, just discernible, read *Massachusetts*. So someone in America did not know that Miss Harriet Gray had never married Captain Dexter, she thought.

Cissy went into the dining room, on her way to the kitchen to hand over the mail. Then, at the kitchen door, she stopped, thinking that this was her chance to find Miss Harriet Gray and talk to her, on the pretext of delivering the parcel. She almost felt emboldened enough to ask directions of the busy staff.

But then, she thought, she could probably find Miss Gray's room herself. The family apartments were where the dress circle of the theatre used to be, she remembered, right above her head. She went back into the lobby and looked about. The tray of tea things was gone, so she left the letters in its place and then, carrying the package, began to mount the stairs. Locating the right area was moiré difficult than she'd anticipated, but then at last she found a door with a notice that said *Private*.

She lifted one hand, ready to knock. When a man spoke loudly from just behind her, for the second time that morning she jumped a foot with fright.

Mr. Will Williams stood there. He was dressed in a Norfolk jacket, breeches, and gaiters, as if he was ready for a brisk morning stroll, a natty cloth cap on his head. He was holding the same tea-tray she had seen in the lobby, but with only one cup and saucer on it.

He snapped, "What in God's name are you doing?"

Cissy blinked, feeling defensive. "I just — "

"That's Timothy Dexter's room."

"*Who?*" Cissy's hand jerked away from the door as if burned. She stammered, "I – I thought it was another room. This package came and..." She broke off and said urgently, "Mr. Williams, I *must* see Miss Harriet Gray."

"I'm sorry. You can't."

"But ... the letter..."

"You'll understand, in due course."

"Mr. Williams, *please*..."

Then, again, she was interrupted. The door to the next room along opened and Jess Williams came out. She wore a pretty pale-blue dressing gown, held closely about her because of the early chill, and her hair was loose. Behind her, Cissy glimpsed a nice, comfortable room, with velvet-curtained windows, a *chaise longue* and a big tousled bed.

Jess said, "Will, where have you been?"

"Out walking." He brushed his moustache with one finger, gazing down at his little wife, holding the tray in his other hand as if he'd forgotten it.

Jess looked puzzled. "With Miss Miller?"

"No," Cissy said swiftly, grabbing her chance. "A package arrived for Miss Harriet Gray, and I came up to deliver it."

"For Mother?" said Jess. She sounded as delighted as a child, and put out her hand so impetuously that Cissy put the package into it.

Then, to Cissy's surprise, Jess started to open the wrapping, wondering aloud who it might have come from. Cissy dithered in embarrassment, trying to summon the courage to remonstrate, feeling very uncomfortable that Jess should open a parcel that was intended for somebody else. Will Williams, standing there watching indulgently, didn't say a word to stop her.

Two women were coming down the corridor towards them, and when Cissy looked up she saw her mother and Miss Fleet. As usual, Miss Fleet looked perfectly splendid. Today, she was wearing a dark green costume with dark brown frilling at throat, elbows, and cuffs, and a small hat embellished with felt flowers and pheasant feathers.

"So here we are," Clara Miller said brightly, coming to a stop. "And what a *beautiful* day it is going to be. I saw the sun break out just as I left the room."

Then, to Cissy's utter horror, she said, "My dear, have you delivered that letter to Miss Harriet Gray, yet?"

Cissy didn't dare look at Will Williams, and though she waited he said nothing to explain why he had refused to let her see his mother-in-law. Instead, she looked down at her walking shoes, and muttered, "I didn't have a chance."

"Oh Cissy, when Miss Minnie Gray put such trust in you!"

"It wasn't my fault, Mama!"

The others had stopped listening, because Miss Fleet exclaimed, "What a darling little box!"

The wrapping of the parcel had been discarded, to reveal a pretty little tin enameled with pictures of flowers. Then Jess opened it, and most unexpectedly laughed. "Oh well," she said, and looked at Will and smiled and shrugged.

Cissy looked from one to the other in some puzzlement, for the tin held six little sweets, shaped and colored into whimsical fruits.

Two little pineapples, two apples and two miniature apricots were set neatly into crimped wax-paper cups. They were bound to be good to taste, as well, as the strong scent of ground almonds told her that they were marzipan, a personal favorite, especially with Christmas cake.

Miss Fleet said, "I didn't know you could get that kind of candy here."

She was studying Jess with her head a little on one side and her lips pursed, rather like a schoolmistress summing up a new pupil, Cissy thought, However, Jess merely smiled.

"The package came from Massachusetts," she said. "By post."

"Then it probably came on the *Royal George*," hazarded Mrs. Miller. "What a charming gift."

"But from whom, I wonder?" said Jess, searching for a card. "It must have fallen out," she decided.

Cissy, unable to bear it any more, said, "But, Mrs. Williams—"

"They would make wonderful *cake* decorations," said Mrs. Miller.

"An elderly cousin of mine was recently sent a box of marzipan just like that one," said Miss Fleet reminiscently. "It came from Boston. She admired the box so greatly that she said she would keep it as a trinket box, once the candy was eaten. And she said the candy was delicious, too. I didn't have a chance to taste, myself, but I am sure they will be much enjoyed by the recipient."

"Look, please, they were meant for—"

Mr. Williams was looking down at the tea-tray as if he'd just remembered he held it. He said, "Excuse me." As Cissy dithered helplessly, he went inside his bedroom and his wife Jess followed him, the tin of marzipan in her hand.

And the bell for early breakfast rang, as Cissy watched the door swing firmly shut in her face.

While eating breakfast, Cissy saw another chance to talk with Will Williams. She sat facing the window that let out onto the yard, and watched the arrival of the procession of hackneys that would take the party to the river steamer. Then Mr. Williams stepped out, evidently to get the drivers into order, and Cissy set down her spoon. Her mother protested, as her breakfast was only half eaten, but Cissy merely excused herself, and dashed through the door that led to the yard.

When she got there, Will Williams had his watch in his hand and was looking a little worried, and Cissy remembered that the party had to be on board the steamer in time to catch the tide, when it turned to run up the river. She didn't have much time, she thought, so without any preamble she blurted out, "It was *stolen*."

He turned. "I beg your pardon?"

"The envelope I had hidden in the bottom of my trunk. It was right under all my clothes, and I made sure of it before we left the *Royal George*."

She told him about finding the bedroom door unlocked, and then how she had immediately checked for the envelope. He listened carefully, looking down at the ground and brushing his moustache in the reflective manner that seemed characteristic. Then he said, "How long had your bedroom door been unlocked?"

"I don't know, but..."

"If Megs left it unlocked after turning down the beds, then it must have been unlocked for quite a long time. Anyone could have taken the letter."

"But—"

"I certainly don't think it's worth upsetting the guests with accusations of theft."

"Well, I can certainly understand that, but I need to explain the situation to Miss Harriet Gray!"

"I've thought a lot about that letter," said Mr. Williams, ignoring this, "and have come to the conclusion that it would cause of lot of unnecessary unpleasantness. It will upset people, and for no real reason at all. Minnie has been nervous and highly-strung lately. She might have made some wild accusations, Perhaps it is better that the letter is lost."

Cissy stared, anger rising. "Mr. Williams, surely Miss Harriet should be the judge of that," she began heatedly, and when he tried to interrupt, she exclaimed, "I promised Miss Minnie that I would do my best to carry her message to her aunt, and I haven't, and I feel bad about it. I insist on seeing Miss Harriet Gray, and explaining it all to her!"

"Insist? He echoed, and reddened. "I told you that isn't possible," he snapped.

And then, while she simmered with frustration, the rest of the party emerged from the Golden Goose.

14

Cissy, sitting mutinously in the foremost hackney, where he had firmly placed her, watched Mr. Williams hurry back into the hotel after handing all the ladies into the string of vehicles. Then the horses were slapped into a smart trot, and off they rattled through the wide streets of Shortland.

Mrs. Miller, in the carriage next to Cissy, with Miss Fleet on her other side, chattered away in her lively fashion, but Cissy, still feeling extremely resentful about Will Williams' off-hand dismissal of her worries, didn't bother to listen. She saw a mown green sward with a pretty picket fence and a band rotunda, and a picturesque little railway station, too, but remained moodily unmoved by the scene. Then the wheels rumbled over the timbers of Shortland Wharf and the hackney came to a stop.

Cissy climbed down and contemplated the steamer that awaited them, bobbing in the first rush of the morning tide. The vessel was the same one she'd glimpsed chugging into port that dawn, a very pretty craft called *Waimarie*, with a tall funnel set forward of a spacious deckhouse. There was quite a crowd of people about, for many of those who were bound for Paeroa had come on the steamer from Auckland, and Shortland was just a breakfast stop for them. Hackneys rumbled up, stopped, emptied their passengers, and rumbled away again, while the Golden Goose party was hassled into a coherent group on the jetty.

Their shepherd was Gladys, who was also their only tour guide. The prospect didn't seem to daunt her in the slightest. She looked perky and brisk, dressed most exotically in a black and red-striped day dress, with a voluminous black mantle thrown over all.

"Good morning, ladies and gentlemen," she cried. With the practiced ease of an actor or a lecturer, she pitched her voice so it carried right to the back, despite the thumping of the stampers, and entertained the passengers lined up at the rail of the *Waimarie,* as well as the Golden Goose group. "The experience of a lifetime awaits!"

She waved an imperious arm, and the Golden Goose group cooperatively shuffled up the gangplank, and assembled again on the stern deck of the steamer. "No place in the Colony is as talked about as the Thames goldfields," she continued, still at the top of her voice. "For nowhere else does the barren rock yield such a richness of gold! Since the first strike, in August 1867, ladies and gentlemen, the name of the Thames goldfields has become celebrated worldwide, and the tour today offers you the unrivalled chance to participate for a little while in a colonial sensation."

Then her voice seemed to lower, just as easily heard, but becoming husky and mysterious. "But all of you from the Golden Goose must never forget that you are taking part in a melodrama at the same time — a play with a victim, and a vicious murderer. The lady in front of you or the gentleman at your side could be a guilty schemer, or the most innocent of souls, and it is up to you to find out which is which. So, I insist that you mingle, and — most of all — *talk,* and never forget for one moment that you are playing the sleuth. Be inquisitive, be curious, forget proper reticence for just a few hours. Ladies and gentlemen, I now give you license to be as plain downright *nosy* as you like! Don't be shy, don't be afraid, ask and learn — and remember, too, that you are allowed to tell as many imaginative fibs as you like, with the aim of creating confusion."

An obedient babble began as the party took up the challenge — all except Cissy, who had just realized that not only was Timothy Dexter missing, but someone else, as well.

Harmony. The American girl. Harmony Bradford. Who might be just twenty-one years old, but flirted like a mature woman. Whose name began with H.

Harmony had awoken feeling poorly, Cissy was told when she asked. And had reluctantly decided against the arduous trip, not feeling up to it. Instead, she would have a quiet day back at the Golden Goose Hotel.

Which made Cissy realize that she'd missed a golden chance.

The sun had come out, and the view was even prettier, but Cissy was mentally berating herself for her lack of resourcefulness. If she had only thought of it, she could have pretended that she was ill, too. A whole day of freedom could have stretched ahead of her, a day in which to find Miss Harriet Gray. But the paddles were churning, and the steamboat was chugging away from the wharf. Cissy was here whether she liked it or not, obliged to take part in the game.

The scenery was *splendid*, as Cissy's mother exclaimed. And, indeed, the river journey presented a remarkable vista, the hills and forests and broad, far-reaching marshlands all in harmonious proportion. The early morning light was wonderful, pale shafts of sunlight highlighting the ferns and rushes on the eastern bank and the speckle of wild flowers in the marsh-meadows beyond. It was all so *flat*, or so Cissy thought. It was as if the steamer was floating in the air, miraculously puffing just above the land. Absolutely dreamlike, she thought. She almost wanted to pinch herself, to make sure she was awake.

Then the scenery became real again, as magnificent trees came into sight, to the west. Tall and black, they were called *kahikatea* — or so Gladys said. Their tall, densely leaved branches were reflected on the shiny surface of the river, which had become very busy. Picturesque scows crested the tide, accompanying the *Waimarie* upstream, almost scupper-deep with the heavy loads of coal they had carried all the way from the north. The *Waimarie* passed a mill where other scows were taking on back-loads of timber for the passage to Auckland, and where tall ocean-going ships were anchored, also taking on timber.

There were canoes on the river, too, padded by Maoris who exchanged loud greetings with the steamboat captain. Good-naturedly, he had a few lines thrown out, so they could be towed bobbing along in the steamer's wake. It was fun for them, and the passengers, too, but scarcely necessary, Cissy thought. Because of the sweep of the tide, every vessel, small or large, was going up the river at a famous rate.

All about Cissy, guests from the Golden Goose chattered and laughed together, evidently taking full advantage of the license that Gladys had given them to indulge their curiosity, and make up lies of their own. Cissy was guiltily aware that she hadn't taken part as much as she should — that she wasn't being a good sport. This was the kind of lively social situation that her mother enjoyed, but which made Cissy's skin crawl with anticipated embarrassment.

And Gladys wasn't making it easy to relax, either. The very moment that Cissy had braced herself to make some kind of conversation, Gladys would command the younger members of the party to change places and sit with yet another stranger. Cissy, being one of the young ones, had to move about and accost people she was sure she had never met before, and then listen to their transparently ridiculous tall stores, when she would have much preferred to sit alone and admire the scenery. At the end of the fifth half-hour, she was feeling tired and mutinous, as well as guilty, as she contemplated her latest companion.

This was an elderly woman who had been ensconced the whole journey on a bench in the shadowy deckhouse. Cissy thought she looked vaguely familiar, perhaps from the blur of introductions the night before. Her silver hair was abundant despite her age, drawn up under a pretty blue hat with peacock feather decorations and a veil that matched the wool costume she was wearing. Her face had the crumpled softness of a fine old kid glove, and was dominated by wide, black-lashed eyes that perhaps had once been a much darker blue.

Those eyes twinkled from behind the veil, while Cissy looked back rather nervously. She did not particularly like old people. Her mother, Clara, had been given to a childless aunt when she was born, and so Cissy had two maternal grandmothers, one adoptive who was really a great-aunt, and the real one, who had never been forgiven for giving her baby away. Consequently, the whole grandmother business was difficult, a sentiment that Cissy had transferred to all elderly women.

The playful glint in those eloquent eyes was reassuring, however, so Cissy was only a little diffident when she said, "May I ask where you come from, ma'am?"

"Of course you can," said the old lady with vigor. "I wondered if you would ever ask. I hail from Ballarat, Victoria. That's in Australia, you know. They have goldfields over there, too. I was a *diggeress* in my youth. And I think I can safely bet that you have never met a diggeress before."

Cissy certainly had not, and she did not believe that they had ever existed, either. She mutely shook her head, waiting for the next wild revelation. People were exclaiming loudly as the mastheads of vessels moored at Junction Wharf loomed into sight above the trees upriver, but the old lady from Ballarat paid no attention, being lost in her fanciful yarn.

"It is not generally known that females can be as resourceful as men in the fortune-digging business," she went on in her lively style. "Men had their digging costume, and we women had ours. It was a leather wide-awake hat with a mantilla draped over, and a well-made suit, which was a trim combination of tight-fitting polka and a good handsome skirt.

"Mind you," she amended, after a pause that was far too short for Cissy to find words to comment, "a lesser kind of women preferred a much more ostentatious show. The servants wore silk! And I remember well the day when I was at the blacksmith's and a digger's woman came in with her horse and the material to have it shod with gold. And there were actresses! Can you believe it? However, even those lesser types were hailed with joy at the diggings, for women were extremely scarce, on the whole. The arrival of a woman was guaranteed to create a mighty stir. 'A woman,' the men would cry as I approached some far-flung settlement; 'a woman, a woman!' And they would run alongside my horse. At one place they had been so starved for the sight of a female that they lifted me up, horse and all, to bear me in triumph into the town."

"Good heavens," said Cissy inadequately, so bemused by this ridiculous yarn that the steamer's arrival at Paeroa seemed mundane by comparison.

That, she decided as she descended the gangway, was most certainly the tallest of all the tall tales she had heard so far that day, and she doubted that she would hear another one to match it.

15

If Junction Wharf seemed not much more than a sleepy little river anchorage that happened to be adorned with big coal hoppers as well as ordinary trees, the horse-tramway ride into the town of Paeroa was definitely enlivening. The Golden Goose party bowled along in style, up the centre of a broad street lined with wooden buildings that included a double-storied balconied hotel, which, while not quite so grand as the Golden Goose, was faithful to the goldfields tradition that had rapidly become familiar.

And Paeroa was surprisingly impressive, decided Mrs. Miller, who was enjoying a first-rate time. She saw good solid public buildings, including a substantial bank, which obviously did a lot of business during the week. By comparison, the railway station looked ordinary enough, being the usual line of wooden buildings. But it had quite a history, or so she was informed. Not only the station but the railway line itself were monuments to civic persistence. The first sod for the railway line had been turned by Prime Minister Sir George Grey, 'way back in 1878, and everyone had expected that it would be completed with a couple of years. But things had not turned out as planned. Every road that crossed the proposed track was given a notice reading, LOOK OUT FOR THE ENGINE, but most of the notices has sagged into moldy sawdust long before any engines had arrived. In the meantime, short bits of track had been laid at long intervals, and every now and then various politicians and dignitaries were run up and down what railway there was, in a train composed of one engine and one very special carriage.

The idea had been to persuade those politicians to hurry up with allotting funds to build the line. However, the publicity gimmick hadn't worked very well, for the original bits of rusted track had to be replaced before the line was at long last finished in

1898 — but the special ceremonial carriage remained, much to the delight of the Golden Goose party, because that was the one that was waiting for them. The line to the mines at Karanghake was not open for the usual passenger traffic yet, carrying freight goods only, but, for the pleasure and convenience of the Golden Goose guests, that special carriage was tacked onto the end of the next freight train bound to Karangahake.

Accordingly, they trundled off at the extremity of a long snake of coal wagons, drawn by a balloon-funneled puffer that chugged along backwards. Meanwhile, the party, exclaiming loudly, examined their accommodations, which, as Mrs. Miller agreed, certainly warranted close admiration. Half the special carriage was divided into compartments, each with two long seats that were plumply upholstered in purple velvet, and with walls lined with fine red Spanish leather. There was a table between each pair of seats, and hot pipes along the floor so the passengers could warm their feet. The other half of the carriage was a plush saloon, with great mirrors on the walls at each end, and smaller ones in the ceiling, mirrors that had cracked and darkened only a little with twenty-seven years of reflecting politicians. There was a great mahogany table, too, where those politicians had seated themselves to be photographed signing meaningless documents. There were many wide windows with pink candles in sconces on either side of each, and the view was tremendous.

The train drew swiftly away from the town of Paeroa, clacked across a bridge and puffed through brightly colored meadow marshes, on the way to a green and grey wilderness of mountains. Then they were in a wild gorge that twisted between hump-topped hills that were riven with valleys and clefts, the track curving through laboriously hacked cuttings, with glimpses of a foaming stream that bubbled about the debris cast off by a multitude of mining operations. The cliffs that rose on either side became blazoned with zigzagging trails and precipitous roads where traction engines labored, and as the train penetrated further into the gorge, Mrs. Miller saw the trestles and head buildings of mines, clinging unbelievably to rock spurs and plunging precipices. It was, she decided, a most wild and *romantic* scenery, and the colonial splendor of the carriage was an appropriate means of viewing it.

Then her quiet enjoyment was disturbed by a slight cough from the only other occupant of her compartment.

Clara Miller turned her enquiring gaze to this person, to see a young woman with wide, wicked, dark blue eyes and a mass of thick gold hair, who was as spectacular as any of the scenery. She was wearing the usual kind of Gibson girl costume suitable for a young woman in her twenties, with a straight Oxford blue skirt and blue-striped blouse with a blue cravat. Her straw boater, however, was embellished with enough silk roses to furnish a large bouquet. And, as Mrs. Miller observed after close inspection, the young lady was *not* wearing a corset. Her form, though slim and firm, was obviously unhampered.

When she met Mrs. Miller's gaze the young woman smiled, her expression as knowing as if Mrs. Miller had voiced her thoughts aloud. Then she said, in a clear, beautifully enunciated voice, "Hello!"

"Hello," said Clara Miller. She gave out her sixth visiting card and the day and explained, "The address is in Devon."

"And I came from Australia," said the young woman, but without handing over a card. Instead, she lowered her voice and said, "Did you notice the lady in the compartment next door? The one with the very pretty blue hat?"

Mrs. Miller whispered, "The person of rather *advanced* years?"

"The very one."

"Ah."

"She comes from Australia, as I do. In fact, she is rather well known there."

"Yes?"

"There is a certain amount of scandal attached to her name. I don't expect you know that her husband was a pirate?"

"Her *husband*?"

"Well..."

The young woman broke off, looking thoughtful. Clara Miller waited a good long moment for the sentence to be resumed, then gave up, saying bracingly, "I shouldn't worry too much about it, if

I were you. The lady in question has outlived any scandal, surely. After all, it isn't so unusual."

"I beg your pardon?"

"For a person from Australia to have a somewhat *questionable* background. One hears such awful stories of men being deported for the most *trivial* of thefts — quilts and pocket handkerchiefs, bread for their starving children and all that, and I am sure he was called a pirate on the most *trivial* of evidence."

"Oh, but he was definitely guilty."

"He was *what*?"

"He stole a ship. Quite blatantly. And that, without doubt, is piracy."

"Good heavens! But," said Mrs. Miller doubtfully, "I don't see how that would be possible, not in this day and age."

"Oh, but he was commanding the ship at the time, so that made it quite easy. He simply neglected to take the ship home."

"Oh," said Mrs. Miller, her voice failing her, rather. "I *see*..."

"You are right, he had an excellent reason for the theft," said the young woman brightly, though Mrs. Miller had said nothing of the kind. "It was an act of revenge. He had just found out that the owner of the ship had stolen his house and his wife."

"His *wife*?"

"Yes. She and the ship's owner were living in adultery."

This free and easy use of the word *adultery* deprived Mrs. Miller of her voice entirely, for the moment. She felt more than a little shocked. Their hostess might have given them license to make up wild stories at will, but young people these days really were *too* frank and forward, she thought.

After that, silence prevailed, until curiosity got the better of her. She ventured, "The owner of the ship was ... living in sin with the lady in the next compartment?"

"Good gracious, no!" It was the young woman's turn to be shocked. "The adulteress was a different woman entirely."

"I see," said Mrs. Miller, not seeing at all. "And what happened to the ship?"

"He sold it at the very next port. Honolulu, I think."

"Well, I should say that would be the sensible course. It would not be a good idea *at all* to keep on sailing about, with that kind of record behind him."

"Oh, but he didn't stop sailing," the young woman assured her. "He used the money from the sale to buy himself a lovely craft of his own, and then he sailed about the Pacific for years after that."

"Until the day he was finally apprehended," Mrs. Miller added helpfully. She had at long last realized that this was part of the murder game.

"Apprehended? I never said that!"

"But I thought you said he was a convict?"

"Certainly not," said the young woman, and had the sauce to wag a finger. "Australians are not necessarily convicts, you know."

"Of course not," said Mrs. Miller hastily, recollecting this young person's place of origin. "But I must say the gentleman sounds a *most* remarkable fellow."

"It wasn't just that, that made him remarkable," the young woman declared with enthusiasm. "He also became very rich. That old lady in the next compartment is worth rather a lot, by inheritance as well as on her own account."

Mrs. Miller paused before replying, gazing at the young woman very thoughtfully indeed. Then she said, "I *see*."

And *see* she certainly did, or so she thought.

16

After taking a glass of the far-famed waters at the Te Aroha hot springs, Mrs. Miller joined Cissy in the gardens. She sat down beside her daughter, enquiring rather plaintively, "Are you yourself, dear, or are you pretending to be someone else? I *do* hope you're you, for I don't know how many more farfetched yarns I can listen to today. Do you think it's just the actors who are telling fibs, or is it a kind of infectious disease that everyone has caught?"

"I expect it's a disease," said Cissy. "I was wondering about Mr. Schuyler Bradford the third. Do you think he is real? He seems to know an awful lot about the business of ships, but he behaves more like a publican than a capitalist."

"Oh, but he is *perfectly* real, Cissy, a very big businessman, and very good at it too, I am sure. Mr. Bradford is one of the directors of the company that owns the *Royal George*, and a lot of other steamers, as well."

"Good heavens," said Cissy, marveling. "So that explains it."

"Explains what, dear?"

"How he can afford to take his family around the world. But have you talked to the old lady with the dashing manner who claims to have been a diggeress?"

"Yes, I did, dear, and I heard a tall tale *about* her, too. But I do credit that she had made a fortune in some way or other, for her costume is really beautiful, in exquisite taste. She is travelling with her nephew, who is after her money, no doubt, for he seems a most disreputable type, not *at all* a gentleman, if you know what I mean. I actually witnessed him drink from a brandy flask, right in front of ladies, and then he had the sauce to offer one of them a swallow. *He* is with a young woman who doesn't look as if she'd all that she ought to be *at all*. She claims to come from Australia, and told me a most elaborate tale about a man who stole a *whole ship*, but was never apprehended. A pirate! She gave a most unlikely name, too, impossibly old-fashioned. *Jasmine*, she said. She and the nephew pretend not to know each other, but it's as plain as the nose on your face that they're in cohorts, and are most likely to be murderers."

"Good heavens," said Cissy, as amazed as ever at what her mother could deduce from social trivialities. "And what is his name?"

"The nephew? Valentine."

"What!" Then Cissy began to laugh. "Isn't that a little unusual and outdated, too?"

"Well, it was quite fashionable in my youth, you know. I remember a certain garden party and a certain *most* handsome and attentive young man by that name..."

To Cissy's regret, her mother abruptly recollected her audience, broke off, and said briskly, "But I must admit I am so pleased we came, such fun, don't you think? Wasn't that a marvelous railway carriage?"

Cissy had no trouble agreeing, for it certainly had been fun — and educational, too. Mr. Daw, who was the manager of the Crown Battery, had met them at the door of that marvelous railway carriage and escorted the party all over the works. It had been a tour of variety and excitement, absolutely fascinating despite the terrible noise and the choking fumes. They had seen the kilns where the quartz was roasted, and had endured the thunder of a whole huge battery of stamps at close quarters, mesmerized by the rhythmic rising and plunging of the gigantic iron heads as they battered the hard rock into sand. There had been an unexpected chemical novelty, too — the Crown Battery had been the first in the world to employ the cyanide process of extracting gold and silver from quartz, and so, as the party had been led past the huge precipitation tanks, Cissy had smelled the deadly poison for the first time ever, like the sickly scent of decaying almonds. Like marzipan gone bad.

Cissy had often heard that miners were a thirsty lot, but the men who worked in the clamor and dust of the batteries must have been constantly dry in the mouth, she thought. When Mr.

Daw had kindly taken them all to his fine wooden home, called Crown House, the tea and coffee he had provided for them all, along with a dainty buffet lunch, had been extremely welcome. Then back to that marvelous railway carriage they had gone, and had been trundled back to Paeroa. They had not had to change transport there, as at Paeroa the special carriage had been hooked onto the end of another train, a very short one this time, that drew just a few closely guarded vans to Auckland, making a stop at Te Aroha on the way, where the special coach was cast off. The vans were closely guarded because they held rough bars of bullion, sent from the batteries of Karangahake for further refining. Mr. Daw had jokingly referred to it as the Te Aroha Express. He was constantly waiting, he declared, for the Golden Goose people to stage one of their murders on that train.

They had travelled without incident, however, and now here they were at the fashionable spa resort of Te Aroha — which, as Cissy had learned, was one of the most favored and most famous places in New Zealand, celebrated for its character and the mountain that overlooked the village. The bathhouse was a lovely long white single-storied building with decorative eaves and witch's hat-capped chimneys, tucked into the base of the pretty fern-tree-clothed mountain, with a graceful flight of steps leading down to the velvet sward of a croquet green.

Shortly the party would catch the 3:20 train — the ordinary train — back to Thames. Meantime, people were strolling around the extensive gardens, taking the waters in the bathhouse, or doing whatever they pleased.

The springs were everything advertised, no doubt, but Cissy hadn't bothered to sample the waters, preferring to rest on a bench in a sheltered spot in the sun. There, she had been lost in deep contemplation, thinking over what she had learned so far, and brooding about the lost envelope and her failure to meet Miss Harriet Gray, until her mother had arrived.

Now, at last, her mother was silent. Having delivered her opinion of the old lady in blue, the flamboyant Australian girl with the rose-burdened hat, and the saucy nephew who was undoubtedly her companion, Clara Miller leaned back on the park bench, holding her lacy parasol poised because it was surprisingly *warm* in the sun.

Then she ruined the return of tranquility by saying, "How *could* you have lost the envelope, Cissy? Miss Minnie Gray made such a *thing* of it, dear, that I really am disappointed that you should be so careless."

Cissy said flatly, "I didn't lose it, and I don't know why you jumped to that conclusion."

"What? But..."

"The envelope in the bottom of my trunk was stolen."

"Stolen?" echoed Mrs. Miller. "But why? And by whom?"

"When I went back up to the room last night, it was gone."

"Cissy, have you just made that up? Are you partaking in this fashion for telling fibs?"

"Mama, I am not making this up, it really happened that way. The door had been unlocked and the letter wasn't there. It was gone without trace," Cissy added, for it was a popular line in the detective novels she read, though she reflected then that it wasn't quite true.

"Who on earth could you suspect of wanting to steal Miss Minnie's message?"

Cissy shook her head. She had her theory, but no way of proving it.

"And who would unlock the door and leave it unlocked?"

"Megs, when she turned down the beds. I thought it might have been a maid, but Mr. Williams told me that the housekeeper does that every night."

"You think the *housekeeper* stole the envelope?"

"Not at all. I'm just pointing out that the door was unlocked. The opportunity was there."

"*Indeed* it was there. *Anyone* could have gone into our room. What a thought! Do you think we should complain?"

Cissy shrugged, and said, "It would be embarrassing for the hotel management. And Mr. Williams didn't seem to think that the message was important."

"Mr. Williams? Did he know about Miss Minnie's letter?"

"Well, of course he did. He's Miss Minnie's set designer and her half-brother, too. She told him about it." And that was why he and Clem Gray had taken passage on the *Royal George*, she thought.

"Then who else did she tell, I wonder?" said Mrs. Miller. "Do you think Mr. Dexter knows?"

"I don't believe so," said Cissy, though she thought Mr. Dexter had been keeping a very low profile since he had arrived at the hotel.

"I can't understand why she didn't give the envelope to Mr. Williams to carry here — or her brother Clement."

"She didn't know they were going to make the sudden decision to come here, not when she gave it to me," said Cissy. And, she thought, the actress had been insistent that the envelope be given to Miss Harriet Gray and no one else, not even any other member of the family. For some mysterious reason, it was absolutely private.

Clara Miller ruminated a moment, and then said, "But even if Miss Minnie Gray didn't know they were coming to Thames when she gave you the letter, surely it would have been easier to post it. It would have been safer, and so much easier, and not nearly so *embarrassing*."

Her mother was right, Cissy mused. The tin of marzipan had arrived safely by mail. From America. From Massachusetts.

A sudden thought occurred to her, and she said slowly, "Didn't you tell me that Miss Fleet had worked as a companion to somebody?"

"That was my *impression*, dear, though I don't know that you could call it a *job*," said Mrs. Miller. "For all I know, she could have been living with an elderly relative, giving her companion-ship in return for room and board and the expectation of a small legacy, maybe, when the old lady died."

Cissy found herself the subject of a rather shrewd look. "She mentioned a *cousin*, this morning," her mother said. "An *elderly* cousin. Perhaps she is dead."

And Miss Fleet wore clothes that had once been expensive, but were outdated, and had to be altered to fit. Cissy wondered how very small a legacy like that might be. Not very large at all, she deduced, or Miss Fleet wouldn't have been driven to all that creative needlework.

She said, "Once, on board the *Royal George*, you made the observation that there must be rich folks in New England, and Miss Fleet seemed to take exception. Do you remember that?"

"Of course I remember," returned her mother with a small sniff. "I'm not *quite* in my dotage yet. And I actually said Massachusetts."

And so she had, Cissy remembered. Massachusetts was just one part of New England, and the Bradfords, who hailed from Connecticut, were New Englanders, too.

"But what made you make that comment? It seemed to come out of nowhere."

"It just popped out of my mouth, dear, you know the way one's mind can run on. It was just a *stray thought*, which signified nothing at all. I'd just thought of something that nice young New York lawyer told me. Gossip, really, but he said it was the talk of all the legal set, and Mr. Dexter found it interesting, too."

Cissy blinked. "*Who?*"

"Mr. Timothy Dexter. It was at the hotel in San Francisco, the same day we went to the theatre. While you were *dithering* with the pianist about what songs to sing, he and I enjoyed quite a pleasant little chat. You know, it was very *odd* that he didn't tell me then that he was sailing on the *Royal George*. Or perhaps he made his booking at the very last moment, like Mr. Williams and Mr. Clem Gray."

"Yes, Mama," said Cissy, who had no intention of confiding her theory that Mr. Dexter had changed his plans when he had found that she and her mother had been to the theatre and talked with Miss Minnie Gray. Instead, she said, "But what were you and Mr. Dexter talking about, that he found so interesting?"

"About what the New York lawyer *told* me, dear. You know, everyone thinks that the practice of law must be frightfully dull and dusty ,but it's not like that at all, for such *interesting* problems crop up. He told me several anecdotes, but this was the one he dwelled on the most, for it had occasioned such a lot of gossip and speculation among the legal set. An old spinster lady had just died in Salem, and the estate was *enormous*, for her late brother had amassed a great fortune by the time he died, but the old lady had only had it in trust, and so the fortune was in abeyance, or whatever the *legal* term might be. There was a hunt on for the heir, as the nephew, the old man's only son, was declared dead when he was young, but the question was whether he was *really* dead, and might be living under another name, completely unaware that *millions* were due to him, if he could only prove his existence. I thought it fascinating that so much wealth should be lying about in Massachusetts, waiting for someone to claim it, and that it might end up not belonging to *anyone*, unless they find a suitable heir. That's why it stuck in my mind," she decided.

"I suppose he didn't tell you the old lady's name?"

"But he did, dear."

"And you've forgotten it."

"No, as a matter of fact, I haven't," he mother said, with a trace of hauteur. "It was Grace, only Grace was not her Christian name. It was her surname. How unusual, don't you think? Her name was Miss Etty Grace. Or perhaps Hetty. You would think that Etty or Hetty would be *short* for something, would you not? However, it was her proper first name. Or so the lawyer told me."

Cissy was staring at her, sitting rigidly, remembering the death notices in the paper she had carried from Miss Minnie's dressing room — the same paper that Miss Minnie had clipped.

She said, "Mama, you remember Miss Minnie cutting a piece out of a newspaper, which she put in the envelope?"

"Of course I do." Mrs. Miller's sniff was audible.

"You didn't happen to see the headline?"

"No, but I did glance at the illustration."

"And what was it?"

"A gravestone. The headstone to a grave."

17

The train, as usual, was a little late. The Thames line was a branch one, and so the train was mixed, carrying freight cars as well as passenger coaches, which always necessitated a lot of shunting about at either end. Harriet Gray was glad to get inside a carriage and find a seat on the western side, in a patch of warm sun. A middle-aged men from Christchurch sat beside her, but instead of quizzing her he promptly went to sleep, snoring slightly and exhaling a strong smell of beer. It was obvious what waters he had been taking, thought Harriet with amusement, and was pleased to lean back and lose herself in drowsy meditations.

The day had been too big for her, Harriet thought, but she had wanted to come. She had come on this tour dozens of times over the years, but each time saw it afresh, through the eyes of the tourists. She enjoyed the excuse for not wearing mourning, too. Jake had always hated her in black, and would have been furious if she'd worn mourning on his behalf, but people tended to gossip if one didn't.

It had all been the usual tremendous fun. She supposed that some folk would consider the murder scenarios somewhat repetitive, but only if they took part in the Golden Goose Murder Experience more than once. But it was indeed repetitive, she thought. As the engine let out a long hoot and all the coaches lurched against each other with a mighty clanging, Harriet idly wondered how often she had played the part of the rich, elderly aunt, who was fated to be murdered by a scheming nephew and his seductive young mistress.

It was the scenario she liked best, replete with passion and greed. How many people envied old relatives and their rich possessions, and begrudged them their grip on life? Too many people — too many greedy scoundrels. It was little wonder that some of them became impatient, and anticipated the dark angel with poison, shot or sword. And no wonder that the scenario had such popular appeal, for it rang with the truth of real life.

The train chugged about a great curve, gradually taking on speed. Harriet swayed with the jogging of the iron wheels, her head feeling heavy. Tonight, she thought, the elderly diggeress would have to be poisoned. She really didn't feel strong enough to face being stabbed or shot. In the seats forward of her she could see people still animatedly cross-examining each other, asking ridiculous questions, and at that moment she envied them all their youth, as relative as that might be. She was mostly envious of their energy, though, for, truth to tell, she felt extremely tired.

Tired? It was more than that. There was a sense of wrongness inside her. As always nowadays, there had been pains lurking about inside her breast when she'd woken that morning. Today's pain, however, had been different, so unusually severe that she had wondered for a while whether she should cancel her part in the murder play. But she had decided against it. It was such a nuisance for Gladys when the scenario had to be changed at the last moment, and, after all, she was an old trouper who had gone onto the stage at far worse times than this. And she knew from experience that the pains went away within an hour, gradually losing their clawing grip.

Those pains had started just a week before Jake had so unexpectedly died, but she hadn't told him about it, and she still hadn't told any of the family, either, though the doctor had shaken his head and frowned. She was old, she thought, and that was that. The pains were just another penalty of the passing of the years. All she had to do was consciously relax and the pains would go away.

Relax. Her eyes closed, and did not open until the engine hooted to a stop at Shortland Station.

Valentine was most assiduous about helping her out of the train and into one of the waiting hackneys. But that was part of the scenario, of course. Harriet could see the English child watching her closely, the one who was so bashful — and no wonder, with a mother like that, who could talk the sun right out of the sky. The English child's large grey eyes were surprisingly intelligent, but if anyone solved the mystery, Harriet thought, it would be the girl's mother, who was a great deal shrewder than her gossipy exterior indicated.

At last they were back at the hotel. Harriet took one look at the stairs, decided she could not face them yet, and went off firmly to the little sitting room at the end of the dining room, the part that had been the stage. There, she could nestle in Jake's big chair, and take off her hat in splendid isolation, for while the tables were set ready for the banquet, the dining room was empty. The guests were all upstairs in their rooms, or in the parlor drinking tea, or in the tavern at the bar, fortifying themselves for the fun ahead.

Valentine said, "A cup of tea, Auntie dear?"

"You know what I want, my lad," she said tartly. And her grandson laughed, and brought her a glass of brandy.

Then Valentine had the sense to leave her alone. Snugly ensconced in the shadowy depths of the big wing-chair that had once been Jake's, Harriet took a long sip, saluting the two portraits. She was vaguely aware of the English child coming into the room, and then sitting down at the piano, unaware that anyone else was there. From the hollows of Jake's chair, Harriet could see the girl with the thoughtful gray eyes sort through her folder of sheet music, but then forgot her, as the silence went on. Instead, she gazed at the paintings.

Jake scowled down at her, the creases in his face highlighted by a dusty band of light from one of the sconces. Jake, oh Jake, dear infuriating Jahaziel, oh, how she loved him still, even though he was dead. He had been a passionate man, with a sense of humor. They had suited each other to perfection, and she had been furious with him for dying before her.

Poor Jess, thought Harriet, why couldn't she and Will have made the same kind of match? Poor Jess, who looked forward to Will's homecomings with such excitement, but then became listless and headachy within hours of his arrival. It was as if each of them looked for something that was missing in their relationship, and never found it.

And yet Will so obviously adored her daughter — had adored and looked after her from the day she was born, when he was still a little boy. Harriet had always hoped that the next homecoming would be different. This one had been unexpected, but had proved no better than the rest. She felt so sad for them, because it had been so very different for her and Jake ... and as the English girl began to play a romantic tune ... something by Lehar, she thought ... she remembered what it had been like when she and Jake were reunited after long weeks of being apart... That time in Sydney, for instance, when Jake had discovered her in a flirtatious mood at the Government Ball.

It had been autumn, and the start of the Season, and...

The girl was playing so well ... she was talented enough for the stage. If only Harriet had found her a few years earlier — or so she sleepily thought — she could have made her famous, at the right time. But now, she supposed, the poor child was practicing, managed by that *very* managing mother.

As the music lifted, filling the room, Harriet relaxed even further, curled into the depths of the chair, her eyes half-closed, the brandy half-finished. Dreamily, she heard the sounds of Sydney Domain again, the rumble of carriages on Hunter Street, the shouts of drovers and seamen on Circular Quay. And then ... the night of the ball. It was all so vivid, as vivid as yesterday. That glittering occasion on that long-ago night was so clear, when half the time nowadays she could not remember what she had eaten for breakfast.

A small orchestra in powdered wigs and satin breeches had sweated at a variety of stringed instruments, while the floorboards squeaked under the feet of vivacious dancers. As the piano notes rose and fell, she heard the sibilant sounds of silks and muslins swishing bell-like over swaying hoops, bare arms and shoulders gleaming as perfumed women were propelled about by men whose frilled shirts shone white as marble from within their black frockcoats. Trilling laughter and guffaws of masculine mirth filled air that was warmed by thousands of candelabra. She herself had been gowned superbly, in a smoky blue silk, the waist cinched in to wasp-like slenderness over the extravagant bell of a crinoline skirt, swags of Honiton lace falling about the hem and veiling the upper swell of her gleaming pale breasts — and then, all at once, she'd seen Jake.

Jake, who made even the most crowded place seem different when he arrived. Captain Jake Dexter, tall and rangy in a splendid black broadcloth suit, the wide lapels of his swallowtail coat faced with silver-grey, his waistcoat a fine tabby silk to match. She remembered how the snowy cravat crisped beneath his clean-shaven chin. The candlelight had showed up the grey sprinklings in his thick dark hair, and shadowed the creasing in his eloquent face — the same face she gazed at now, in the portrait.

Jake had been greeted by the Governor, Sir John Young, and was deep in conversation. Then, as if he had sensed her gaze, he slowly turned his head. She remembered how his expression became intent, green eyes narrowing. He had stood poised the whole length of the ballroom away, but in that instant as they gazed into each other's eyes, it was as if the room was small, and they were the only ones there.

For a wild moment she had thought he would commit the unthinkable social blunder of abandoning Sir John — the Governor of New South Wales! — mid-sentence, and push his way through the throng towards her. Jake had much more sense that that, though, so Harriet had been the one to move slowly, with perfect poise, in his direction. She arrived at the end of a mazurka, she remembered, her hand still resting on her dance partner's arm.

Sir John had bowed and grinned with pompous gallantry, and she remembered how his voice had boomed. "Captain Dexter," he cried. "Allow me to introduce you to the Rage of the Season!"

Providence alone knew how she had managed it, but she had met Jake's dancing eyes without losing her composure. She even said demurely, "You've just arrived in Port Jackson, Captain?"

And so he was, from Auckland with a cargo of timber and kauri gum, she remembered.

"I've been eight weeks a-coasting," he said. "Obviously," he added dryly, "much has changed in the meantime."

"Much indeed!" the Governor exclaimed, completely unaware of conversational undercurrents. "You missed the opening of the theatre season! Miss Harriet Gray, I assure you, is the celebrity of the day! By thunder, sir, you should have seen her tonight, you should curse yourself for missing such a triumph. Shakespeare, it was, and Miss Gray made a most splendid Shrew."

"That," Jake said, straight-faced, "I can readily believe."

At that moment the orchestra had piped up into another dance, and without another word Harriet had found herself in Jake's arms. Some young fop pushed up and bleated something about it being his dance withal, forsooth, he truly declared it. Jake gave him one brief look, and the boy wilted. And then they were safely together, in the midst of the crowd on the floor.

As always, it had felt like melting, and she'd almost forgotten his scent of salt and fine leather. Her crinoline skirt pressed against his thighs and her hair brushed his face as she whispered demurely in his ear, "Lord Alfred truly had booked this dance with me, Captain."

"H'm. A lord, is he?"

"As blue-blooded as a blackberry, fresh out from England."

"Then I guess the correct thing, ma'am, would be to call him out for a duel."

She had laughed aloud, at that. Then he murmured danger-ously, "It is a most unexpected pleasure, to find Miss Harriet Gray in Sydney Town."

"Would you prefer me in Ballarat, Captain?"

"I'll let you be the judge of that, as you know the state of the theatre there."

"Manager Coppin has made an offer of one hundred thousand English pounds."

"To purchase? Without conditions?" When she nodded, his lopsided eyebrows shot up. "You beautiful rogue! And you signed the sale?"

"No, of course I did not. The theatre is held under your name, remember."

"So?"

"I rented it to him — at a *very* good rate, pending your return."

"And came to Sydney?"

"I received an offer that was too good to refuse."

He smiled. "Your performance tonight sounded as magnificent as ever. You're working for Manager Buckingham?"

"Foley."

"Well, he must be hugely gratified that he lured you here. But surely such a triumph was fatiguing? I'm surprised to see you at a ball and not at your lodgings, resting instead. In bed."

"I appreciate your concern, my dear," she'd demurely murmured. "But you might never have found me, since you evidently have not received my letter ... and, in any case, you must understand that after such excitement one does not necessarily want to go to bed."

"No?"

"Or, at least ... not yet."

Jake had smiled like a tiger. "And were you surprised to see me here?"

"But of course! But I am sure you didn't come without a pressing invitation from the Governor himself, Captain. And what else surprises me is that I didn't notice you for such a long time. Perhaps you were late?"

"I couldn't find a confounded cab prepared to bring me here for anything less than fifteen shillings."

"Oh dear! It's the effect of the gold, I'm afraid. The cabmen are so used to free-spending miners on the spree that you're lucky to get anything under two pounds. So, did you walk?"

"Jehovah, no. When it's not muddy out there it is dusty, and it's like a brickyard out there tonight. No, I finally shook one up a little, and he carried me here for half a crown."

"Captain Dexter!" They had both been fairly shaking with laughter when they were interrupted. The English lordling arrived, his courage all summoned up to claim his rightful dance, his fresh young face flushed with righteous rage.

Jake sighed, "Is your card quite full, Miss Gray?"

"Quite, I'm afraid," she sighed back in response. "I was booked for every dance *long* before you arrived."

"I see." And he had relinquished her. "But," he informed the self-righteous young lord, "*I* am escorting Miss Gray to her apartments tonight."

18

Jake, who had passed many more hours in backstage dressing rooms than the average well-raised Yankee boy should expect, had been resigned to not being the only one to see Harriet home on that long-ago night. And he was right. A full party escorted her to the rented apartment near Circular Quay, travelling in a carriage that had been summoned by the Governor himself.

Her lodging place was on the bottom floor of a tall brick building, underneath a coffee house and alongside a hatter's shop, and they all trooped down five stone steps to her entrance below the street. Jake followed the horde, looking around. The sitting room inside was good and large, but cluttered up beyond belief, with half-unpacked trunks with their lids wide open, spilling gowns and hats. Obviously, Miss Harriet Gray had only just arrived in town.

In the midst of this chaos sat a gnarled little twig of an Irishwoman, accompanied by a tall, starved-looking servant girl, who had deepset, disturbingly frightened eyes. They at first appeared to have no role in this late drama, save that of chaperone, but then Jake found out that the Irishwoman was the wife of the coffee shop owner, for the girl was sent up for a great tray of cold lobster and bread, and several decanters of wine.

Never had an après-theatre party been so convivial, never had men been so slow to leave. Then at last — at near cockcrow, damn it — the party picked up their hats and straggled out to the carriage. Jake went with them as far as the street. When he looked back over his shoulder he saw Mrs. Gavitty and the girl emerge from Miss Harriet Gray's doorway and disappear up the stone stairs to the coffee shop — and then at last, at very long last, the carriage clattered off.

The actress's door was still half open. Jake slipped inside, kicked it shut with his heel, knocked the bar down into its socket, and hauled the celebrity of the day into his arms.

"Confound it," he said. "Were you determined to tease me to death?"

Harriet merely held his beloved face between her hands and kissed him soundly, leaving him no breath for further scolding. Long, delirious moments later, she pulled away as he bent to lift her skirts, laughing and evading his hands, laughing still more as he pursued her into the bedroom. "Stop, stop," she gasped. "I refuse to be tupped like a wharfside doxie, so you'll have to help me undress .... unless you wish me to send for Mrs. Gavitty."

Jake did not deign to answer, removing his coat and waistcoat instead. Her hair was already down, tumbled and disordered about her shoulders, and the heavy lace about her breasts was rumpled. Then she turned, and Jake surveyed the formidable task before him.

Her gown was secured with a multitude of buttons and lacings down the back, but his fingers were experienced and swift. His dearly beloved mistress murmured breathless endearments as he methodically worked, but he said nothing, fully involved in unwrapping this delectable parcel. Away went the elaborate gown, thrown into a corner, and his long-fingered hands rested on her shoulders, turning her about to face him again.

Undoing more little buttons at the front relieved her of her lacy camisole, so that her round breasts, thrust upwards by the busks of her corset, were revealed. Then more cream lace foamed as he unbuttoned the waistband of her rich taffeta petticoat-skirt. Her crinoline frame went next, tossed side in a singing of wires, and she stepped out of long lace-trimmed drawers. Then Jake crouched to untie ruffled garters and tug off her white silk stockings, revealing long, white, slender, endlessly beautiful legs.

When he stood over his mistress again, she was clothed only in her corset. Those confounded stays, such an appalling monument to fashion ... such an iron impediment to passion.

The laces of that terrible corset were tied in demure little bows up the middle of her back. As he undid them and released the whalebone contraption, Harriet groaned with pleasure, and wriggled with a relief that he found highly understandable. Women, he thought, women! They might be adorable, but he really did wonder.

The contraption joined the crinoline in the corner with a weighty thump. And then the Rage of the Season, nymph-naked, her white skin streaked with pink creases where the whalebone had bitten in, had thrown herself into Jake's arms and commenced tugging at his shirt. Once naked, he slid his hands down, down and lifted her slowly against him, shivering with ecstasy as their bodies merged. And then ... and then, slowly, by degrees, linked as one, they tumbled gasping onto the bed. And oh dear God, he had almost forgotten the brilliant sensation — the piercing delight as he lost himself in Harriet.

When at last they collapsed together, the sun had risen behind Harriet's window, laying squares and triangles of purple and red and a peculiarly vicious green on the quilt and the pillows. The effect was weird, like bedding down at the bottom of the sea.

"Jehovah," Jake had remarked, rolling over. "What the devil kind of windows are those?"

"Stained glass window, of course, and it was not Jehovah, or the devil. It was Mr. Gavitty," she had yawned. "He's a truly horrible man, but useful in some things. And lodgings in Sydney are terrible to find, did you know that? But the windows have proved to be a blessing, truly, for they prevent my admirers from peeping in on my privacy."

"Admirers? Good lord, so you really are the Rage of the Season?"

"You are too ungallant, Jahaziel Dexter!"

But, she remembered, she had laughed.

The music had stopped. The English child had packed up her music and gone back upstairs, leaving Harriet alone with the portraits. "Oh, Jake, darling Jake," she thought, and raised her glass in a fond salute, then wondered where the portraits had been when she was in Sydney. On board the brig, or hanging somewhere back in Ballarat, where the portraits had been painted? She could not remember, so turned her dreams to the time after that reunion, instead. She had been signed for the whole season by Manager Foley, and so Jake had spent all the time that he could in Sydney, breaking the habit of a lifetime by sending the brig out under the first mate. And, how wonderful that had been.

In June, Jake went to Ballarat to sign the document of sale, returning complacent with the draft for one hundred thousand silver dollars in his wallet. "So," he had said as she placed a celebratory glass of wine before him, "what do we do once the season is finished?"

"Oh, there is bound to be another gold rush somewhere," she had prophesied blithely, not realizing at that moment that they were about to quarrel.

"Oh, yes?"

"And we could build another theatre there."

"Oh, God."

"What's wrong with that?"

"If you want to know the truth, I'm sick of the whole damn business. I'm heartily tired of sailing about while you're enchanting the crowds from the stage."

"But why?" She had blinked in surprise. "We've lived this way for years, and very happily, or so I believe, and we're certainly not the only couple to do it. Manager Foley and Mrs. Foley both work in the theatre, and yet they are apart a great deal of the time. He's here in Sydney and Mrs. Foley — or so I believe — is managing the Theatre Royal in Christchurch. No doubt, between them, they are prosperous — and after the sale to Manager Coppin, you must feel quite happy with the money we've made."

He shouted, "But Foley and his wife are married!"

She blinked with surprise. "And it makes such a difference to you that we are not?"

"You know it makes a difference! Oh, perhaps I did enjoy our flirtatious game at the ball," he angrily allowed. "It gave an extra spice to being as randy as a billy goat — but I don't enjoy it when men like Sir John Young don't have a notion that we belong together. I don't enjoy having to trail around after you like a lovesick pup, waiting for your admirers to pack up and go and leave us alone, because you insist on being *Miss Harriet Gray* and never Mrs. Jahaziel Dexter."

"Oh dear," she'd said, amazed by his vehemence.

For many years they had been free to marry each other, but Harriet had refused to do it. Her first husband had been a cheat, a bully, a fake, and a sadist, who had savaged her and abandoned her. Jake was the absolutely opposite of all that, but why bother with the farce a second time around? Anyway, she'd murmured naughtily, tumbling about in bed might have turned into just a marital duty. It had been a shock to realize how he really felt, after all this time of drifting about the Pacific as lover and mistress, but the decision, then, had been easy.

"Am I to take it, Jahaziel," she had enquired, "that all this grumping is the prologue to a proposal of marriage?"

Curtly, he'd nodded.

"Well then, it's an uncommon uncourtly one, sir, but I accept."

"You *will*?"

"Don't sound so surprised. It's impolite. I would have made you marry me years ago, if I had known you felt so strongly about it."

Now, sadly, she remembered the way his face had lit up, with an eagerness that was almost boyish.

"You'll marry me right here, and now?"

"Oh, now that we have decided to make the plunge," she'd said. "Let's make a proper do of it. Let's have a ceremony in New Zealand, with Royal to give me away. It'll be fun."

It had to be New Zealand, because Royal, her brother, was ensconced in Auckland with his wife, Constance, and a growing brood of children. There he was not just managing a theatre, but was a popular attraction on the stage as well, often with his older children beside him — and that brood included the daughter Harriet had given Jake fifteen years before. Young, lovely, fragile Jess, who was in Auckland for her schooling, and who loved to sing to whatever audience would stay around to listen.

"But what about Jess?" Jake's voice had been sardonic in his disappointment. "You don't think she'd be too embarrassed to attend her parents' wedding?"

"She'll think it romantic," Harriet had roundly declared. "As a matter of fact," she had added reminiscently, "I think I was quite fourteen before my parents got around to getting married. It's the way of the stage, you see."

Looking back, Harriet realized that had been the moment when Jake had decided to use Coppin's money to settle down and adopt a more respectable life. He had taken the brig to Auckland, and told Royal to get ready for the Great Event — the party that Harriet wanted, with all the family gathered to witness their belated nuptials. That was when, not knowing it, he had made the decision to spend the rest of their lives in the Thames. Jake had died at the Golden Goose, and it would be here that she would gladly join him ... if fate allowed it.

Upstairs, the guests were becoming noisy, as they visited each others' rooms to show off their fancy costumes. Harriet stretched in Jake's cavernous chair, thinking that she had better make a move before Will came down in search of her. When he was home he insisted on making her a glass of warm milk to go with the bromide the doctor had prescribed, and she knew he would fuss is he arrived at her room and found it empty. But one of the maids had told her that someone kept on trying to see her ... and she greatly feared that it was Timothy. Did she have the strength to face his demands? No matter how tired or worn out she had felt, strength had flowed into her as she stepped onto the stage — and the confrontation with Timothy was going to as demanding as the most passion-ridden drama.

Timothy. Harriet's lips set tight.

In July, while she had worked out the last three weeks of her contract with Foley, Jake had sailed back from his little conference with Royal, and their reunion had been as ecstatic as ever. She supposed that was why it had taken Jake a week to get around to telling her that while he was in Auckland a young man had called on the brig — to hail him as his father.

Harriet remembered the jealous rage that had filled her. She had asked in low, dangerous tones, "And how old is this pup?"

"Twenty." Then Jake had added dryly. "Or so he says."

"You don't believe him?"

"I don't believe much of what he told me at all, though he's a plausible rogue. He arrived on board the brig as I sailed into Auckland, before the anchor was even dropped. Somehow, he had found out that the *Gosling* was mine. He'd come from California, he said, having worked his passage on the old *Rolling Moses* — and before that, Kentucky, Mississippi. He had fought on the Union side, the last few months of the Civil War. Or so he said."

Jake had paused before saying tightly, "He claims to be the child of the woman who used to be my wife, and states that I fathered him before I sailed off. My wife's lover was his stepfather only — or so he says, and, he says further, that his stepfather has disinherited him since."

I wonder why," she said caustically, because the boy sounded a rogue indeed, and with obvious motives.

"So he hopes to be recognized as your legal son and heir instead," she mused. "What does he look like?"

"Not like me, I assure you!"

It was a shout. She had paused, and then said, "So you are absolutely sure he isn't yours?"

"I promise you he isn't mine! There's no way he could look like me!"

"Oh Jake," she had said, distressed by his fury and mortification. And then he had showed her the old letter, kept for years in the back pocket of a wallet.

He had received the letter in Macao, he said, while he was a-coastering in China, in charge of his first command. The letter, dated eleven months after he had sailed from Salem, had been written by the ashamed and distressed old man who happened to be his father-in-law. Addressed to the son-in-law he liked and admired, it was to break the news that his daughter had betrayed her husband — that just days after the ship had sailed the writer's daughter, Jake's young wife, had moved in with the ship's owner.

Not only that, but the ship's owner had stolen Jake's cottage — the cottage he had built with his own hands, honor-built as only a seaman could do it, with a shell wreath on the front door — and sold it, and pocketed the money. That the ship's owner had taken everything, had robbed Jake of all that was good in his life. The old man who wrote the letter said that he felt driven to break the humiliating news because his daughter had just given birth to the son of her adulterous lover.

Jake said grimly, "And then is when I *stole* the ship that belonged to the bastard who had made a cuckold of me. I sailed to Honolulu, and sold it to the highest bidder."

"Yet, despite the evidence of this letter, this young rogue..."

Jake snapped, "Oh, he tried to spin a story of a deluded grandfather and hard usage at home, but I did not believe a word of it. I warrant I know more about stepfathers and ill-treatment than that ill-conceived pup could imagine in a month of midnight watches."

"Oh Jake..." she had whispered, because she had heard the story that haunted him so several times before, and it always moved her to tears.

"My father died at sea when I was eight, and my mother remarried — as happens often. In New England, at that time, it could be impossible for a woman to live — and bring up a child — without a man to support her. And, as also happens often, my stepfather did not like me. He apprenticed me out to a farmer and I never saw my mother again. I dreamed of her one night, Harriet. I was eleven years old and I dreamed that she came to me and told me she was dying. In my dream she said goodbye to me ... gently. I told the farm couple about it next day, and sure enough, a letter arrived a few weeks later to say my mother had died on that date. And so, as soon as I was old enough, I went to sea."

He stopped, and Harriet had heard him swallow hard. "All I ever wanted was to make enough money to build a home of my own and have a wife and family, all the things I had missed since the age of eight. Can you understand why I married before I was twenty-one years old, can you understand why her unfaithfulness hit so hard? Can you possibly believe that I would have abandoned her, if there had been any chance at all that the child was mine?"

Instead, as Harriet knew, that wife had divorced him — she had divorced Jake on the grounds that he was a pirate who had brought dishonor upon her. She found herself shivering, all these years later.

Jake had been telling the truth, she knew that beyond a shadow of doubt.

But then he had changed his mind and recognized Timothy as his son.

They had come back to New Zealand, and dropped anchor just in time to hear the news of the goldfields on the Thames River. Knowing time was critical, Jake had moved fast. Leaving Harriet on board, he had gone on shore to register his arrival at the Custom House and bring Jess back on board, before making haste for the Firth of Thames.

But, instead of their daughter, he had brought a plausible rogue on board, and Harriet shivered again as she remembered the look on his face. Jake Dexter's expression was as grim as death, and he carried the news that he had changed his mind about Timothy.

Timothy no-name. Now recognized as Timothy *Dexter.*

Harriet's eyes were shut tight and stinging. She had punished poor Jake, she thought bleakly now. She had refused to listen to his explanations, and refused to share his bed for a week. And she had refused to marry him — ever. And because of that stupid, blind, callous refusal to marry him and make Jess legitimate, she had endangered the whole family.

Harriet opened her eyes, made an enormous effort, and managed to get herself upright again. The stairs loomed like a mountain ahead of her, but she climbed them doggedly, determined not to call out for help.

This was her problem, and she had to solve it herself. Timothy was back with a lawful claim to the Golden Goose, and Harriet was prepared to do anything — anything all, to make certain that he would never usurp her family's rightful inheritance.

19

When Cissy returned to the bedroom, it was empty. Undoubtedly, she mused, her mother was one of the happy throng that was rushing about upstairs showing off their masquerade and sipping champagne.

She was pleased to be alone, as it still felt awkward to dress up as a man. After slipping her music folder into a drawer, she braided up her hair, shed her clothes, slid into the supple cool silk of the Harlequin costume, drew on the floppy cap and put on the mask. Then she contemplated the reflection that gazed back at her from the looking glass.

It was Harlequin who stared back at her, illuminated by the last light that slanted in the window, like a stained glass figure in his eye-deceiving motley. At that moment the sense of being back on board the *Royal George* was overwhelming. Just as Will Williams had described, the distant thunder of the batteries was like the never-ending thump of the ship's turbine engines. Then the sun went down and the light dimmed, so that Harlequin's suit turned to white and dark grey. Pierrot, the white clown, Cissy thought, listening to the sounds of excitement that echoed from the bedrooms along the passage. That, too, was like the surprisingly successful masquerade ball on the *Royal George*, a thought that gave her the courage to make yet another attempt to find Miss Harriet Gray.

After the long day in the goldfields, the layout of the big hotel was almost as bewildering as when she had first arrived. People were passing along the corridors, too, which made her feel self-conscious. At length, however, she found the door marked *Private*.

That, she knew now, was Timothy Dexter's room, and definitely to be avoided. It was right at the end, abutting onto the balcony, and was as silent as ever. The next door, the one closest to her, belonged to Mr. and Mrs. Williams.

The doors were just a few feet apart in the short passage with its glass door that led to the balcony, and there were just the two of them, while Cissy had hoped to find a third, which presumably would belong to the owner of the hotel, Miss Harriet Gray. Well, she had to face it, there were just two doors, and she was disappointed, but she was certainly not going to knock on either Mr. Dexter's door or that of Mr. and Mrs. Williams, either, and so she turned back. Within a few steps she had reached the end of the short passage, and two long corridors stretched on either hand.

Both long passages were as empty as the short one had been. She could hear laughter and chatter filtering up the stairs, so guessed that most, if not all, of the other guests were down there, admiring each others' costumes and getting fired up for the evening's entertainment. Someone had been here very recently, though, because there was a tray on a small table that was set in a little niche at the corner.

The tray held two tall glasses of gently steaming milk. Each one was covered with an initialed napkin — H and J. Jess ... and Harriet. So Miss Gray was certainly in one of the rooms nearby — and the windows to the rooms on the corridor to her right had windows that opened onto the balcony.

Inspiration led to immediate action. Cissy ran along the corridor, thrust open the balcony door at the end and went out into the chill dark night.

Outside, the stampers hammered on in the distance. When she touched the balcony rail the wood was cold and damp, and mist felt like cobwebs on her cheeks. She turned and leaned backwards, scanning the row of windows for lights and silhouettes, seeing nothing. Trying another ploy, she ran along the long balcony to the corner, where the French door to the painted parlor interrupted the neat line of bedroom windows. And there she saw a light, and a moving shadow.

Without even thinking about it, Cissy rapped on the pane. The figure stilled and then came over and pulled down the handle, letting her in. It was Megs the housekeeper, still in the black dress that was greenish with age, her apron as white and stiffly starched as the one she had worn the evening before. Behind her, the door to the corridor was half-open.

She was holding a hearth-brush and shovel, and said rather sharply, "Hello?"

The big, raw-boned woman with her gaunt face and scraped grey hair had made Cissy feel nervous from the first moment she had seen her. She didn't have the courage to ask for Miss Harriet straight out, so ventured, "I heard a ... noise, and wondered if I could have another look at this lovely room."

"Lovely?" The housekeeper emitted a queer bark of laughter. "I guess some folks might admire it, but I don't think it was paint-ed with that intention."

"But the paintings are splendid. Last night I wondered if they were pictures of real ships, and Mr. Bradford assured me that they were."

"He was right," the housekeeper said, with an odd trace of pride. "And Timothy, Mr. Dexter, could tell you a great deal about each one. He knew all the voyages and the profits and the sales, right down to the very last cent. That one, there," she said, pointing at a clipper with all sail set, "was stolen. By a pirate."

Stolen? Cissy blinked, remembering something her mother had told her, and she went up to the wall to inspect the ship closely. It really was a beautiful painting. The house flag and the Stars and Stripes almost seemed to flutter in an unfelt wind. She could read the name on the side — *Thomas Grace* — and remembered that Mr. Bradford had told her that all the ships were owned by the Grace Brothers Shipping Company.

The room, she thought, was like a little maritime museum. A round table in one corner was covered with a tasselled cloth that was embroidered with fouled anchors, and carried two elaborate ship models inside glass domes.

She said impulsively, 'It's like a ship's cabin — or a shipping merchant's private parlor."

"Some folks might agree. Captain Jake used to keep his log-books in here, after Timothy had gone back to America."

"Logbooks?" said a quick voice.

Cissy jumped with surprise, and Megs turned rather sharply, too. A tall woman stood just inside the open corridor door, clothed in a voluminously skirted black gown. She had a blood-stained dagger stuck in her belt, and her hands were artistically streaked with drips of red. A black lace mantilla had been thrown over her head, veiling her face, but Cissy had no trouble recognizing Miss Fleet. Even in masquerade, she was elegant.

Cissy, wondering how long she had been standing there, said rather blankly, "Who are you meant to be?"

"Lady Macbeth," this apparition explained, but the veil was turned enquiringly at Megs.

"Logbooks?" she said.

"Logbooks," Meg repeated. "Captain Jake Dexter's record of all his voyages. They were here, but when Captain Jake died Miss Harriet took them away and put them in her bedroom. She ordered this room shut up, and we haven't used it since."

That had a most ominous ring, Cissy thought uneasily. It was like closing up the parlor after the corpse had been taken away.

Miss Fleet said, "When did Mr. Dexter leave?"

"Just over a year ago, the same day as the fire."

Fire? Cissy stared at the empty fireplace. Then she realized that Megs was talking about the fire that had damaged the old theatre so badly that a near-miracle had been needed to restore the Golden Goose.

So her hunch had been right, she thought, and Timothy Dexter had taken no part in the restoration. Then she heard the housekeeper click her tongue irritably.

"I wish I knew who done it," she said.

Miss Fleet said, 'I beg your...?"

"I laid a fire in here last night with paper and kindling, intending to bring up wood today and warm and air this room. Mrs. Williams is out of health again, and she frets if she don't have the sitting part of the double room, so I was going to shift a day bed in here, to give her a change of scene, but when I came up this morning someone had gone and burned all the paper and kindling. I ask you, why would a body wish to do a thing like that? So I put that down for a clean-up job when I found time to do it."

The housekeeper sounded quite aggrieved rather than relieved, when she added, "But look you, someone had cleaned it up already, and taken the ashes off. But if they wished to be helpful, why didn't they lay another fire?"

Cissy shook her head, at a loss for an answer. Her own room did not have a fireplace, and she didn't believe she had seen one in any of the guestrooms. Anyway, the Golden Goose had only three chimneys.

She ventured, "Do any of the other upstairs rooms have fires?"

Megs shrugged, evidently dismissing the strange question as an eccentricity. "The double room has one, and then, of course, the owner's room has to have a fireplace."

"Double room?"

"Mrs. Williams' apartment, as I told you," the housekeeper snapped. "It's a double room, with a bedroom and a sitting room, but the sitting room has been furnished as a bedroom for Mr. Dexter, Timothy, while he is here." Then she added angrily, "What bothers me is how that person got in here to do it. It was locked when I came in this morning, and I locked it again when I went out, and none of the servants has a key."

The word *key* triggered another thought. Cissy said, "Do you remember going to my room to turn down the beds last night?"

"*What?*" Then, before Cissy could answer, the housekeeper began to laugh, making a coughing kind of noise. It was weird. Cissy felt the hairs rise on the back of her neck, but then she saw the reason and felt quite a fool.

She looked down at her costume and said, "How silly of me. But it has been a long day, which has addled my brain. My name is Miller, and my mother and I have room number three."

"That man's costume don't make it easy to guess who you are."

"I know, and I am sorry." Cissy remembered how the waiter on the *Royal George* had easily mistaken her for a young man. It had been quite liberating, at the time.

She persisted, "So you don't recollect going into our room last night?"

"Perhaps I do, perhaps I don't." The housekeeper's tone had become brusque again. "If I do remember, then I certainly recollect seeing the trunks there, and stuff. Was something not brought up?"

"No, all the luggage was there." Cissy hesitated, very aware that Miss Fleet was listening, but took the plunge. "But, when you arrived, was the door still locked?"

The housekeeper's face soured. "Miss Miller," she said, "over the years I have learned a philosophy, and that is to take no risks. I knock on the door, and if there's someone to answer, then I call out and tell them I'm there. I ask before I enter. If there ain't no answer I try the door. And if it ain't locked, I go away. If it is locked and I have had no answer, then I unlock it, knock again to make sure, go in and turn down the beds. And I wouldn't advise anyone in the same position to do any different."

"And most laudable, I am sure!" Miss Fleet applauded. "I wish the stewards on the *Royal George* had been that conscientious."

"So," said Megs to Cissy, ignoring this, "any complaints?"

Oh, lord save me, thought Cissy. She said hurriedly, "I agree with Miss Fleet that your behavior is exemplary."

"I know it is." Her tone was flat and dismissive.

"It seems to me that you have worked for the Grays a long time."

At that, Megs stared at Cissy so combatively that she took an involuntary step back. Then a bitter expression crossed the housekeeper's face, and she said, "So no one told you."

"I beg your...?"

"I'm Timothy Dexter's wife."

"You're *Mrs. Dexter*?"

"That I am, Miss Miller, that I am."

The silence was frozen. Cissy was aware that Miss Fleet was standing as rigidly as herself, startled beyond belief. Then Megs spoke again, saying with a most unexpected smile, "It's hard to guess, I know. That a smart, handsome, clever fellow like Timothy Dexter should hitch himself up with a woman like me — for I was never what you would call pretty, even as a girl. He could have had anyone, for the girls threw themselves at him, and still do, but I was the girl he married, and though he might go off for a few months now and then, he always comes home to me."

Oh dear *lord*, thought Cissy, for she was stricken not just with embarrassment, but terrible sadness, too. She remembered the savory-smelling meal on the tray that Megs had carried up to Timothy Dexter the previous night, and how carefully — *lovingly*, she realized now — Megs had selected and opened a special bottle of wine. As bizarre as it seemed, Megs worshipped her neglectful husband.

And then she remembered what she had overheard in Timothy Dexter's cabin, the night of the ball on the *Royal George*, and felt her cheeks flush under her mask.

"I'm sorry," she blurted meaninglessly, and escaped through the balcony door before either Megs Dexter or Miss Fleet could say another word.

20

Cissy ran around the corner of the balcony, and then, safely out of sight, went to the rail by the end wall and hung over it, peering sideways into the darkness, working out directions in her head.

The hotel, she realized, was U-shaped, with the kitchen and dining room in one arm of the U, and the tavern in the other, with the lounge and lobby in between. There was a cobbled yard between the arms of the U, at the back. She looked for a drainpipe, and found a fire-escape. Without a second's hesitation she swung herself over the rail and onto the narrow cat-walk.

She was naturally athletic and agile, and the Harlequin suit helped considerably. Cissy landed on her hands and feet in the yard, only slightly out of breath. The dustbins stood in a neat row in the moonlight, alongside the outdoor privy, which, mercifully, was empty. She lifted lids and began to rummage.

Ten minutes later she abruptly drew back into the shadow of the privy, for a man came out into the yard. In the light of the moon and the reflected lamplight from a kitchen window, she saw that he wore a kind of uniform. He went into the privy and Cissy froze, trying not to listen to undoings of buttons and so forth. The cold had made her clumsy, however, and just as he was coming out she knocked her knee against a bin, making a small clang that echoed even though the night was full of the noise of stamping machinery.

The man stopped and said loudly, "Hello?"

Cissy's heart bumped. She felt terribly conscious of carrying the result of her rummaging, though it was tucked into the waistband of her pantaloons, and hidden by the overlapping tunic.

Reluctantly, she stepped out of the shadows. The man was a perfect stranger, a burly fellow with a small moustache.

She said in a gruff low voice, "Good evening, sir!"

"Ah." He peered at her closely. "I see you're a guest, sir. You are part of the Murder Experience."

"An excellent deduction." Miraculously, Cissy managed to chuckle in a comradely fashion, feeling quite the actor. She could see the faint glint of braid on his shoulders, and the reflection of the bright buttons on his jacket, and went on, "Are you a real policeman, or are you dressed up in masquerade, too?"

"An excellent deduction of your own, sir! But I am real, I assure you. Allow me to introduce myself — Sergeant MacDonald, of the Hauraki Police Force. You'll be making my acquaintance later, when the murder has been done. I'm off-duty, really," he explained. "Gladys hires us for acting duties, as it were. There's an excellent dinner awaiting in the kitchen inside, and the Grays are always most generous donors to police charities. The volunteer fire brigade will be along before the night is out, too. Quite a festival occasion, a murder is, here at the Golden Goose! And your name, sir, if I may be previous? For I will be cross-examining later, I warn — unless, of course, you turn out to be the victim."

He laughed merrily at his little joke, while Cissy thought about a name. She looked down at her costume, started to say, "Mr. Har—" and stopped.

The stark moonlight had bleached all the color from her motley, so that she was clothed in black and white chequers. She was the White Clown, she thought, and said, "My name is Mr. Pierrot, who—"

And she stopped again, for that didn't sound quite right.

"Who?" said Sergeant MacDonald.

"M'sieu Pierrot," said Cissy, and nodded, thinking that it sounded much better. "I'm a clown. I'm cleverer than I look, though I make people laugh."

And he laughed. Then, suddenly, he silenced, as a woman's laugh echoed from one of the windows that overlooked the yard.

This laugh was very different, so contemptuous that the hairs on the nape of Cissy's neck ruffled up. "Jake finally showed it to you, did he? The same day that he threw you out?" the woman who had laughed exclaimed then. "You really want the evidence of the perfidy of your background? Have it, and welcome — and be gone with you. And have this, too! — I know it was not intended for me, unless you want my demise, as well!"

A man's voice replied. It was impossible to recognize who it was, or even distinguish the words. Whatever he said, however, the effect on the woman was obvious.

"Oh, ye gods," she cried, in a voice that had once been pitched to hit the back wall of a theatre. "Don't stand up for bastards — for they have enough arrogance for themselves! But here you are," she spat. "Take it, take it — on the understanding that you get back to America and never come to leech on the family again. We would have given it to you years ago, if it had guaranteed never seeing your face at our door again. So take it, and go!"

Whatever the man said in reply was bitter. Evidently stung, the woman shouted, "You think we hate you? And clannish, are we? Dear God, it wasn't ever hate, not ever — it was pity, you poor wretch, *pity*! You will never have the slightest notion of how we've pitied you all these years, trapped by your own greed in a place where you did not belong — because we were family, and you, by God, were not. So take what you want and get out!"

Cissy, staring up at the window and the chimney that soared against the stars above it, heard a door slam. The third chimney, she thought, *the third chimney*. When she looked at the policeman he was standing as frozen still as she was herself, shooting little sideways glances in her direction.

The woman's voice had belonged to the talkative diggeress, the elderly person with the lovely hat, Cissy was sure of it. Feeling extremely rueful that she had talked with Harriet Gray on the tour without even a suspicion of it, she said to the policeman, "That was Miss Harriet Gray."

He didn't deny it. Perhaps he thought the tirade was part of the Murder Experience, she thought, for he merely said, "I sup-pose my dinner is getting cold," before heading off to the kitchen door.

The door shut with a decisive snap, and Cissy whirled and began to run, because she now thought she knew where to find Miss Harriet Gray.

She sprinted out of the yard and along the dark street, and burst through the main entrance, to find the lobby crammed with a jovial crowd, bringing her to an unwilling stop. She had to push through people who were queuing for the dining room, many of whom called out to her, forcing her to answer and slowing her down still further. The atmosphere was hectic. The party had entered into the spirit of the masquerade wholeheartedly, many of the gentlemen looking overburdened with liquor already.

Ghosts in white drapery hung on the arms of black-masked hangmen. Mr. Schuyler Bradford III was dressed as Count Dracula, flourishing his red cape and dribbling greasepaint blood from false fangs. Patience and Harmony were both present, Cissy saw, which seemed rather strange, though she didn't have the time to think about it much. Both, appropriately, were dressed as devils in fire-red and orange satin. The poised and beautiful blonde Australian woman was there as well, in a slim green silk dress with an enormous rose-colored silk velvet robe thrown over it, all printed in silver and gilt, looking absolutely gorgeous, even if Cissy couldn't work out what kind of costume it was meant to be. She was with the elegant fellow called Valentine, who was dressed in sateen breeches and a flowing silk brocade coat, a white periwig on his head and a violin in his hand. Then Cissy saw two of the smallest Gray children dressed up as the little Princes of the Tower, escorted by a nurse in mob cap and apron.

This person called out gaily, "Cissy, Cissy, where have you been? That's the dinner bell ringing, you know. You've been outside," she answered herself, before Cissy had a chance to frame a word. "Your cap is all misty, quite wet, I declare, and your hands are *dirty*. For goodness' sake, dear, get them cleaned and then come to dinner, or everyone will start without you."

Cissy escaped upstairs. At the top she began to hurry again, running along swiftly in her silent slippers. Then, as she rounded the bend in the passage that led to the private family quarters, she froze to a stop.

Mr. Williams was there, carrying the tray that she had noticed earlier. Surely, she thought, the milk must be cold by now. This time, however, there was only one napkin-covered glass upon it, and then she saw that the glass was empty.

Will Williams turned and saw her. When she said his name she saw he recognized her voice, for he frowned and said, "I wish you wouldn't persist in disturbing my wife. She has a headache and needs to rest."

Cissy gazed at him resentfully, for she hadn't intended to disturb Jess Williams at all. She said, "I am still concerned about the package getting to the right..."

Though, she thought now, the package had not been intended for Miss Harriet Gray. It had been addressed to *Mrs. Dexter* — who was Megs, the housekeeper. But who would be sending *her* marzipan sweets?

Will Williams was barking, "Forget the package! And I wish you would forget about that confounded letter, too. For heaven's sake, go down to the dining room. Dinner has started, and it's an excellent meal, I assure you. You're here to have fun, not to interfere in the family's private affairs."

"Am I?" said Cissy wryly, thinking of Miss Minnie's strict injunction. However, she made an appearance of obeying him, going back along the corridor, pausing only when he pushed past her, and headed down the stairs. She was still at the corner when her attention was caught by a faint metallic scraping sound, and she looked back up the short passage, to see the flick of a black, voluminous skirt as someone went into Timothy Dexter's room. Megs, she thought, but the housekeeper was gone before she could call out and forestall her, meaning to tell her about the package that had been given by mistake to Jess Williams, to hand on to Miss Harriet Gray.

It was more difficult to find her way to the room beneath the third chimney that she had hoped. Stopping, she counted in her head, remembering what she had seen from the yard. Three chimneys. One belonged to the fireplaces in the lounge below and the painted parlor above. The fireplaces to the second chimney were in the kitchen and the double room where Jess Williams was nursing her headache. The third chimney ran from the tavern stove ... up to the owner's room, which also overlooked the yard.

At last she found it. The door looked the same as all the others, and had no notice or number, but Cissy was almost certain it was the right one.

Holding her breath, Cissy tapped, and waited. Nothing, not a movement, not a sound. She knocked again.

No reply. She knocked more loudly, the sound sharp and imperative even with the muffled thump of the stampers in the distance. Nothing. When she put her head against the wood she heard the bump of her own pulse in her ears, echoing the never-ending thump of the stampers. When, greatly daring, she tried the handle, the door was locked. She paused, slumped with defeat, and then gave up and trudged away.

The door to her own room was locked, too, but she had a key on a string round her neck. The bedroom was a mess, a testament to her mother's change into masquerade, and the beds had not yet been turned down. Cissy was more interested, however, in the booty she was carrying in her waistband, retrieved from a bin outside that had held the ashes of a small fire.

Slowly and carefully, she drew it out.

It was the corner of a yellow envelope. Though it was greatly scorched, she recognized it immediately. Cissy held between two fingers, holding it up to the light as she wondered whether the person who had stolen it had read what was inside, before setting it on fire.

21

When Cissy slipped into the dining room, she found she was not the last one, rather to her relief. One noisy group took a long time to come out of the lounge, and it was not until then that the meal was served, and everyone could set to.

Once started, the dinner seemed endless. Cissy's adolescent appetite was healthy, and the food was delicious, but her mind was elsewhere. The noise was becoming distracting, too. One of the Gray grandchildren was playing salon music on the piano, but it was almost impossible to hear her, over the din. When Cissy looked around after finishing dessert she was that quite a few people had taken off their masks so they could drink wine more easily, and many had dropped their cloaks and capes on the floor. Most of the faces were flushed, and the room, indeed, was hot.

One set had pulled a number of tables together to make a separate group, which was becoming quite rowdy. They were mock-introducing themselves, she noticed, according to the costumes they wore, along with much jeering and laughter. Harmony and Patience waved their gilt pitchforks aimlessly, and giggled, sounding much more like children than young ladies. Miss Fleet, flourishing her Lady Macbeth robe, quoted a long piece of Shakespeare, but unfortunately from the wrong play. Her cheeks were hectically flushed, Cissy saw, and her eyes were unnaturally bright, as if in the throes of great excitement.

Mr. Bradford introduced himself as Dracula, but seemed to think he was a werewolf. Mrs. Bradford wore a crinoline that was decorated with dangling rubber spiders, and her hilarious husband described her, with a lot of rather salacious detail, as the courtesan actress, Lola Montez.

"But *au contraire*," his dear wife hollered, in an execrable French accent, "I am Hortense Spencer Bradford!" And stood up and curtsied, rather wobbily.

"Spencer?" said Cissy to her mother, who was still beside her. "Isn't that a strange middle name?"

"Not in America," said Mrs. Miller wisely, before flitting off. "One's mother's *maiden* name is a very popular choice, over there."

"Mother's maiden name?" Cissy echoed, though no one was listening. She frowned, her head on one side.

It was hard to think, because the party was becoming so loud. The Bradford girls were singing *Come along, ducky* at the tops of their voices, while their jolly father rumbled with laughter. It was all rather undignified, Cissy thought. But of course, she realized, it was due to excitement, as people wondered openly when the murder was going to happen, and the suspense began to mount.

Cissy pictured Sergeant MacDonald waiting in the kitchen, quietly digesting his dinner, and perhaps a second glass of beer, and she wondered if he knew the script, or came into the drama perfectly unprepared. She wondered if the firemen were in the kitchen, too, or were shivering outside with their horses and pump-cart, and began to feel the suspense herself.

But it was ridiculous, she suddenly thought. The murder could not happen while everyone was in the room, as everyone would have an alibi. A *cast-iron* alibi, she thought. It was a popular phrase in the murder mystery books she read. Then, almost as if the girl at the piano had picked up the thought, she packed up her music and left the room, using the door to the yard.

It was like a signal. First one group left, and then another, and then the dining room was almost empty. Even the two Little Princes had gone, though their nurse sat back down next to Cissy.

"Well, the food was even *better* than advertised," said Mrs. Miller. "A *most* entertaining day and evening, don't you think? Tell me, Cissy, do you think it's worth getting undressed and going to bed?"

"I doubt it," said Cissy, who had no intention of retiring. Then she said, "Mama—"

"But it's almost *midnight*. The murder might not happen for *hours*."

"Mama, did you know that the housekeeper, the woman they call Megs, is Timothy Dexter's wife?"

"Of course I knew it, dear. When you're old enough to go to country parties — and that won't be long at all, for I anticipate many invitations when we finally get home, as everyone will have forgotten that I am supposed to be in mourning — you will find that it always pays to *make sure* of name and station before drawing conclusions. Otherwise, it is all too easy to mix up the butler with the lord of the manor, the servant being ever so much more pompous, and a dowager with her nicely spoken lady's maid. Lady Postlewaite, for instance, is quite *addicted* to gardening, and almost invariably receives her guests in a sacking apron, with secateurs in her hand. However, while gossip can be most useful, one should not pay too much attention to it."

Cissy blinked. "Gossip?"

"Well, people do *talk*, your know."

"About Lady Postlewaite?"

"Don't be ridiculous, dear, though I *do* know a story about her..." And Clara Miller laughed happily to herself, while Cissy waited with growing impatience.

"No, I am talking about Mrs. Dexter, of course," Mrs. Miller went on, at length. "Mr. Schuyler Bradford was telling me about it, for he and his wife heard it from a Shortland Town resident, *such* a sad tale. Back in the mid-1860s, or so they were informed, the Australian government was *paying* people to bring in female migrants, for women were so very scarce in the colonies. And so, at the age of fifteen, Megs was taken from an English orphanage and set aboard a ship for Sydney, just so that *somebody* could get the bounty. No better than slavery, so shocking. And then, as if that wasn't bad enough, she was contracted out to a terrible couple who ran a coffee house and who treated her horridly. Then, one day, when she had done some sewing work for Miss Harriet Gray, who was lodging below the coffee house at the time, Captain Jahaziel Dexter tipped her a sovereign. It's so like a sailor, you know, to be so open-handed, generous to a fault, if you know what

I mean. The man who as good as *owned* her found the coin, took it away from her, and then beat her, for he claimed that she must have stolen it. Captain Dexter found out about it, and he and Miss Gray saved her from that dreadful fate by buying out her contract and then bringing her to New Zealand."

Cissy gazed thoughtfully at her mother, remembering Will Williams' rather similar history. Captain Jake Dexter and Miss Harriet Gray had been quite the philanthropists, she thought.

She said, "Mama, what is sad about that? It sounds like a happy ending."

"And so it was, dear. But then Timothy Dexter, who was Captain Dexter's son by an earlier marriage, arrived — and Megs fell in love with him. *Besotted*, they say. He is quite good-looking even now, and was quite the Greek god at the time, or so I hear. And such a gallant manner, too. And the natural outcome..."

Clara Miller's voice trailed off, and she looked with deep meaning into Cissy's eyes. For the first time in her life, Cissy exchanged a look of complete understanding with another woman.

"And Captain Jake made him marry her?"

"Of course."

"Yes," said Cissy. It was easy to picture Captain Jake Dexter's fury when he found that Timothy had taken such advantage of a naïve young girl's adoration. The man in the portrait would have made no bones about forcing Timothy to face his responsibility.

'Quite a tragedy, really," Mrs. Miller said musingly. "Mrs. Dexter's little boy died from drowning when he was just ten years old, and they had no other children. But still ... still she refuses to hear anything to his discredit, even when he is away for *months*. And while she waits, she works for the Grays, knowing that he'll come back one day. Love can be so *blind*, Cissy."

"Mama—" said Cissy.

But she never finished the sentence.

Because the gaslights flickered and flared, and then went out. People screamed and ran about in the dark, and sirens wailed in the street.

Firemen rushed through the hotel with their hoses, shouting out stagily to each other. Gladys, stationed in the doorway of Miss Harriet Gray's bedroom, let out yet another piercing scream. Sergeant MacDonald and his constable blew their whistles in the lobby. It was a scene of most marvelous consternation, Gladys decided with great satisfaction.

No guest, ever, loved the melodrama more than Gladys herself. The family had often declared that Gladys had had a gift for creating panic and chaos from the moment she was born, a sentiment that was echoed by Gladys's adoring but practical-minded husband, and Gladys thought that they were probably right. As a child, she had treated life in cavalier fashion, running through puddles on the way to school, kicking her toes up against walls, rocks and fences with her handstands and cartwheels, tearing the knees out of her stockings, ripping her aprons and dresses on branches and fences palings. Gladys had been the despair of her mother, and her actor-father's favorite chick of the brood.

And, like a true Gray, she had grown up with greasepaint in her blood and the gleam of theatre gaslight in her eyes. From the age of nine, Gladys had been a regular on the stage of the theatre her father managed, as clever with a banjo, a song, a comic reading or an impassioned bit of melodrama as any of her brothers, but where she had excelled was at dance. The blackest moment of her life had come during the slow months of recovery after Timothy's horse had bumped hers during a race, and she had crashed. It was the moment when the doctor had told her that she would never dance again.

The hotel and the Murder Weekends had made up for all that. It was impossible to imagine what life would be like if Timothy took the hotel away from the family. But Gladys staunchly refused to think about it, for she had already made up her mind that it would never happen.

And so, instead of thinking, she let out another yell.

Guests were thundering back and forth all over the hotel, women shrieking and giggling, and men guffawing ghoulishly. It looked and sounded as if it was unmanaged chaos, but Gladys had more control over this "murder" than was apparent to the casual observer — control that she exerted as the mob arrived at the door. Standing stalwart in the doorway, she refused entry to an assortment of pirates, courtesans and courtiers, allowing them only as far as the threshold of the room for a brief tantalizing glimpse of the "corpse" of the diggeress, before ordering them off down the corridor again.

It was an intriguing glimpse, the stage set very well. There was only one candle lit, and the curtains were adjusted so that just one moonbeam lay across the bed. Miss Harriet Gray reclined on the pillows in a particularly effective pose. One hand was slightly uplifted, as if to caress a man's unseen face, and the other was trailing on the floor. The silvery head was turned, so her face was hidden. Like Titania the Faery Queen in *Midsummer Night's Dream*, Gladys decided with a dash of romance, Aunt Harriet gracefully reclined in her flowery bed. There could have been a hitch — Gladys had come to the murder scene late, as there had been a small crisis with a temperamental cook, and Megs had been mysteriously missing. But, as Gladys had known all along, there was no need to fret, as Aunt Harriet had set up the scenario.

It was time now to let half a dozen inside to view the scene at closer hand and provide more detailed evidence at the "enquiry." Over the years, Gladys had found that this was the best way to do it, so that all the guests did not have the same information when the policeman cross-examined them. This was carefully timed so that those favored ones, save three or four, were members of the cast. And tonight it went exactly as planned.

At first.

Six latecomers were allowed into the room, including Jasmine, the seductive young siren from Australia, and her "swain," young Valentine, who was in fact Jasmine's brother. Then Gladys frowned as a figure from pantomime slipped silently in with them.

He was wearing a costume of tunic and trousers in supple many-colored silk, a velvet eye-mask over the upper part of his smoothly youthful face. Gladys knew the character immediately. Harlequin — Arlecchino, the character in Aunt Harriet's portrait that had fascinated little Minnie from the first day she saw it. Arleccino, the enigmatic manipulator from commedia dell'arte, his motley shimmering eerily in the light of the candle. It was as if he had stepped right out of the background of the painting — come to play an important part in this mock-drama. Gladys felt an unexpected shiver down the back of her neck.

She watched him look about the room, taking in the single candle that threw a deceivingly shadowy light over the bed, and the moonbeam lying over the draped figure on it, then turning to scan the row of books in the case on the wall. Who the devil was he ... and why did he seem so serious about his inspection? With years of watching guests in masquerade, Gladys usually had no trouble in telling one from another, but this one had her mystified. Then she realized that because of her preoccupation, he had been in the room longer than the script allowed for, and she hurried the group out.

Then, just as the Harlequin figure reluctantly followed, she realized who "he" was. The English girl, the Miller girl, the one who had innocently informed Minnie that Timothy was coming back to the Thames.

Another shiver ran down her spine. The costume belonged to Minnie.

It was not just a message, it was a warning.

Everyone had gone, and the room behind her was silent. Harriet, reclining on the bed, had not moved. Gladys took a quick look around, and then started to shut the door, ready to go down and help Sergeant MacDonald with his part in the play. Just before the door shut completely, however, a faint gleam of light caught her eye.

It was something vaguely shiny and round, and reflected back the candlelight. It gleamed at her from under Aunt Harriet's bed.

It felt wrong. Something was wrong.

Gladys opened the door again, and went inside to see what it was.

22

The same air of hilarity dominated the dining room, along with a distinct impression of relief. The guests were pleased that the "murder" was over, Cissy deduced. Now that the "victim" was safely dispatched, they could relax and get down to some leisurely sleuthing.

The gas lighting had been restored, and shone brightly down on ruddy, jovial faces. A few of the men — including Mr. Schuyler Bradford — had evidently changed for bed in the interval, for brocade dressing-gowns vied in splendor with the fancy dress that many still wore. Some of the ladies were extremely disheveled. Cissy thought it was undoubtedly because of the fun they had had rushing about in the dark when the alarm had been sounded. Patience Bradford was particularly so, her hair fallen down about her gilt horns, and there was a smudge like soot on one cheek. And where was her sister, Harmony? Cissy's eyes searched the room, but the other imp was definitely absent. Perhaps Harmony was sick again.

The mock cross-examination was well underway, but it was hard to keep listening, though Sergeant MacDonald was making a splendidly humorous job of it, surely earning his good dinner. As the long minutes crept by, Cissy's attention kept on straying to the door that led to the lobby, and, as she noticed, he kept on shooting glances that way, too. She felt certain that Gladys was supposed to preside over this mock-melodrama, but the door to the lobby kept firmly shut. So what, she wondered, was Gladys doing?

Then she abruptly sobered, listening to sounds from outside. Footsteps, quick, urgent footsteps. Out on the street, someone was running. Two people. Cissy heard the faint echo of breathless, agitated voices. Then, with a double thud, the entrance door to the hotel opened and shut. She heard the footsteps hurry through the lobby and disappear up the stairs.

The happy crowd didn't seem to notice, and certainly didn't share Cissy's sense of something gone wrong. "I reckon," called out a rather tipsy-looking hangman, "that we ought to narrow it down to all those what come from Australia." Then he added darkly, "*Particularly* if they happen to be convicts."

"Because the victim was Australian, herself?"

"Well, they told me she made quite a fortune there, digging up the gold and all that. I'd like to know who expected to take over all that gold and stuff when the old girl expired."

"Ah!" said Sergeant MacDonald, and all eyes shifted to the man who called himself Valentine. He flourished his feathered hat and executed a little bow. "You claim to be the victim's nephew, do you not? And tell me, are you a convict, sir?"

"No, no, I am Dr Hastings, the famous quack of Harley Street."

The beautiful young woman in the rose-colored silk velvet robe, the one called Jasmine, cried out, "He lies! He lies!"

"And on what grounds do you make that accusation, ma'am?"

"The bald spot on the top of his head, that you will discover when you remove his wig. It's as plain as a tonsure that he's a runaway priest."

"What I want to know, Sergeant," called out a woman's voice, "is how the old lady died."

The voice was American. Miss Fleet, still garbed as Lady MacBeth, looked as if she was having an exhilarating time, as her eyes were still as brilliant.

"She was poisoned, ma'am," said Sergeant MacDonald, and nodded emphatically. "Poisoned with cyanide, by a cold-hearted villain."

So he did know the script, Cissy thought, or at least he knew it well enough to carry on, even though Gladys hadn't arrived to prompt him.

Then she found the policeman's mock-officious frown focused on herself. "I think I know your name, do I not?"

"Pierrot, M'sieu Pierrot."

"And you are Australian?"

"No, no."

"You're French?"

"Perhaps."

"Aha," he said. "A French convict, huh?"

And everyone laughed again.

"What I want to know," called out Mr. Schuyler Bradford in his Yankee accent, "is who else had a motive for the murder."

"You do, do you? And who may you be, sir?"

Mr. Bradford began to say, "Count Dracula," looked down at his dressing gown, and changed his mind.

"Tom Thomas, if it please you, Sergeant, or Peeping Tom, as you may wish to call me."

"What? You mean you peeped and saw the murder happen?"

"Well, what if I did?"

"I would consider it highly suspicious, sir, that you should be in such close proximity to that foul criminal act. What I want to know is what motive *you* had for dispatching the old lady."

"None, sir, none at all."

"And what were you doing, sir, at the time of the crime?"

"Ah, that'd be telling," giggled Mrs. Bradford, and jostled her droll husband with a meaningful elbow.

He nudged her back. "You keep your mouth shut, my innocent bride. You know a wife can't testify against her husband, Horty."

Everyone had another good chuckle, including the policeman.

Then all of a sudden the door behind him opened, and a short stout man Cissy had never seen before poked his head into the room, took the sergeant's arm, and whispered in his ear. A second later, without a word of explanation, Sergeant MacDonald was gone.

The door shut, gently, without a sound, as the laughter slowly died in the room. Then everyone was silent. People looked at each other, but said nothing.

It was a waiting kind of silence, Cissy thought, and she supposed that everyone assumed that this was part of the murder play. Then a man coughed, somebody whispered, and somebody else giggled.

"Well," said Mr. Schuyler Bradford to no one in particular, "who was the poisoner, do you reckon?"

Cissy's mother said very firmly, "*He* did. He poisoned his aunt so he could inherit her fortune." She was pointing at Valentine, who clapped his hand to his forehead and waved his arms, but didn't bother to protest his innocence.

"And," said Clara Miller, swinging her pointing finger, "*she* helped him."

"Me?" cried the wickedly lovely young woman in a tone of perfectly offended virtue, and swept her rose-colored robe about her. 'I assure you, madam, that I have naught to do with priests, and particularly not with fallen ones."

"You were probably the brains behind the crime," said Mrs. Miller, undeterred. "No doubt you tempted him away from the cloisters. And you were hoping to marry him once he had inherited his aunt's fortune, no doubt."

At that, the blonde bowed her head in respectful defeat, and everybody clapped and cheered. They had solved the murder, and without even the policeman to lead them. All the faces all about were smiling, all of them looking pleased with themselves.

"So that's that, then," said Mr. Bradford, and stood up and stretched. "Well," he said. "I'm off for a nightcap."

And everyone shifted at once. Obviously, now that the crime was solved, the party could get back to whatever socializing they had been about when they had been rudely interrupted by the murder. Ladies chattered as they gathered their costumes around them. Men drained their glasses. Mr. Bradford led the way out of the door, followed by his wife, Miss Fleet, Patience and the others. Within moments the dining room was empty as everyone moved through the lobby towards the parlor and the bar and the late supper that awaited. Cissy, under cover of the confusion, slid through the stage door and outside into the yard.

The yard was empty, exactly the same as the last time she'd been there. The stampers hammered on, relentless in the star-specked blackness. The curtains of Miss Harriet Gray's room were still drawn, but Cissy could see a chink of light. So the actress, she thought, was still awake.

The guests were still milling about inside. Instead of going back into the dining room, Cissy went to the bottom the fire escape ladder, made a mighty leap from the top of a barrel, and swarmed up it and along the catwalk to the balcony.

And the stampers stopped.

Cissy froze with fright, and her skin crawled. The whole night seemed to freeze to a stop, as silent as the far-off stars.

And the night was rent with a gunshot.

23

Cissy knew exactly where the shot had come from. She clambered over the balcony rail, ran to the nearest door, and tore it open.

Then she pelted along the corridor. The passage was dim and the upstairs part of the hotel seemed deserted, but when Cissy arrived at the door of Timothy Dexter's room, Sergeant Mac-Donald came running round the corner. He said nothing, but lent his strong shoulder to help her hammer down the locked door. Between blows, Cissy could hear people downstairs calling out to each other.

"Wasn't that a gunshot?"

"Is it part of the game?"

"Isn't the murdering over yet?"

Then, a patter of footsteps, coming up the stairs. As Cissy and the policeman burst into Timothy Dexter's room, a crowd arrived in the corridor — and came to a halt, all bumping into each other as the ones at the front stopped frozen in the doorway, staring.

The room was large, with a bed and a sofa, both with plenty of cushions. A big wardrobe had been pulled away from the wall, to expose a door that connected to the next room — the room where Jess Williams had been sleeping off a headache, Cissy remembered. That communicating door was shut.

Timothy Dexter was sprawled on the hearth rug, face down, one arm thrown out, a grotesque form in the trembling firelight. His face was turned away, but there was a gaping hole in the parting of his hair. A large pistol lay by his outflung hand, and there was a nasty dark red puddle under his head. The air stung with gunsmoke.

The people in the passage all started shouting out at once, the ones at the back demanding to know what had happened, and the ones at the front shouting back at them to be quiet and make room. Sergeant MacDonald dropped to his knees beside the body, and lifted and turned the head. When he stood his normally rubicund face had gone pale and grim, but it was obvious already that Timothy Dexter was dead.

He turned and snapped at the crowd, "Everyone out of this room. Somebody fetch the constable. The rest of you, go down to the dining room."

But no one moved. The crowd stood as if paralyzed. Just about the whole of the Murder Experience party was there, but not a single person obeyed. Then, before the sergeant could open his mouth to shout again, the door in the wall beside the wardrobe opened, revealing Megs Dexter.

She stopped short, bracing herself with a hand on the doorframe, staring down at the corpse of her husband. Her face was white and frozen, and she seemed unaware that an eerie keening sound was coming from her wide-open mouth. Then, slowly, she came forward, and Cissy could see the room on the other side of the communicating door.

The other half of the double room, she thought. She saw a rumpled bed, almost hidden by a *chaise longue*.

The soft keening wail stopped. Meg's face was a ghastly white, completely bleached, except for the eye-sockets, which seemed black.

She said numbly, "My husband ... dead? Shot?"

Sergeant MacDonald cleared his throat. "I'm sorry," he said, and when she made a sudden rush to drop to her knees by the corpse, he put out a hand to stop her. "I'm sorry," he said again. "It appears that he put an end to himself."

"That's not possible!" Cissy cried.

Heads from all around jerked about to stare at her. The look in Megs Dexter's deep-set eyes made her flinch.

Then she heard Sergeant MacDonald say firmly, "Please don't interfere. We will need a coroner's investigation, of course, but the judgment of suicide is inevitable. As you know perfectly well, the door to the corridor was locked."

"But it can't be suicide!"

"Sir!"

She winced, but said doggedly, "It was murder, I'm sure of it."

The sergeant paused, looking at her very thoughtfully indeed. Then he said, "You have a reason for saying that, sir?"

"A good reason — the pistol on the floor by his hand is not his. Surely he would have used his own weapon? See, he is fully dressed, and the gun he habitually carries is much smaller than that big pistol."

"*What!*"

"Please, sir, look inside his jacket."

Sergeant MacDonald took a long moment to move, staring at her thoughtfully all the time. Then he dropped to one knee and gingerly felt through the big pockets in Timothy Dexter's Norfolk jacket.

A surprising amount came out, one thing after another — a handkerchief, a ring of keys, a pen, a Harland watch and a tin of cigars were placed one after another in a pile on the floor. Then, with his eyebrows high, Sergeant MacDonald placed a fancy tin beside the rest — a tin enameled with pretty flowers, exactly the same tin that had been posted to Mrs. Dexter. When he opened it briefly, it looked from that glimpse as if there were still marzipan fruits inside.

Then Cissy abruptly forgot it, glimpsing something that the policeman had not noticed. There was something clutched in the dead man's right hand, a scrap of blue paper.

She opened her mouth, but Sergeant MacDonald forestalled her, saying in a tone of vast surprise, "You are absolutely right — there *is* a gun."

Megs Dexter said in an unexpectedly strong voice, "My husband had several guns. He was mad on them, collected them, and stored them all over the place. How could it be murder? You had to break down the door to the passage because it was locked, and I swear that this connecting door was locked, too."

Cissy gazed at her in surprise, thinking that the housekeeper had made a very fast recovery from her shock and grief, and wondering why Megs was so determined that it was suicide. Then she heard Sergeant MacDonald say musingly, "And wasn't the connecting door covered by that wardrobe, there?"

Megs' tone became cautious. "Maybe it was, or maybe it wasn't. It depends on who was using the room. But it makes no difference, anyhow, for no one could get through that connecting door without a key — this key here."

And she held it up between two fingers of a clenched hand. Then, in a lower voice, as if on an afterthought, she added, "Will and Jess Williams have the other one, of course."

"Of course?" Mr. MacDonald said swiftly.

"The two rooms are usually together, making a double room. They give up the day room if we need a place for a guest."

"And that is why the wardrobe was put over the communicating door?"

"Of course," she said again.

"So who moved the wardrobe away?" the policeman asked.

But then he was interrupted, as someone ran from the corridor into the other bedroom. It was Will Williams. He was in shirt-sleeves, his appearance disheveled. Looking confused, he walked towards them, then stopped short in the connecting doorway, staring at the corpse and the crowd.

His mouth opened, but before he could say anything, Megs cried out, "It's Timothy — he's killed himself!"

It was like a warning. Cissy frowned at her, trying to work her out. How fond of the Gray and Williams family was she? Captain Jake Dexter and Harriet Gray might have rescued her from an awful existence, but Cissy had not had the impression that there was much love lost between her and the rest.

Then Cissy forgot it — because there was a slight movement, and she realized that there was someone in the bed of the other room. Jess Williams was so slender and lay so still that the rumpled blankets had hidden her.

One hand lay curled on the pillow, not far away from a tall glass on the side table, one of the same glasses Cissy had seen on the tray much earlier, in the passage. It was empty now, but still covered with a napkin. She said to Will, "Is your wife all right?" and he spun around, coming out of his stupor.

He ran to the bed, bent, and scooped Jess up in his arms. Her body drooped, as if she was dead. His expression was tortured, and anguished tears ran down his cheeks. Then Jess Williams moved — she was alive! She struggled groggily awake, and then clung to her husband.

She twisted around, and Will tenderly let her slide down his arms until she stood, still clinging to him, befuddled, but definitely alive, looking with dazed incomprehension at all the staring faces.

"Will," she whispered. "What happened? Why are these people here? Will ... I feel so sick."

"Sick?" Cissy said quickly.

Jess frowned, and then looked up at her husband. "The milk," she said plaintively. "It made me feel so sick."

And then her voice was drowned out by a deafening commotion of sirens, Bells clanged, and urgent voices cried out, "Fire! Fire! Get out, get out! Fire, fire, fire!"

Perfect chaos reigned. Instead of listening to orders to get downstairs and outside, and sensibly obeying them, the guests ran about everywhere, many of them in a total panic. Not only had they been embroiled in a fake murder, but then in a real one, too, and now a fire had happened, and their wits were totally addled.

Women screamed, and took dreadful risks to get back to their rooms to rescue silly things, and some had to be forcibly carried downstairs. Cissy grasped her chance to disappear, dropping through an upstairs window onto the balcony, and then down the fire escape to the catwalk. She waited under the overhang of the balcony, the stage door to the yard directly below her. She was undetected, the chequered pattern of her Harlequin costume concealing her in the mingled moonlight and dark shadow. There, she crouched like a gargoyle, observing the crazy scene.

The rest of the guests had somehow arrived out in the street, milling about in the chilly darkness, talking loudly into the strange silence, some of the more overwrought ladies indulging in fits of hysteria. Firemen rushed about with hoses over their shoulders, and buckets in their grip, while their horses snorted and stamped with excitement. But then, within a surprisingly short time, the guests were informed that that fire was out, and it was safe to return to their rooms. The firemen straggled out the front door, having returned from checking all the rooms, looking as if they were ready to return to their homes. The crowd dispersed, and Cissy slithered back up onto the balcony, and sidled into the room where the fire had blazed.

It was the painted parlor, Timothy Dexter's old room, the one with the lovely mural of ships. By great good fortune someone in the street had heard glass shattering, and had stopped to stare upwards. Then he had seen flames billowing out of the shattered French door, and had raised the alarm. The room stank and the ceiling dripped with water, but because the fire had been put out so fast, the firemen being right on the spot, it was surprisingly unscathed — except for the paintings. Cissy felt a pang of regret. Only fragments of line and color remained where the ships had progressed about the walls. The maritime panoply that had made this room unique and distinctive was utterly gone.

But why? It was weirdly easy to see the narrow progress of the fire. Someone had carried a brand around the walls, with the deliberate intention of obliterating the paintings. The smashed glass from a lamp lay in the hearth, and the smell of the kerosene that had been splashed along the walls was as strong as the stench of burned plaster. It didn't take much experience of fires to see what had happened, she thought. The arsonist had smashed the lamp, tossed the kerosene along the paintings, then crumpled a newspaper in the hearth, set it alight, and lit a spill from that to ignite the flash of running flame.

The ashes of the newspaper that had been used to start the blaze were lying about on the hearth and on the rug in front of it.

Some of the pieces were quite large, Cissy saw. The sudden rush of wind down the chimney when the fire sucked the air out of the room had sent the pieces flying away from the grate, and the arsonist had not had a chance to brush them up, as the alarm had been raised so quickly by the person out in the street.

Providentially, Cissy was still alone. She knelt carefully among the shards of glass and dabbed at the ashes with a damp finger. She was out of luck — the pieces collapsed into black dust whenever she touched them. Then she found a more fire-resistant scrap, evidently from a paste-on label, with the letters ROY— and BOS— plainly legible. It was the remnant of the paper she had searched for unsuccessfully on the *Royal George*.

Holding her breath, she inserted a fingertip underneath it, and lifted it up entire — and underneath was a twisted piece of blue paper. It was scorched at the open edge, but the twist had preserved the rest. This, she thought, scarcely daring to breathe as she tipped it with a finger into the palm of the other hand, was what remained of the spill that the arsonist had used to start the fire.

Crouching there, she stared at it, too scared to try to untwist it. Then, gathering her nerve, she started at the open corner, and unraveled it very carefully and slowly.

It was a fragment of a letter, a very old letter on old-fashioned blue paper, the kind that was waxy, designed to withstand sharp steel pen-nibs. The date — "—*uary* 184—" was just discernible, along, with the words, "*My dear Jahaziel, it is with an aching heart—*"

It matched the scrap of paper she had glimpsed in Timothy Dexter's dead hand. Obviously, the old letter had been torn out of his grip, some time before the arsonist had used it to start the fire. This was too much knowledge to keep to herself. Cissy jumped to her feet and ran back along the balcony.

No one stopped her as she hurried along the passages towards the stairs. Most of the bedroom doors were open and many of the rooms were empty, while others were very crowded. The guests had gathered in groups for the reassurance of company, and to talk out the unexpected tragedy that night. Then she arrived at the door of the room that she now knew belonged to Miss Harriet Gray.

Cissy stopped short. The door was open and the room was brightly lit. Gladys was standing at the end of the bed, talking to Sergeant MacDonald, apparently unaware of the tears that were streaming down her face. The man who had drawn the policeman away from the dining room was there as well, and she saw that he was a doctor, because of the stethoscope hanging round his neck. But most of her numb attention was focused on what lay on the bed, and her mouth was too dry to say a word.

Miss Harriet Gray was lying exactly as she had posed for the murder scene. This time, however, the sheet had been pulled up to cover her face.

With a dreadful sense of shock, Cissy absorbed the terrible fact that Miss Harriet Gray was dead. And that she may have been personally responsible.

24

Sergeant MacDonald held his enquiries at a table in the raised area off the dining room that had once been the stage. It was close to the old stage door, which he left open so that he could keep an eye on what went on in the yard. It was the best he could do, strapped as he was for resources. Volunteer fireman had been set on guard at all the other outside doors, and the constable kept watch at the lobby door, and fetched witnesses in the order requested. The sergeant took his own notes.

Will Williams was the first member of the family to be interviewed. He arrived reluctantly, not just because Jess was still groggy, and being attended to by the doctor, but because he, like the rest of the family, was struggling with grief at the news that Harriet Gray was dead. He scrubbed his face with a weary hand as he sat down, and then looked at the policeman, seated on the other side of the table.

Sergeant MacDonald, he thought, looked a very different proposition from the jovial fellow who was so good at vaudeville-style cross-examinations. Will had never considered the round-faced, burly countryman very quick-witted or shrewd, but now he was forced to revise his opinion. The policeman had a formal, determined look, betraying a dogged, methodical intelligence.

Will watched silently as Sergeant MacDonald wrote down his name at the top of a page.

The sergeant then looked up and said, "My condolences on the loss of .... of ... your mother-in-law?"

"Miss Harriet Gray was my wife's mother, yes," Will said.

Then he mopped away the tears on his cheeks, blew his nose, and added, "But she was much more than that. She rescued me and my mother when I was very small and my mother was very sick. She saved our lives, and more than that, she made our lives exciting. Because of her — and Captain Jake Dexter — I became someone special, instead of someone ordinary. To be fanciful, she is — was my fairy godmother."

The policeman cleared his throat, sounding embarrassed, and muttered, "My deepest regrets."

"Thank you. She was old and frail, and missed Captain Jake most terribly, but still it is an awful loss."

A pause, while the policeman squared his pad, aligning it neatly on the table. Then he looked up again and said, "Where were you when you heard the shot?"

Will hesitated. While it was less than an hour ago, so much had happened and his emotions were in such a mess, that it took a moment to sort his thoughts out.

Then he said, "I was down in the cellar, shifting a beer barrel. I like to do what heavy work I can, while I am here."

"Had you been down there very long?"

"It's hard to remember. I was down there off and on all day." Will scrubbed his forehead with one hand, trying in vain to get rid of the nagging headache. "The stampers were certainly going that last time I went down, and I had a job to sort out which barrel was needed. Then it was midnight, because I heard the stampers stop, and shortly after that I heard a shot."

"So what did you do then?"

"I waited, in case somebody shouted out to explain what had happened, but when I heard nothing more, I finished my job, and then went up to check on my wife. Which was when I found — when I found that Timothy..."

"Do you have any witnesses to the time you were down in the cellar?"

Will frowned, beginning to feel very uneasy. He said, "Do I need them?"

"Yes," said the sergeant heavily. "Yes, Mr. Williams, I believe you do."

There was a knock on the door that led to the lobby, and the constable came in, his hand on the housekeeper's elbow.

"You asked for Mrs. Dexter, sir," he said.

MacDonald nodded, and said, "Thank you." Then he turned back to Will, and said, "That will be all for the moment, Mr. Williams."

"So I can go upstairs to check up on my wife?"

"No, sir, I am afraid not. But worry not, she is in good hands. Please wait in the lobby until I call for you again, as I need to ask you more questions."

Very reluctantly, Will stood up, and gave his chair to Megs Dexter. The gaunt woman's eyes were dry, but her hands were clenched so tightly that the knuckles stood out like blue stones. Her face was dead white, so that the shadowed bags under her red-rimmed eyes looked like dark bruises. She said nothing, looking up at the two portraits instead of thanking Will or nodding to the policeman. The only sound was the thud of the door as the constable ushered Will into the lobby.

Finally, Megs turned her contemplative stare from the portraits to a study of the sergeant, thinking how different he looked from the fellow who had enjoyed the good dinner she had given him. He had liked the beer, too, she remembered. She had never taken him seriously, considering him an amateur stand-up comic who pandered to the Gray family, but now he looked serious, and unexpectedly efficient. She blinked, and made an effort to focus her mind.

He looked down at his pad as he wrote her name at the top of a fresh page. Then he looked up again. He said, "My condolences on the loss of a husband. It must be hard for you to carry on, right now, but I am afraid I have to ask some questions."

"Go ahead."

"Where were you when you heard the shot?"

"In my room."

"*Your* room?"

"Of course," she said defiantly.

"It was midnight, remember," she went on, though he only lifted a surprised eyebrow. "I had been up since four in the morning. Working. The guests had to be fed at six on the dot, and so the stove had to be lit well before that. Then there were the pitchers of hot water to be taken up, tables to be set, and maids and cooks to organize. I tell you, it's never easy. And, once the guests were gone, there was all that to be cleared away. Beds to be made, bathrooms to clean, floors to be swept and polished. You think I don't deserve my rest?"

Then she returned to her bitter thoughts, not even bothering to listen to his questions, because, oh dear lord, how she worked.

The Murder Experience weekends were bad enough, but every day was a challenge. On weekdays the breakfast was no sooner served and cleared away that bells began to ring, as laundry-women, butchers, fruit and vegetable sellers and other sundry trades-folk came and went, all of which demanded sharp super-vision, and sharp bargaining, too. And there were the sundries — the glassware to polish, the tavern to clean until it didn't stink of beer, soup stock to be made from the sack of bones the butcher left at the door on Wednesday. Gladys and Oscar and their young'uns did their bit, Megs had to allow it, but unremitting hard work had been her lot at the Golden Goose — and she had put up with it, because of her blind loyalty to her husband, knowing without doubt that one day he would return.

Yet on Friday, when Timothy had finally come back to her, she had slept in *her* room, not the one made up for him— and she had not complained, though it was her right to spend the night with her spouse. She had served Timothy his roast dinner and wine, taken his jacket and then his trousers, and brushed and cleaned them as he ate.

And then he had sent her away. He was too tired, he said — as if she wasn't tired, too. Instead of objecting, she had gone to her room, collapsed on her bed, and tossed and turned all night, asleep yet dreaming so agitatedly that it had been no kind of rest.

She had dreamed about the men in top-hats and frock-coats who had come to fetch her from the orphanage, and now she had a headache, because the echoes of the nightmare had nagged in her head all day. They reminded her of her humble beginnings, and how she was still humble now.

Up to the time those men had come for her, Megs had known, without question, that she was worthless, a liability to the grudging charity of others, but then she had found out that she was worth a fortune, the immense sum of five pounds sterling. Not for herself, but for those men in frock-coats, who had been desperate to fill the berths in the steerage quarters of a Sydney-bound ship, and earn their bounty. The minimum age for a female migrant was eighteen, but at fifteen she had been tall, if thin, According to the rules, she was supposed to own at least one change of clothing and pay six pounds towards the cost of passage, too, but that, of course, had been a joke.

When she had been man-handled into the stuffy, foul-smelling steerage of the vessel there had been a few respectable women there, true, and some of those had even had children. They were farmers' widows, maid-servants who had been unfairly fired without a reference, and country girls wishing to better themselves, but there had not been enough of them, and so the quota had been made up with orphans like Megs and the scrapings of the city streets. Those last had been the ones who had jeered and sung as the anchor was weighed, while the legitimate migrants wept, And then they were off on a five-month voyage, left to the mercy of the captain, the officers, the crew and the surgeon.

As Megs remembered it, the surgeon had been the worst.

Arriving in Sydney Town had been a short-lived relief. The female migrants were housed in the old barracks at Hyde Park, a place that had been originally built for the reception of four hundred male convicts. When Megs arrived there were more than a thousand women and girls crammed inside. There was an exercise yard where the dirt was still stiff and black with the blood from hundreds of floggings in the past, but no other amenities. The authorities, they were informed, were anxious that the girls should not feel temped to stop at the barracks for more than twenty-four hours.

Megs had stopped much less than that. Within half a day an old Irishman named Gavitty had come to buy her. He had worked her like a skivvy, to make sure that his purchase turned a profit, and his wife had treated her like her personal slave. There had been no joy in those days, just grim endurance. But then Miss Harriet Gray and Captain Jahaziel Dexter had shown her decency and kindness. They had bought her from Gavitty, and taken her to the Thames, and there she had at last found joy, because Timothy Dexter came with them. Such a handsome cove, he, with such lovely manners, and how miraculous it had been that he had chosen her for seduction, and that he had done the decent thing and married her when she fell pregnant. Timothy, her Timothy, had robbed and cheated the family, and often he had gone away, but her loyalty had never failed ... because no matter how far he went, no matter how long he stayed away, he always came back. To her.

But now, Timothy Dexter was dead.

A widow, Megs thought numbly. She was a widow.

Which meant that now she was free to leave the Golden Goose. She was freed from her endless thrall to the Grays.

The policeman was still talking. Making an effort, she paid attention.

He patiently repeated, "Can I take it, then, that you and your husband slept in different rooms?"

"Didn't you hear what I said?" she demanded. "I get up at four. My husband is — was — a gentleman, sir. He never rose before nine. It was then I carried him his breakfast tray, his coffee, and a pitcher of hot water for his shaving. I'd already made his suit nice and clean, and it wasn't until he was washed and shaved that he got dressed."

"H'm," said the policeman, while his pencil busily scratched away. "And he ate lunch in his room?"

"I took it up to him, yes. He preferred to be alone."

Will and Clem and Oscar had been in the hotel, along with Donald, the local lawyer who was Gladys's husband, and the father of her brood. Not only was Donald the man who was going to represent the Gray family when Timothy contested Captain Jake's will, claiming his right as the legitimate heir of the hotel, which made any confrontation difficult, but Megs knew from long experience how badly her husband got along with all that lot, who made no effort at all to hide their contempt. It was perfectly understandable that he wished to keep himself to himself.

"And in the afternoon?"

"He walked, but mostly stayed in. He was anxious to see Miss Harriet Gray, but she had gone on the tour with the Murder Experience Party, so he had to hang about until she returned."

That said, Megs pressed her lips together. The long, frustrating wait had made Timothy irritable and snappish, but she had no intention of revealing how bad-tempered he had been. She had not understood his angry impatience to see Miss Harriet, and did not want to describe it, or try to explain it now.

"So you were in and out of your husband's room all day?"

"When I had the time, yes. He needed his meals, his hot water, his coffee and whisky and wine."

"So, when you heard the shot, how did you know that the door was locked?"

"Because it always is locked, when the other half of the double room has to be used for a guest. It's the only way of making sure the two rooms are private. And apart from Will Williams, I have the only key."

"I'm talking about the door from the corridor to your husband's room, Mrs. Dexter, not the door between the two rooms."

"But you told me yourself that the corridor door was locked."

"I did?"

"Yes. You said it must be suicide, because the door to the passage was locked."

"So I did," he agreed, but did not smile. "But, Mrs. Dexter, you did not know that when you ran to his room."

"I don't know what you are talking about."

"After the door was broken down, you were first on the scene. When you heard the shot, you ran straight to his room. How did you know the shot came from there?"

"I knew that Timothy had guns, and ... and, well, it seemed obvious. I don't know anyone else here with a gun, and ... well, he had been acting strangely."

"Strangely?"

"I knew he had come here to contest Captain Jake's will, and claim the Golden Goose as Captain Jake's firstborn child, his only son, and his natural heir. The whole family knew it. But when I asked him if he had hired a lawyer, he looked at me so strangely. And then — he laughed."

"Lawyer?"

"Well, he needs one, don't he? The family's lawyer will be Gladys's husband, but he's only local, and not so sharp as a Boston lawyer would be, so it was natural to ask if he had hired himself a lawyer before he came back. But he laughed — he said nothing, just laughed at me. And it seemed so strange, too, that he was so anxious to see Miss Harriet. It was as if he had come all this way just to talk with her. He had a proper legal case, so he did not need to see her, but all he did was wait and wait for her to come back from the Mystery Tour."

"So when you heard the shot, you jumped to the conclusion that he was disturbed in mind?"

"Either that, or he was killed by one of the family, to make sure he couldn't take the hotel away from them. But to think that would be disloyal."

"Indeed," said MacDonald neutrally, and made a note on his pad. Then he looked up and said, "So that's why you went straight to his room?"

"Of course."

"But instead of coming down the corridor, you went to the Williams's room, intending to use the communicating door."

She shrugged, and said, "Why not?"

"How did you know the communicating door would be open?"

"Sergeant, it wasn't open. It was locked! But it makes no difference if it were locked or open. I had a key. And even if I didn't, Will and Jess had a key."

"And what about the corridor door? Why didn't you go to that door, instead of invading Mrs. Williams' privacy?"

"I knew it would be locked," she said grimly. "And I don't have a key to that one."

"You don't? Yet I thought, as housekeeper, you were entrusted with all the keys to the house."

"And after all these years, I should think I would be trusted, too."

"Yet you don't have a key to the room where your husband was sleeping, even though you had to carry his meals and hot water there?"

"He took my key away from me."

"*What*? Why?"

"He took it from me on Friday night," she snapped, neglecting to add that he had given her a smart slap when she objected. "He liked his privacy. He liked people to knock before he let them in."

"Even his wife?"

"Even his wife," she expressionlessly agreed.

25

Clem Gray was the next to be interviewed. Sergeant MacDonald studied his young, fresh face, then noted his name at the top of a new page, offered the same condolences on the sad loss of an aunt, then asked the same question.

"Where were you, sir, when you heard the shot?"

"Down in the cellar, shifting a barrel."

"You were alone?"

"No, sir, I was not. Will Williams was with me. It's not a job for one man."

"You both went down, even though your aunt was dead?"

"We had no idea the poor woman was dead! As far as anyone knew, she had played her part in the Murder play — she was pretending to be dead! It wasn't until Gladys went back into the room that she found the worst had happened, and the fake death was real."

"How long had you been in the cellar, sir?"

"Rather a long time — most of the day, on and off. The gas lighting system had been acting up while I was away in Europe and America. I suppose you do know that I am the lighting and effects technician for my sister, Minnie Gray?"

"I believe your effects are famous, and that people marvel that such a young man should have accomplished so much," the policeman said, but did not look up from writing his notes.

"And of course I had to be down there during the staged murder, to dowse the lighting, and then bring it up again. And," Clem went on, his tone aggressive, "I'd noticed the night before that some of the gentlemen liked to have a glass before retiring. Gladys had told me that a fresh stock had just come in, so I thought it was a good idea to get another barrel ready for tapping, seeing I was down there."

"*I?*" said the policeman, with heavy emphasis.

"We, then," said Clem, flushing.

"You are quite certain that Mr. Williams was there? That you were not alone."

"I was not alone!"

"And how did you feel, sir, about Mr. Timothy Dexter contesting your uncle's will — that there was a good chance he would take the hotel away from your family?"

"You're accusing me of killing Timothy?" Clem exclaimed. "For God's sake, man, remember who I am! I'm a technician, sir, an expert in both gas and electricity! If I *was* going to kill him, I certainly would not need a gun!"

"So you are pleased he is dead?"

"I did *not* say that, but now that you mention it, I am not particularly unhappy."

"Perhaps you were so delighted when you heard he had been shot that you wanted to protect the person who killed him — if you thought you knew his identity."

Clem went from red in the face to utterly white. "My God, you are trying to twist my words so you can charge Will with the murder."

"Isn't he the killer you have in mind?"

"Most certainly not!"

"So you are prepared to swear that Mr. Williams was in the cellar when the shot that killed Timothy Dexter was fired?"

"I am."

"Perjury is a crime, sir. Are you absolutely certain that Mr. Williams was in the cellar at the time?"

The silence dragged on as the words rang in the air, but then Clem nodded. "Absolutely," he said.

The doctor had decided that Jess Williams was fit to be questioned, so she was the next to be summoned. She arrived at the sergeant's desk alone, as requested, though the constable murmured that Mr. Williams had angrily protested. Then Sergeant MacDonald wondered if the doctor had been premature, and Mr. Williams's objections had been justified, because she looked so pale and heavy-eyed. A thick shawl was hugged tightly about her shoulders, and her fingers clung to the fringing.

Feeling obscurely guilty, the policeman made a great fuss about helping her into the chair. Then he sat down on his side of the table, and wrote down her name at the head of the page. When he looked up he said, "Dr Springer said you had been administered a hefty dose of bromide. Do you have any idea how it happened?"

"The doctor said it was in my glass of warm milk."

"Which your husband brought to you in bed?"

"Yes. I had a terrible headache, and had retired early. Whenever he is home, he brings me a drink of warm milk, because it helps me to sleep, but—"

"The maidservant told me that he keeps a bottle of bromide of lime in a special medicine cabinet in the kitchen. She said he often added it to a glass of warm milk."

"But not for me! It was for my mother, to help her sleep. Ask Dr Springer — he was the one who prescribed it! When Will wasn't here, Gladys always made sure of that dose of bromide. It was because — because she had a heart condition, which gave her bad dreams. And she missed my father so much! But we didn't know how bad her heart was..."

Tears were pouring down her face. "If only we had known, we would never have allowed her to exert herself so. She was determined to go on the Mystery Tour, and we made no effort to stop her at all. Valentine — poor Valentine — he could kill himself, he says. He brought her into the hotel — into this room — after the tour, and — and she sat down and asked for brandy. But she seemed cheerful enough, just a bit tired, and she wanted to sit and look at the portraits and mull over old memories ... and he took her at her word, and left her alone, and so — so she was left to climb all those stairs. By *herself*."

The last word was a wail of grief. Sergeant MacDonald silently passed her a handkerchief. Then, when the sobbing had stopped, he said, "Was it usual for your husband to put bromide in your milk, as well as your mother's?"

"No, of course not. I have no idea how it happened. Somehow, the glasses must have been switched — though he always made sure to cover them with napkins, each with an initial so they would not be confused."

"Do you remember the exact time you drank your milk?"

"After the dinner downstairs had started, I think. Just after I drank it, I remember my husband telling someone in the corridor to hurry up, as the dinner was being served, or something like that."

"And you fell asleep right away?"

"I remember feeling sick ... and then, nothing, not until my husband woke me and — and I found out about Timothy and — and my poor mother..."

"So if someone walked through your room, opened the door, and went into Mr. Dexter's room, you would not have noticed?"

"I didn't even hear the shot that killed Timothy!"

The policeman tapped his pencil, looking down at his notes while he waited out another spate of tears. Then he said, "I suppose your name — Jess — is short for Jessica."

"Jessica? No, no, though a lot of people make that mistake. It's Jasmine. Jasmine was my father's mother, who died when he was only eleven years old, and so I never knew her, but he gave me her name. He said it was a good choice, too, as I take after her in looks. And so Will and I christened our own daughter Jasmine, as well. But she turned out to look like *my* mother, instead."

And Cissy, crouched like a gargoyle on the edge of the fire escape, directly over the open stage door, stood up and grasped the balcony rail, and swung herself over it. As soon as she was indoors she began to run.

Cissy did not find the rose-robed blonde from Australia, but she did find her mother. Mrs. Miller was sitting in their bedroom, a cup of tea on the dressing table beside her. She had changed out of her costume and was attired in a fluffy blue dressing gown.

Cissy said without preamble, "I didn't know that Mr. and Mrs. Williams had children."

"But *of course* they do, dear," said her mother, blinking but still amiable despite all the excitement and the late hour. "There's a son who is a *dress designer*, believe it or not, in Auckland, and a daughter who is following some kind of stage career in Australia. I hear they are both very successful in their fields, becoming quite *famous*, or so they say."

Cissy took a deep breath, sat down on the edge of her bed and surveyed her mother very earnestly. "Mama, what exactly did Jasmine tell you when you sat with her on the train?"

"Jasmine?" her mother repeated thoughtfully. "The young lady from Australia who was the villainess in the murder mystery? H'm," she said. "How shrewd of you, Cissy. So she is the daughter and Mr. and Mrs. Williams, and that dress designer must be her brother."

"Exactly," said Cissy. "So, what was the story she told you?"

"The one about the *pirate* — the fellow who stole a ship?"

"Yes."

"H'm," said Mrs. Miller again, and pursed her lips. "It was not a very *proper* story for a young woman to relate to a stranger, but I suppose it was part of the play, as it was really too *sordid* to be true. Are you sure you want to hear it, dear?"

"I certainly do," said Cissy.

"Well, that young woman declared that the ship the pirate stole belonged to his wife's *lover*, and that the theft was an act of revenge. A tall tale, surely, though she seemed quite *positive* that he never went back to Massachusetts again, which does seem to indicate a bad conscience. One would *think* that a sea-captain would visit his home every now and then, especially a man who had the freedom to go where he wished, for he owned a brig, purchased with the proceeds from the sale of the ship he had stolen. But then, perhaps he was *embarrassed* to do so, knowing how people back home were talking about his errant wife's indiscretions. All in all, I suppose that it is not all that surprising that he limited his seafaring to the Pacific after that."

"The vessel was a brig?"

"Yes, that's what she said." Then Mrs. Miller put her head on one side, her expression alert. "Didn't Captain Dexter own a brig?"

"Yes, the *Gosling*."

"The baby Golden Goose," said her mother, and Cissy found herself the object of another searching look.

When Clara Miller spoke, though, it was merely to say, "Cissy, have you any idea of the hour?"

"Late, I imagine."

"It most certainly is. Don't you think it's time you got out of that costume and retired?"

"Oh, no, I have far too much to do."

"I *thought* it might be like that," said her mother.

26

Cissy was forestalled from another search for the rose-robed Jasmine, as the constable hailed her when she came down the stairway, and she found it was her turn to be questioned by Sergeant MacDonald.

But, when she arrived at the double door to the dining room, where he was holding his investigation, she was told that he was busy, and she had to wait in the lobby. When she protested, the constable merely waved her to a seat, and so she folded herself into one of the big soft chairs, alongside Will Williams, who was slumped with his elbows on his knees.

He looked sideways at her as she settled her folder of music sheets on her lap, and said, "How long is that damn policeman going to keep me here, do you know?"

Cissy shook her head.

"Then would you mind going upstairs and checking on my wife? She looked dreadful after the sergeant questioned her, but I'm not allowed to talk to her. And I'm going frantic."

Cissy looked at the constable, who was stationed in front of the double doors to the dining room with his boots planted apart. "I'm sorry, I can't. I'm as trapped as you are," she said. "I'm sure Gladys is looking after her."

This was followed by a silence that dragged on until Cissy said diffidently, "Can I ask you a question?'

He snapped, "No, you cannot! You have poked your nose into our family affairs far too much already!"

"But it's not my fault!" As she gazed at him reproachfully, she saw that his eyes were bloodshot, and that his expression was haggard.

Then she saw him change his mind, shifting in his chair with impatient movements, crossing his legs the other way.

Sarcastically, he said, "Ask away, why not? For some un-fathomable reason, Minnie trusted you, so maybe I should, too."

"I just wondered why you had decided that Minnie's letter wasn't important any more. You seemed to think differently on the ship."

"Because I thought Timothy would steal it! But then I realized that he didn't even know it existed."

"But that doesn't mean it was unimportant."

He sighed, "Why do you harp on about it? Minnie has become tense. She's driving herself too hard, and where Timothy's concerned she's prone to wild accusations. She was only a small child when Timothy Dexter joined the family, and she hated him on the spot, and has hated him ever since. It's a natural resent-ment. The family was shifted from Auckland to the Thames just a short time afterwards, and Minnie hated that, too, as she had just started school and had several little friends. And her favorite brother, Robert, whom she looked up to and adored, was killed when the brig blew up, you know. Timothy survived, and Minnie accused him of causing the accident. She became quite hysterical at the funeral, and made wild allegations."

"That the explosion was ... deliberate?"

"That's what she said."

"So, did Captain Dexter blame Timothy for the loss of his vessel?"

"No, of course he didn't. He was an experienced seafarer, who knew the dangers of the business."

"And how did he feel about Timothy, generally?"

Will Williams paused, staring into space. It was as if he had forgotten she was there, and for a moment Cissy thought he wasn't going to answer. Then he said in a low, intense voice, "Jake loathed him."

"I beg your pardon?"

"Can't you understand? Jake *loathed* Timothy. He and Timothy were absolute opposites in nature. Both were attractive, in their own different way, and both of them certainly had style. Like Jake, Timothy didn't lack courage, either, but nonetheless the fellow was an utter blackguard. He always had another sharp scheme to make himself a fortune, and Jake would *lend* him the money to get going, just to get quit of him for a few weeks or months. Then, when Timothy came slinking back broke and in debt, as always happened, we would put up with him in Golden Goose, while Megs indulged his every whim, lavished him with our best wine and food, and then another scheme would boil up in his brain, and Jake would fund him again. Anything to get rid of the leech."

Cissy frowned. "Then why did Captain Dexter put up with him at all?"

Will shouted, "Because he was his *son*, damn it!"

But, she noticed, feeling puzzled, his eyes had become evasive. He slumped down again, his elbows on his knees, as if to avoid her questioning gaze.

After a moment, she said, "Many men have disowned their sons."

"Well, Jake was not like that."

The door to the dining room opened, and the sergeant put his face through the gap, evidently disturbed by the noise. Both Cissy and Will straightened up and looked silently back at him, and he went back inside and shut the door again. The constable shifted his feet, his hands firmly clasped behind his back.

Cissy said curiously, "When did you first meet Timothy Dexter?"

"I think I've told you that already. It was just before I joined Jake here in the Thames."

"And — before that, did you have any idea that Timothy Dexter existed?"

Will was silent, and when she looked at him his lips were pressed tightly together. She persisted, however, saying, "For, if you did not know that Captain Dexter had a son in America, it must have come as quite a surprise to the family."

"That," he said with unexpected grim humor, "is quite an understatement."

"So surely everyone must have wondered if Timothy Dexter was a fraud."

"Jake believed him," he said, and shrugged. "Jake knew the background, and we did not, so we were forced to believe him, too."

But, thought Cissy, Minnie Gray did not. She said, "Your wife, Mrs. Williams, spoke of Miss Minnie Gray as *my dear little Minnie*. I imagine they were very close?"

"Not particularly."

"Really?" she said, surprised.

She thought he was not going to talk any more, that this was the end of his confidences, but then he shifted in his seat, and said, "My mother was poorly for a long time after Minnie was born, so Jess took over Minnie, which was quite a responsibility for a girl who was only ten years old. She was Minnie's little mother, which meant that she missed out on a lot of the fun that her friends were enjoying. I was with the family, too, as you know, and I did my best to help, but when I turned fourteen I was apprenticed to a cabinet-maker. And then, when I was nineteen and Jess was fifteen, she met Timothy..."

He stopped, his expression brooding. Cissy waited, but he said nothing more, so she ventured, "Did you meet Timothy at the same time that Jess did?"

"How interesting that you should ask that," he said, giving her a restless look. "You are really very perceptive."

Minnie had said something like that, too, Cissy recollected. Encouraged, she asked, "So how did you meet Timothy Dexter?"

Will paused for a long time, while Cissy waited, watching his expression become faraway, as if he had lost himself so far back in the past that he had forgotten he had an audience. Then he said, still staring into space, "It's impossible to explain it to someone who wasn't there — someone who doesn't know what Jess was like at the age of fifteen. Fragile, so lovely, and so vulnerable ... and very, very romantic. *Stagestruck* is the term, I think. She wanted most intensely to go on the stage, and was angry and rebellious because she wasn't allowed to join her mother in the theatre in Ballarat. But then, she changed. There was a sort of aura ... and it became obvious that she had fallen in love."

His voice had become flat, with a harsh hint of past pain. "She had a certain glow. She was more beautiful than ever. She would get up early and sneak out of the house, to avoid having to take Minnie with her ... and then Jake came back from Sydney. He'd sold the theatre in Ballarat, and was ready to invest in some other likely place. That was his way of life, you see, and his investments were usually in theatres, because of Harriet's talent. And because they made a lot of money.

"Jake had left Harriet on the brig, because it was supposed to be just a brief call. He had come ashore to collect Jess ... and you have to understand that he idolized her. He indulged her like the only child we all believed her to be, spoiling her to make up for being away so much, but he expected perfect loyalty from her, as well.

"But she was out — as usual with her, at the time. He waited, but she did not come home. Then Minnie — who was naturally jealous — blurted out that Jess had a young man. She had followed her one day — had spied on the couple. Jake became anxious, as any father would, and after I came home from work he took me with him when Minnie led us to the place on the waterfront where she had seen them together. It was ... evening ... and..."

He broke off. Cissy saw him swallow. "The last golden light was on her face..." He stopped, and swallowed again, "They didn't see us coming, though we were only a few yards away, because they were so absorbed in each other...

"And I *felt* Jake's shock as he recognized the young man, it was like a tremor in the air — and I will never forget the expression on his face, of not just shock, but horror, and a kind of disgust. Then his face smoothed out and he stepped forward with his hands held out and he hailed Timothy as his *son* — the son he'd had by his wife in New England."

"And was Timothy surprised?"

"I've never seen a man so amazed — or ever seen such a display of conflicting emotions cross a man's face. He wavered, I swear it. He looked at lovely Jess, he looked at Jake, and I swear he looked at the brig as well, anchored out in the stream. Then he smiled, and embraced Jake with well-played delight at being united with his birth father after so many years. Twenty, he said."

"And Jess?"

"She said nothing, but her face, her *eyes*, as she realized that she had fallen in love with her *brother*..." Will stopped, taking a long shaking breath. Then he said in a low fierce voice, "She must never *ever* be allowed to wonder if Timothy made a deliberate choice."

"Or she would realize that he was greedy — that greed won over whatever love he had professed?"

"Exactly."

"And is that why you burned the letter, Mr. Williams?"

"What?"

"The letter that you stole from the bottom of my trunk. I heard you burn it, in the room that had been Timothy's, the only fire-place where you could destroy it in private. "

"Dear God," he said, shaken."Minnie certainly didn't under-estimate you."

"Did you read what was inside before you burned it?"

"I didn't need to. I knew exactly what Minnie had written. She had guessed beyond doubt that Timothy was coming to Thames to contest Jake's will and seize the Golden Goose from the family, and so she was repeating her old accusations that Timothy was not Jake's son at all."

"I see," said Cissy. She paused, and then said, "How did Miss Harriet Gray receive the sudden news that Captain Dexter had a son?"

"Jake went back on board, taking Timothy along with him. I don't know exactly what happened, then, but Harriet's temper was notorious."

"And Jess? Did she go too?"

"No, she came back home with me."

"And after that — did she run off to join an acting troupe?"

"Dear lord, how did you guess? My God, girl, with the instinct for human motivations you have, you should be writing novels — but you are right, for that is exactly what she did. Jake was a stubborn New Englander, and refused to go after her — but he knew all along that he could leave the quest to me. I was only nineteen years old, for God's sake, but he was right. As soon as the hotel was built, I packed a bag and pursued her. It took me three years, but I found her."

Then Will added bitterly, "It took that long because she had been such a failure that her name had never appeared on any theatre bill. I'd even hunted for her in Australia, but in the end I found her in Dunedin, in the cold south of New Zealand, in her dressing room in the so-called Theatre Royal. It was an ill-lit, flea-abounding rat hole, and she was sharing it with two other aspiring actresses."

"And you brought her back?"

"I did more than that," he snapped. "I married her."

"But what about Timothy?"

"What do you mean, *what about Timothy*? He was married to poor, patient Megs, and wasn't around very often. He even disappeared the day of their little boy's funeral! I told you how Jake used to stake him to money, just to get him out of the place. He weaseled his way of many fraudulent schemes that went wrong, but last year the law finally caught up with him. Jake bailed him out, and paid compensation to the people Timothy had cheated, then ordered him to get out of the country and never come back. And Timothy went — but we scarcely noticed, because it was the same night that the hotel caught fire."

"By accident?"

"Oh, that was probably in Minnie's letter, too. She swears that Timothy set the place ablaze in revenge."

"And what did you think?"

"I don't know. We were all too busy to think. I imagine we all just hoped we had seen the last of the blackguard."

"And it was indeed the last you saw of him — until you boarded the *Royal George*."

"Again, you are right. When he didn't turn up at Jake's funeral to make a fuss about the inheritance we began to think we had seen the last of him. Then, when your mother's card was brought to Minnie's dressing room we wondered if he had gone to England, and whether you had met him there. We didn't think it was important, as Dexter is a common name, but of course Minnie agreed to see you, just to make sure. Then, when she talked to you and found out that he was on the way to New Zealand, it was a terrible shock, for his motives were so obvious."

"Were they? Are you sure that he knew that Captain Dexter was dead?"

Will stared at her. His mouth opened, but he was forestalled by the opening of the dining room door.

Sergeant MacDonald came out, trailed by Clem Gray and Harmony Bradford. To Cissy's astonishment, they were holding hands. Clem was grim-faced, and Harmony was most unusually subdued.

Cissy heard Will Williams mutter, "*Goddamnit,*" but heard no more, because Sergeant MacDonald beckoned her over.

"We need to have a long talk," he said.

27

Sergeant MacDonald preceded Cissy into the room. After sitting down, he watched her closely as she approached the table, evidently comparing her with his memory of their conversation in the yard, and she abruptly wished she had changed into a dress, or at least a dressing gown.

She sat down, and he said, "I remember you said your name is Pierrot."

"It's Miller, actually, Cissy Miller," she confessed. "I am wearing a Pierrot costume, you see, though it is Harlequin when I am in the light."

Ignoring this last, he exclaimed, "You're a girl?"

"I'm afraid so."

He blinked, shook his head, and then said, "So, Miss Miller, what did you do when you left the yard?"

"Well, you remember the quarrel we overheard?" He nodded, and she said, "It gave me the location of Miss Harriet Gray's room, because I recognized her voice, you see, and so I went inside and then upstairs, on the way to her door."

"Did you see anyone else upstairs?"

"I saw Mr. Williams, coming out of his wife's bedroom."

"Ah." The policeman looked very alert. "How did he seem?"

"He was worried about his wife's headache. He jumped to the conclusion that I intended to disturb her, and he scolded me, rather. And then he said I should hurry up and get downstairs, as dinner was about to be served."

"Was he carrying anything?"

"Yes — an empty glass that had held milk. It was on a tray. I had seen the tray he was carrying before, you know, on a little side table, only it had two glasses on it then, covered with initialed napkins. But when he came out of his bedroom, he had only one glass."

More scribbling. Then: "And?"

"He went back downstairs and I went off down the corridor."

"You saw no one else?"

"Well..." She put her head on one side, struggling to remember, and then said, "I heard a key turn, and when I looked back I saw someone go into Mr. Timothy Dexter's room. I didn't see the woman's face, but I saw the flick of a long black skirt, so I am sure it was his wife. Mrs. Megs Dexter."

"A key?" He was looking more alert than ever. After he had finished writing this down, he underlined it heavily.

Then he said, "According to Gladys, ever since you arrived, you have been very anxious to see Miss Harriet."

"Yes — because I had a message for her, in a yellow envelope that Miss Minnie Gray had given me. And then," she added, "there was a parcel, apparently addressed to Mrs. Dexter, which I very mistakenly thought was for Miss Harriet Gray. Mrs. Williams opened it, and I think she delivered it to her mother. The package held a pretty tin — the same tin you found in Mr. Timothy Dexter's pocket, after he was shot, the one holding fancy marzipan sweets — and I think Miss Harriet gave it to him during that quarrel. Or she maybe even threw it at him! Do you remember what she said? — *And take this, too! — I know it was not intended for me, unless you want my demise, as well!* Oh, Mr. MacDonald, sir, do you think she ate one of the marzipan sweets, and was poisoned? Because if she was, then it is largely my fault, because I made a mess of getting it to the right person."

"Good lord," said the sergeant, extremely startled. "What on earth made you think the marzipan is poisoned?"

"When we were at the Crown mines, I smelled the cyanide they use to extract the gold, and while it stank, it also reminded me of almonds, which they use to make marzipan — and in the Murder Play, the old lady was poisoned by cyanide..."

"Set your mind at rest," he said, and in the midst of her flood of relief Cissy almost had the impression that he was amused. "Miss Harriet died of natural causes. She had a bad heart. And the tin was full — there were six places for sweets, and six sweets there. Believe me, no one who knew the quartz-gold business would eat anything that smelled of almonds! But," he added thoughtfully, "I will certainly send those sweets to the School of Mines for testing."

There was silence for a moment, save for the scratching of his pencil. Then he said, "So, what happened when you found Miss Harriet's door?"

"Nothing. No one answered my knocking, and there wasn't a sound." She hesitated, and then said, "Do you think she was dead already? That nasty quarrel we overheard would have set anyone's heart racing, and..."

"Perhaps," he said neutrally.

Cissy, however, was thinking again. "No, she can't have died so soon after the quarrel, as she had time to arrange herself. When I went into her room after the pretend murder, she was very prettily laid out, like Titania on her flowery bed. In fact," she mused aloud, "she might not have been dead even then, because she looked so wonderfully peaceful. She may have passed away after the viewing party left."

This time, one of his bushy eyebrows rose, but his tone was professional when he said, "We'll leave the time of death for the doctor to decide, shall we? But tell me, who were the others in the viewing party?"

"Gladys was at the door, regulating who was allowed in and who was not. I am afraid I sneaked in, rather. That made seven inside the room, when I think she wanted only six — Miss Fleet, Mr. Schuyler Bradford, and his two daughters, Harmony and Patience, all of whom came on the *Royal George* to New Zealand. I was rather surprised to see Harmony," Cissy confessed. "As she had been too ill to come on the Mystery Tour, so had rested at the hotel all day. I suppose the rest had done her good," she mused, though she remembered that Harmony had looked pretty sick just now, when she had come out of the dining room with Clem. Or had it been guilt? It certainly made her wonder what Harmony had been really up to while the others in the party were on the Murder Mystery tour.

She went on, "And then there were the two actors who were playing the murderers in the Murder Game. They're Grays, of course, as I have worked out since — Jasmine, who is Miss Harriet's granddaughter, and Valentine, who is her brother. He's a *dress designer*," she added in a hushed voice.

She thought there was another twitch of his lips, though it was hard to see the sergeant's expression, because he was busily writing down the names of the people who had been allowed into the room. Instead, he said, "Miss Minnie Gray had given you an envelope for Miss Harriet Gray?"

"Yes!" she said, and described meeting the actress. "That's when she gave me this costume," Cissy said, gesturing at her tunic. "She said I was to be like Harlequin in a medieval drama, and watch and listen to unfolding events. And then she cut a piece out of a Boston newspaper, and put it in an envelope with a message, and instructed me to give it to no one else but Miss Harriet Gray."

"But you weren't able to give it to Miss Harriet Gray?"

"No, of course not. I only met her once, and then without the slightest idea of her real identity. Though she was a very attractive person, quite charismatic, really, and I do wish I had known her better," Cissy added wistfully. Then she gathered her wits, and said, "Miss Minnie must have told Mr. Williams about the envelope, because he accosted me on the *Royal George*, and was most insistent that I should give it to him, as he expected it to be stolen — by Mr. Timothy Dexter, or so he strongly hinted. But I remembered my instructions, and refused, so when he argued I deposited it in the purser's safe, to keep him happy, and then I bought an identical envelope, put a message to Miss Harriet inside, addressed it to her, and when we left the *Royal George* I hid it in the bottom of my trunk. And to be sure, it was stolen! On the very first night! And the thief destroyed it! I found the ashes in the bin in the yard."

"So you had left the original in the purser's safe on the ship?"

"No, no, of course not. I have it right here," she said, and opened her music folder, and slid it out.

Sergeant MacDonald took the envelope with his eyebrows hoisted very high indeed.

Without opening it, he asked, "And what were you going to do with it, now that Miss Harriet has passed away?"

"Give it to her granddaughter, Jasmine. It seemed the obvious choice, as Mrs. Williams — Miss Harriet's daughter — is far too distressed. But you forestalled me, when you ordered me to wait in the lobby."

"But you are happy to give it to me?"

"Well, you are the arm of the law, Sergeant."

Another twitch of the lips. He turned the envelope over in his hands, and then observed, "You haven't opened it."

"Of course not!" She was quite shocked that he could suspect her of such impropriety.

"Then we shall open it now, shall we?"

It was a rhetorical question, so Cissy didn't answer. Instead, now that it was proper to find out what was inside, she half-stood and leaned far over the desk as he slit it open, so eager was she to see what the newspaper item might be. And, cooperatively, the sergeant turned it so she could read it, too.

At first, it seemed nothing more than an item of casual interest.

The heading read DID THEIR CRIMES DIE WITH THEM? Underneath was a gossipy piece about ne'er-do-wells who skipped after cheating various people, and who were declared dead soon afterwards by their embarrassed families, who put up gravestones to prove it.

The writer's interest had been aroused, the story went on, when he had been given information that a local lawyer had been hired to prove that at least one of the gravestones was misleading, the person named on it being not just alive and well, but also the rightful heir to a family fortune. And it was illustrated with a picture of a headstone, commemorating the death of a certain Timothy Grace.

And then Sergeant MacDonald read the message Miss Minnie Gray had written. The policeman stood up so fast that his chair fell over with a clatter, and with no hesitation at all, Cissy pursued him as he ran upstairs to Miss Harriet Gray's room.

28

When Cissy ushered her mother into the lounge next morning, she was startled to see other people there. On one of the settees, Harmony Bradford and Clem Gray were sitting holding hands, still looking sheepish, though rather less guilty. Evidently they had declared their romance, and so did not feel so furtive. Jasmine was perched on the arm of an easy chair, while her brother, Valentine, was slumped — though elegantly — inside it, his long legs crossed at the ankle. Jasmine looked as outstanding as ever, and Cissy wondered if her brother had designed her outfit — a magnificent black and white Russian blouse with voluminous demi-gigot sleeves, over a narrow black skirt that had been pleated from the knees down. Her feet, also long and slender, were encased in short black patent leather boots.

Then Jess Williams walked in. She was alone, and looked terrible. Huddled in a shawl, her dark hair uncharacteristically untidy, she looked too fragile to be cross-examined — if that was the reason Sergeant MacDonald was sending people into this room. She said nothing, and looked at no one. Instead, she went to an armchair in a corner, and sank exhaustedly into it. She looked so unlike her two children, and behaved so differently, Cissy thought, that it was almost impossible to credit that they were related.

Jasmine, obviously, took after Harriet Gray. Indeed, she was so like her grandmother that she could have stepped down from the portrait. Blonde, poised and beautiful, she looked ready to play any romantic or melodramatic part, and it was easy to believe that she was enjoying a brilliant career. Valentine, too, was flamboyant — dark, lithe, lean, and matador-like, very like his grandfather. All the dash and charisma, Cissy meditated, had skipped a generation. Then she wondered how Jess Williams felt about it. And why was she here? She had not been in Miss Harriet Gray's room, and had not taken part in the Murder Play.

Then Mr. Schuyler Bradford III came in the door, his wife and Patience at his shoulder, and waved at everyone before he and his wife and daughter settled on a settee. Cissy noticed that all three avoided looking at Harmony. Evidently, she had let the family down by becoming romantically involved with Clem Gray. But was it such a bad match? He might be ten years older than their daughter, but he was very successful in his field. Then Cissy remembered that Mr. Bradford was a shipping mogul. He probably had a society wedding to a rich associate planned.

Then came Miss Fleet, garbed in an elegant gown made of pale brown cashmere, a black, brown and white silk scarf about her neck. Forgetting the Bradfords, Cissy leaned forward and said, "I think you dropped this, Miss Fleet." Casually, she handed her a handkerchief. The American woman flipped it out of its folds, looked at it briefly, nodded thanks, and tucked it into her reticule.

Gladys came in with a trolley that was loaded with a teapot, a pot of hot water, milk, sugar, cups and saucers and spoons, along with a plate of cake, which was handed around by the expression-less Megs Dexter. That done, the two women sat down.

Ominously, the trolley had been followed by the constable, who shut the door and then stood in front of it, evidently to deter people from either coming in or going out. Silence, except for echoes from the kitchen. Unearthly silence, really, because it was the Sabbath, and the stampers were still.

Then Will Williams walked in, followed closely by Sergeant MacDonald.

The sergeant stood so close to Will, and Will's demeanor was so subdued, that it seemed obvious that he had been arrested. Jess, huddled in her chair with her shawl gripped in both hands, looked at her husband as intensely as if she had never seen him properly before. He wore a lounge suit with his newest single-breasted waistcoat, and was freshly shaved, as brisk as if he was about to go off on the paddle-steamer *Wakatere*, back to setting stages for Minnie in Munich or Vienna or New York. But when he turned his head to smile wanly at her, Jess saw that his eyes were rimmed with red.

Poor Will, she thought with terrible guilt and pity. He had been just four years old when she was born, but she had no memories of him as a carefree lad. Life for Will had always been serious, she thought, a constant endeavor to make up to Harriet and Jake for rescuing him and his mother from the hell of Little Adelaide. Her uncle, Royal Gray, had told her all about it. Harriet had nursed Will's mother back to health, and her brother, Royal, had married the winsome, blue-eyed girl who had emerged from the sick bed, adding to the heavy obligation that Will already felt.

And Jess herself had been part of that debt. When Royal Gray had set up the family in Auckland, leaving Harriet and Jake to manage the thriving theatre in Ballarat, little Jess had gone along, too, as she was now five years old, and ready for school. Jake and Harriet had been heartbroken to see their only daughter go, but, as Jake had said, there was always Will, to make sure that she was safe. And though Will was only nine years old at the time, Jess had known it was true. As far back as she could remember, Will had looked after her. It was an obligation he had taken seriously, which was typical.

Will had never changed from the way he had been at the age of three, when Harriet had discovered him with a pitcher half as large as himself, hunting for water for his sick mother. He had grown up sturdy, earnest, and hardworking, so different from the frivolous Grays and the swashbuckling, opportunistic Captain Jake Dexter. Jess had often wondered what he made of them all, particularly his incurably romantic actor of a stepfather — Royal, who was a charmer, but not a practical man at all.

As a lad, Will's only pleasure, seemingly, was to ramble off into the countryside. Hours would pass before he arrived back with his satchel full of twigs, flowers and leaves, looking sunburned and happy, but now that she thought back, no one seemed to notice. Perhaps Will would have liked to tell them about his latest botanical finds, but none of the effervescent Grays ever wanted to stop and listen, and so, instead of talking, he had filled sketchbooks with lovely paintings — paintings that no one had known about until much later, when he became famous.

Then Jess flinched, jerked out of her meditations as Will swung about at Sergeant MacDonald, who had settled on a sofa next to Miss Fleet. He snapped, "I don't want my wife to be any part of this investigation. As you know, she was unconscious during the murder, and can't give any kind of evidence. So please let her go."

Sergeant MacDonald said, very calmly, "Mrs. Williams is here at her own request, sir. After all, the victim was her brother."

Her brother. Her *brother*. Jess flinched again. After all these years, the word still hurt. And *victim*? Timothy had never been *the victim*. The Grays were the victims. Timothy had made victims of them all — right from the first day she had met him, though she had been too young and too foolish to understand that the world held men like Timothy.

She remembered it now with a queer sense of detachment, as if it had happened to somebody else. In her mind she could smell the way Queen Street, Auckland, had smelled back then. It had been a penetrating stench of damp, for mud ran freely down the steep street, much of it coming from the taps on the junction with Wellesley Street, where the housewives gathered with their wooden pails.

The taps were busy that morning, Jess recollected, so it must have been Monday, blue Monday, wash-day. Some of the women stood impatiently in line as they waited for their turn at the pumps, while those with more leisure sat down to rest on the low walls that set off the boardwalk from the houses. Jess had always fancied that they looked like pullets on a stony perch as they sat, talking as animatedly as a flock of hens, their skirts gathered up into their laps to keep the hems out of the mud, their pails set down beside them.

Instead of joining the line, she had begun to cross the street towards them, to sit down for a while herself, for once she had filled her pail and got back home, the nasty job of washing greasepaint-stained shirts awaited.

Halfway across, she heard the screeched warning.

Instead of running, Jess had stopped and looked around. She saw the women who had been standing in line all scattering away, but only dimly, with no sense of understanding. Then she screamed herself, as she saw the horseman come plunging down the hill, completely mad and out of control.

The rider was hollering drunkenly, perfectly uncaring about the women who were fleeing out of the way of his dangerous rush. Jess at last began to run, but tripped in her panic. She fell in a muddle of white petticoats, right in the maddened horse's path. And a young man whirled off the sidewalk and dived into the road, right under the razor-sharp hooves.

He landed on his shoulder, rolled, grabbed her, and rolled again. She had felt his tight arms. Hooves slammed down, close to his head. Gravel spurted into her face. Then, with a last yell, the horseman was gone.

The arms let go. Jess scrambled to her feet. She was trembling violently, bruised and scratched, but at that moment she had felt no pain, her whole attention on her savior. And what she saw, all those years ago, was a handsome young man, about twenty years old, wearing a black suit and a white ruffled shirt with a black string tie. His eyes were a glittering brown, and his straight brows were black, but his hair was as blond as straw. His face folded into a triangle shape when he grinned — and Jess remembered now that he had smiled a lot as he gazed down into her flustered face.

"My compliments," he had drawled, scooping up his hat, and she remembered how his American drawl had surprised her. Then, flourishing the battered hat, he had bowed very deeply, and taken her hand. And then he kissed her fingers.

As Jess, flame-faced, had snatched her hand away, she heard a burst of laughter. The women had gathered around to watch. One called out, "Where be your manners, Jess? You should thank 'im, Jess, thank the 'andsome young man. Give him a nice little kiss."

Her blush had deepened, until she felt hot all over, and it was impossible to say a single word. "Cat run off with your tongue, Jess?" another woman teased. "Thank the sailor kindly, Jess, afore he runs back to sea."

"Sailor?" Jess echoed, finding her wits at last. "Surely not!" she said, and even managed a giggle.

"What, you don't believe it?" he cried, amid more laughter. "I've stood my watch and taken my trick at the wheel, miss, and I can prove it, too!"

And with another flourish he had ripped open his ruffled shirt, to reveal a pale wide chest, complete with a tattoo of a ship in full sail.

Jess, her mouth hanging open, heard half-scandalized laughter all about, and had had a job not to giggle again. Then Timothy reached out and slyly tugged the end of her thick braid of dark hair.

"Jess?" he had said. "Do I hear bells, sweet Jess?"

And she had fallen in love, without even knowing his name.

Oh God, she thought now. What had she done?

29

Sergeant MacDonald, sitting next to Miss Fleet, cleared his throat, ruffled the pages of his notebook, then looked up and said, "I apologize for the early hour, but many of you are scheduled to leave this afternoon, and I need to get all the evidence possible before that happens."

Mr. Schuyler Bradford shifted heavily. "But what kind of evidence can we provide, sir? We had nothing to do with the victim. I know he was on the *Royal George*, but I can't say I ever saw him. And ever since he got here, he kept as close as a mole in his hole. We didn't exchange a single word, sir!"

"But the time on the *Royal George* is important, sir," the sergeant said calmly. "First, there is the matter of a letter that went missing."

Cissy, startled, sat upright. This was the last topic she had expected to be discussed. Mr. Bradford was confounded, too, because he said, "What letter? This is the first time any letter has been mentioned."

"I think Miss Miller can explain it," the sergeant said, still very calm.

Cissy said, "*Me?*"

"Just tell them what you told me last night."

Oh dear lord, thought Cissy. Will Williams was staring at her with gathering alarm and hostility, and everyone else was staring, too, including her mother, who made a clicking noise of dismay, saying, "*What* is this all about, Cissy?"

"It was the letter Miss Minnie Gray gave me to deliver to Miss Harriet," she said, looking at her mother, because that was easiest. "Surely you remember that?"

Gathering courage, she looked at the other staring faces, and explained, "It happened in San Francisco. Mama and I were lucky enough to get tickets to *The Merry Widow*, and when my mother's card was sent to the star, she very kindly consented to see us. Unwittingly, however, we carried bad news — that Mr. Timothy Dexter was on the way to the Thames. Miss Minnie Gray became quite alarmed at that, and wrote a letter to Miss Harriet Gray. Then, after putting it in an envelope with a newspaper clipping, she handed it to me with the *strictest* instructions to deliver it to Miss Harriet Gray and absolutely no one else, not even any of the family."

Cissy paused, shyness overcoming her again, but then she saw Will's hand tighten into a threatening fist, and, emboldened by anger, she said, "But then, after I boarded the *Royal George*, I was warned that the envelope could be stolen! So of course I became very curious about the contents."

Will snapped, "So we are here to listen to your imaginative guesswork."

Cissy looked at Sergeant MacDonald, but he made no response to her silent appeal, so she said quietly, "It was easy enough to guess that the letter was a warning — a warning to do with the inheritance of the Golden Goose, because I had learned that in Captain Jahaziel Dexter's will, he had left the hotel to the family, even though Timothy Dexter was the rightful heir, being his son."

Clem shouted, "How do you know about Jake's will? It's none of your business, miss!"

"Perhaps not," Cissy allowed. "But I couldn't help overhearing when you accused Timothy Dexter of travelling to the Thames to contest Captain Dexter's will. You were quarrelling very loudly, you know."

"But that was exactly what the b— blackguard intended," Clem blustered, going bright red. "And if he had done the decent thing, accepted Jake's will as his rightful intention, he would have stopped in America, and none of this would have happened."

Sergeant MacDonald said quickly, "You mean that Timothy Dexter would still be alive?"

"I did *not* say that — but it's true!"

A pause, and then the policeman said, "If you would continue, Miss Miller?"

"Well," said Cissy, feeling self-conscious again, "learning that Timothy Dexter had been cut out of his father's will made me feel very interested in their relationship, and after I arrived here at the hotel and saw Captain Dexter's portrait, I became more intrigued than ever. They didn't look at all alike, have you noticed? And I also heard from my mother that she had been told a very interesting story about Captain Dexter, and how he had stolen a ship."

"Hearsay," snapped Will Williams.

"She heard it from your daughter," said Cissy, and looked at Jasmine, who inclined her blonde head, not at all embarrassed at becoming the focus of attention.

"I thought everyone knew the story," she said.

"But I know no more than what my mother related to me, and Sergeant MacDonald hasn't heard it at all. Would you mind repeating it?"

"Not at all, Miss Miller. It's quite a simple yarn, really, though with plenty of human interest. My grandfather, Captain Jake, had just got married, 'way back in eighteen-forty-whatever, when the ship-owner who employed him sent him off on a long, long Pacific and China voyage. Six or seven months later, when Captain Jake touched at his first South American port, some friend kindly informed him that he was a cuckold."

"A ... what?"

"A man whose wife has been enticed into bed by another man. As often happens, I believe. What was particularly galling was that his wife's lover was the owner of the ship, who had deliberately sent him out of the way. Captain Jake didn't want to believe in such perfidy, or so I was told, but after that every Salem captain he spoke had the same story to tell. And then, after he had been a few months or so a-coasting in the South China Sea, he learned that not only was he a cuckold, but there was a cuckoo in his nest — a baby boy had been born, after he had sailed from Salem."

Cissy said, "Did this news come in the form of a letter?"

Jasmine frowned. "I don't know. When my grandmother told me the story, she didn't say. Does it matter?"

"Yes, I think it does. When Mr. Dexter's body was being searched, I noticed a scrap of blue paper clutched in his right hand, as if he had been holding it when he died, and his killer had torn the rest away. And when I took a look at the room where the fire had started, I found another piece of blue paper in the grate — the remnant of the spill that had been used to start the blaze."

"Meaning that the person who started the fire was the same one who shot Timothy?" Valentine Williams said quickly.

Cissy looked at Sergeant MacDonald, who lifted his brows, but then motioned to her to continue, without commenting on this. She said, "The piece I retrieved from the grate was the first part of a letter, starting, *My dear Jahaziel...* and with a date that was either January or February in the year eighteen-forty-something."

She looked at Sergeant MacDonald, who slowly and portentously unbuttoned the flap of his top pocket and pulled out a small envelope and an even smaller Bible. Then, just as slowly, he set the Bible down on a table, and drew two scraps of blue paper out of the envelope.

Valentine, who was suddenly taking an intense interest, said, "Do the two scraps come from the same letter?"

"It certainly seems that way," said Sergeant MacDonald. "I'll need an expert to confirm it, but the paper is the same, and the writing looks the same."

"And is anything written on the second piece — the one that Timothy was clutching?"

"One word," said the sergeant, and paused before saying, "Bath-sheba. With a dash between 'Bath' and 'sheba,' just the way it is written in the Bible."

"*Bible?*" said Jasmine. Her arched brows were very high.

"Are you a Christian?"

Jasmine merely smiled.

"Well, you should know the story of David and Bath-sheba," said Sergeant MacDonald in reproving tones. And, picking up the little Bible, and turning it to a marked page, he began to quote:

And it came to pass in an eveningtide, that David walked up on the roof of the king's house, and from the roof he saw a woman washing herself, and the woman was very beautiful to look upon.

And David sent and enquired after the woman, and one said, Is not this Bath-sheba, the wife of Uriah?

And David sent messengers, and took her; and she came in unto him, and he lay with her.

And the woman conceived, and sent and told David, and said, I am with child.

And it came to pass in the morning, that David wrote a letter to Joab, and sent it by the hand of Uriah.

And he wrote in the letter, saying, put ye Uriah in the forefront of the hottest battle, and retire ye from him, that he may be smitten, and die.

And the men of the city went out, and fought with Joab; and there fell some of the people of the servants of David; and Uriah the Hittite died also.

And when the mourning was past, David sent and fetched Bath-sheba to his house, and she became his wife, and bare him a son.

Sergeant MacDonald concluded, "Samuel two, eleven, verses three to twenty-seven," then brushed his moustache with one complacent finger, and smiled at them all.

Everyone was gazing at him with utter bemusement, and it occurred to Cissy that he must have been a model Sunday School pupil.

Then Jasmine said, "The ship's owner didn't have the means to send Captain Jake into the heat of the battle, so he sent him off on a very long voyage, instead. Which means that he didn't die, like whatsisname, Bath-sheba's husband—"

"Uriah," said Sergeant MacDonald helpfully.

"Thank you. Uriah died before he learned that he had been made a cuckold, but my dear grandfather did not. Instead, he received that letter. And so he took his revenge by selling off the adulterer's ship and pocketing the money. As a matter of fact, he used the money to buy the brig *Gosling*. I, for one, do not blame him. He certainly did not deserve to be treated like that. Right up to the day he died, he still believed it was a fair exchange, his house and wife for the adulterer's ship — and I think so, too."

"But," said Valentine very thoughtfully, "doesn't it raise some doubt about Timothy Dexter's heritage? As Miss Miller pointed out, Timothy and Captain Jake did not look at all alike."

Will Williams was growing very tense, Cissy saw. He blurted, "But I was there when Jake hailed Timothy as his son!"

Jasmine said thoughtfully, "That, when you think of it, is very strange indeed. Had anyone in the family ever heard of Timothy before he arrived in Auckland?"

Gladys shrugged. "We were all very young at the time."

"But how did my grandfather know that the ship-owner was not Timothy's father? After all, he had received that letter, and unless he had totally forgotten it — which seems very unlikely — he must have held deep suspicions."

"In his place," said Valentine, "I would have asked a lot of very searching questions."

"About dates and so forth?" asked the sergeant.

"Precisely."

Cissy said, "I think Miss Harriet Gray was quite certain that Timothy was not Captain Dexter's true son. Last night, before dinner, both the sergeant and I were out in the yard, and we overheard a quarrel, between Miss Harriet and a man. She sounded terribly angry, and she called him—"

She had to brace herself to say the word, very conscious that her mother was listening. "She called him a ... a *bastard*," she said, in a very low voice.

She saw Jasmine smile. "People often do that in the heat of a quarrel, Miss Miller. My grandmother was an actress — an actress with a famous temper. She was known to be free with her tongue when roused."

"Yes, yes, I have thought of that — but it sounded more like a quotation. It ran, *Oh ye gods, don't stand up for bastards* — or something like that."

Jasmine lifted an eyebrow at her brother. "*An honest woman's issue?*" she murmured, and nodded. "*Lear*," she said.

"Well," said Cissy, thinking she must look it up, one day. "At first I thought it was just an insult, and then I remembered that other quarrel I overheard, the one between Clem Gray and Timothy. Mr. Dexter referred to Miss Harriet Gray as a *harlot*, which sounded like a vicious, but meaningless, insult, just as the word *bastard* does. But then I found it was technically true, because Miss Harriet and Captain Jake were never married. And I think Miss Harriet meant the word *bastard* literally, too."

There was dead silence, and then Sergeant MacDonald turned to Jess, who had the fringe of her shawl twisted around her fingers, and said, "And what do you think, Mrs. Williams?"

Will said harshly, "Leave her alone."

"No, Will, it's alright."

Jess leaned touched her husband's hand, then turned to the policeman and said with remarkable calmness, "I was devastated when my father hailed Timothy as his son — and I rather think that Timothy was shocked, as well. But that shock, for him, was overtaken with pleasure. My father was rich, by the standards of the time. He owned a brig. As things turned out, Timothy was able to lay his hands on a great deal of the family money."

Mr. MacDonald said, "How long had you known Timothy?"

"Two weeks, maybe three — not long enough to know him very well, to tell the truth, as he told me very little about himself. I didn't even know his last name! Looking back, I think he was running away from something, but I was too blind — too *romantic* —to think about it. He had saved me from being trampled by a horse, a very dramatic way for a girl to meet a young man, and I never thought to look beyond that. I kept on encountering him, as he found out where I lived ... though he never knocked on the door, or introduced himself to my uncle, who was my guardian at the time. I know I was stupid, I *know* it, but I let myself fall in love."

"So, if your father hadn't revealed that Timothy was your brother?"

Will said, "Don't answer that, Jess."

"No, Will, I must." She looked at the sergeant and said steadily, "I was just fifteen. I came to believe that this handsome young man who had saved me in such a dashing manner was in love with me, just as I was in love with him. I knew nothing about him, but I would have run off with him. My father was strong-minded, very stubborn, a true Yankee. He might never have forgiven me for running off with this stranger.

"I loved my family, Sergeant, but if I had never found out that Timothy was my half-brother, I would have run off with him, and perhaps lost my family forever."

30

Instead of running off with Timothy, Jess had run off alone. When Jake took Timothy on board the brig — to introduce him to Harriet, for heaven's sake! — he had left her behind with Will. Jess, hurt, angry, confused, had refused to speak to the poor fellow. As soon as Will had taken her home she had shut herself in her room, and that night she climbed out the window, and then she was gone, off to the southern port of Lyttelton, without even leaving a note.

For as long back as she could remember, she had wanted to be an actress, but, much to her chagrin, her mother had refused to allow her to come to Ballarat to play on the stage, and so her dearest wishes had never been fulfilled. And so, in the throes of hurt, confusion, and rebellion, she took the steamer for Lyttelton, where an operatic troupe was advertising for an accompanist, hoping to shine so well at the piano that she would finish up on the stage.

And it could have worked. A golden future as a singer and actress would have made life bearable. Instead, her sentimental illusions were dashed. Now, Jess mused, it would have been so much better if she had been able to work off her romantic ambitions in Ballarat, but undoubtedly her mother, recognizing her utter lack of talent, had wanted to spare her the inevitable hurt and disillusionment.

And, back in 1867, she had chosen the worst time possible to find it out for herself.

There was no lack of actors, as New Zealand was full of them, mostly from Australia. The goldrush era in Australia was over, and the entertainers had flooded over from South Australia, Victoria and New South Wales. In Lyttelton, Jess had only been taken on by the operatic troupe because she was using her mother's family name, Gray, and the only job offered to her was as pianist in the pit, rattling weatherworn keys for ten shillings a week.

A gleam of hope arrived with a small part in *Lady Audley's Secret*, staged for His Royal Highness the Duke of Edinburgh in Dunedin, but His Royal Highness got the lion's share of mention in the papers, and young Jess got no attention at all. In Auckland, now vacated by her family, who had all joined Jake in the Thames, she landed another tiny part. "At the end there was no curtain call for the author," the paper reported the day after the première, "and the audience appeared relieved that the play was over." The theatre closed, and the play was never staged again — and again, Jess had not been mentioned. Jess, as she now wearily reflected, had had none of the magic that made critics sit up and pay attention, not even to say something bad.

She had inherited her father's obstinacy, however, and so she had struggled on for three years, going as far as Melbourne before returning to New Zealand, trudging from theatre to theatre. There had been a walk-on part here, a session as a pianoforte player there, and occasionally she had been able to sing. And then had come that final, dreadful, season in Dunedin.

The winter was atrocious and the streets were full of snow and mud. The program was the usual kind that had gone down well so many times before — an interlude from Shakespeare, and then a round of songs, and after that the inevitable farce or murder melodrama. This year, the timeworn system didn't work. They played to nearly empty houses night after night. The manager dropped his prices all the way down to a shilling, and cut their wages to compensate. He even struck up an arrangement with a bottle merchant, and advertised that a place in the pit could be bought with an empty stone ginger beer bottle. That brought a small rush of urchins to make sure the theatre wasn't absolutely empty, but nothing better than that. Jess was playing three sessions a day, working until midnight every night, on the very verge on being paid in empty ginger beer bottles, when there was a knock on the stage door.

She answered the knock, and found Will standing on the snowy stoop.

He looked at her, and she looked at him. And he said in a matter-of-fact voice, "You look a lot better than I expected."

With the rain and snow dripping off his hat and his shoulders, his boots planted in icy mud, his nose bright red and his fingers blue, Will looked pretty bad himself. Jess had wanted to laugh and cry and hug him hard, but instead she echoed insouciantly, "Better than what, pray?"

"I thought I'd find you as skinny as a rail."

And, indeed, despite the poor fare, she had not lost weight, simply because the poor fare was mutton. In other parts of the world only rich people ate meat. In Australia and New Zealand, by contrast, sheep meat was the cheapest food. It was invariably fatty, and always tough, but it was cheap and there was a lot of it.

"Are you calling me *fat?*" she'd exclaimed.

"No, of course not. And to prove it, I will buy you a meal."

Then he had peered past her, into the dark and musty depths of the theatre backstage. Turning back to her, he said, "Where are your lodgings?"

She had spread her hands. With two other minor but aspiring actresses, she had set up camp in the curtained cubicle that served for their dressing room. They had done it often. That way, they could save money for the times they could not find employment. Will made no comment, but promised to pay for lodgings for all three of them at Buckingham's Hotel.

He had come to see the show as well, sitting in splendid isolation in the middle of the block of most expensive seats, muffled up in scarves and his Ulster because it was freezing cold in the theatre, and then he bought them a meal. Jess remembered that supper well. Soup, roast beef, the luxury of vegetables, and warm red wine to wash it down. All three girls had blossomed with the warmth of the fire and the good hot food, and had laughed a good deal. They had even felt hopeful again, for those few hours. However, there had been only one extra room to let at the hotel, and Will had given that to the two other girls.

Then, gallantly, he had given his own room to Jess, declaring he would manage perfectly well with a chair in the public lounge.

"Oh Will," she had said, "oh, don't be a fool." And she had drawn him inside. She remembered how his big hands had trembled.

The next day they'd got married, and began the journey home to the Thames.

Jess looked about at the sergeant, the English girl and the company. She met Will's eyes, then, and said very clearly, "Yes, if I had never found out that Timothy was my half-brother, I would have run away with him"

And then she added with deliberation, "I was very young and foolish. It would have been the worst mistake of my life. I would have missed out on marrying the dearest man in the world. Will is the man I truly love, and though he has never said so, I know he loves me, too." And she reached out and gripped Will's hand, and heard him sigh deeply. His eyes were tight shut for a moment. She heard the sergeant's pencil scribble briskly.

Then he looked up, and said, "We seem to have established good grounds for believing that Timothy was not, in fact, Captain Dexter's son — and that Captain Dexter was perfectly aware of it. Mrs. Williams, is it possible that Captain Dexter guessed that you were likely to run off with this young man, a prospect that horrified him so much that he was prepared to recognize Timothy as his son, just because it would make your union impossible?"

Jess shuddered, and said, "Yes. That Timothy *preyed* on us is all my fault. That's is how he managed to take so much from us. That's why he kept on coming back, and begging for more money for yet another wild plan, and then came back for more."

And Megs said in a loud flat voice, "Aren't you forgetting something?"

Everyone stared. Megs said grimly, "Despite what folks say about him and Jess, he was my lawful husband. I was the one he married. He had the right to come back."

Jess flushed, and looked down at her knee, where her hand rested, still linked tightly with Will's strong fingers. She heard the sergeant clear his throat, and then he said, "Did you ever feel any doubt that your husband was not, in fact, Captain Dexter's son?"

"I never thought about it, and Timothy said nothing," Meg retorted. "But it makes no difference, anyway."

Cissy's clear English voice said, "I think it made a difference to Miss Minnie Gray. She certainly doubted that Timothy was Captain Dexter's son, and because she knew that doubt would make a big difference in the court when Timothy contested Captain Dexter's will, she wrote that letter to Miss Harriet Gray — the letter that Mr. Williams thought Timothy would try to steal. And, interestingly, an envelope was stolen out of my room."

"Well, it wasn't Timothy! And it wasn't me, neither, so don't you go accusing me, Miss."

"I'm sure it wasn't Timothy, because he didn't know the letter existed. But *someone* took it out of my trunk. And I *did* discover the loss after I found that the door to my bedroom had been left unlocked."

"If it was unlocked, it was your own fault, or your mother's. I've told you before, and I'll tell you again, I am unfailingly particular about locking doors behind me."

"No, I'm sorry, Mrs. Dexter, but the fault was yours. I know it was you who left the door unlocked, because the lock had been blocked by the corner of a room list that you carried. It fell out when I opened the door, which proves that you were the last one in the room."

Megs' flush was dark with anger. She snapped, "Be as clever as you like, Miss, but it makes no difference. Today is the first I have ever heard of any letter, so you can just set your mind to finding another thief."

"I agree that it could be anyone, since the door was unlocked, but I know already who stole it."

And she looked at Will Williams.

He started upright, exclaiming, "You have no grounds for that accusation!"

"But I do," said Cissy, her voice remarkably firm and steady. "That first day on the ship, you tried so hard to get the letter away from me that it was natural for me to start wondering. Now, I know that you had a good idea of the contents, and wanted to spare your wife the shame of knowing that her father had lied to save her, but at the time I just felt curious. And then, when I told you that the envelope had been taken out of the bottom of my trunk, you claimed that anyone could have stolen it, even one of the guests, which was ridiculous, as they didn't know the letter existed, either."

She paused, arranging her thoughts. "The obvious suspect was Megs, who had the key to our room, but she was another who didn't know about the letter. So I was left with only one name, and that was yours, Mr. Williams. Added to that, when I informed you that the envelope had been stolen, you told me it wasn't important any more. And of course it wasn't — because you thought you had destroyed it."

Clem shouted, "That's ridiculous! You're dreaming, if you think Will would do anything like that!"

"I'm sorry, but he did. He took it to the only private fireplace, which was in the painted parlor, and burned it there. He couldn't burn it in his own bedroom, because Timothy was in the adjoining room, the one with the fireplace; and he couldn't burn it in the lounge, because there were people in and out; or in the tavern, for the same reason. So he was forced to go to the painted parlor, where, fortuitously, Megs had laid a fire."

Will said grimly, "You have no evidence of this."

"I was with you before breakfast when Mrs. Williams asked where you had been. You told her you had been out walking, but your jacket and cap were perfectly dry. No, you were the person I heard in the parlor as I walked along the balcony just a few moments earlier. I even heard you striking a Lucifer to get your little fire going. Unluckily for you, I tried the door, forcing you to get out in a hurry, which is why the grate was not cleaned out, and I was able to retrieve this."

And she held up the charred corner of a yellow envelope.

Will buried his face in his hands and said, "Oh, God."

"But I know you did it to save your wife from reading what you thought was inside. Did you look at the contents before you burned the envelope, Mr. Williams?"

"Of course not." He sounded extremely insulted at the slur on his propriety.

"I thought not, or you wouldn't have bothered to burn it. You see, it merely held a note from me."

"What!" The sofa rocked as Will lurched upright.

"Yes. It was a note from me to Miss Harriet Gray, apologizing for the deception, and promising to deliver the real envelope to her as soon as I could. I was most unsure of the situation, you see," she explained. "You had unwittingly put me on my guard. So I bought a matching envelope, and put it in my trunk. That was the one that you stole."

"So what the devil happened to the real letter?"

"Oh, I have it here," said Cissy, and drew it out of her music folder. Then, as everyone tensely watched, leaning forward, she stood up, walked over, and handed the envelope to Jess.

"You are the right person to have it," she said. "It was meant for Miss Harriet Gray, and you are her daughter."

Will said sharply, "Don't open it."

"But we have guessed what Miss Minnie wrote already," Cissy pointed out. "And when Mrs. Williams reads it, she will find that the guess is right. Miss Minnie had evidence that Timothy was *not* Captain Dexter's son, and advised Miss Harriet Gray to produce that evidence if Timothy persisted in contesting the will. She also recommended a study of Captain Dexter's logbooks — and when Sergeant MacDonald, Gladys and I went to Miss Harriet's room last night, we found the first logbook, the one he kept on that first, very long China trade voyage."

Then she looked at Mr. Schuyler Bradford, and said, "The name of the ship — the one he stole and sold — was *Thomas Grace*."

Mr. Bradford leaned forward, abruptly intrigued. "But that is one of the ships that was painted on the walls of what you call the painted parlor," he said. "All the ships painted there were Grace Brothers ships."

"So you told me," said Cissy. "And that makes a clipping from a Boston newspaper that Miss Minnie included with the letter very interesting indeed — and not just for what it implies. The same Boston paper was stolen from the library of the *Royal George*. Miss Fleet borrowed it, but did not return it, as she reported it stolen."

"Perhaps," said the sergeant, signing to the constable, who nodded, and left the room, "Miss Fleet has some idea who stole it."

"Indeed I do," Miss Fleet snapped. "It am positive it was Mr. Williams."

31

Will buried his head in his hands and groaned, "Oh, for God's sake, this is a nightmare. I swear this is the first I have heard of any newspaper. Minnie told me about the letter — but not about *that*."

"But the paper did arrive in the Thames," Cissy said. "And it was burned in the painted parlor, where I found *this*." She held up the charred label. "It's the remains of the tag that the librarian pasted on the paper, so that borrowers could see that it came from Boston. The papers from other places had similar tags."

Jess cried, "Are you accusing Will of burning the newspaper, too?"

Sergeant MacDonald cleared his throat, and said, "We have strayed from the important subject. Two people have died, and my job is to find a savage killer, not a mere burner of newspapers."

Valentine protested, "But my grandmother died of natural causes, poor woman. Her heart condition was far worse than any of us suspected. If anyone is to blame, it's me — because I left her to climb those stairs by herself. And I am certainly not a savage killer!"

"That may be so, sir. But there are questions to be asked about what happened before she died. As you already know, Miss Miller and I overheard your grandmother in the throes of a violent quarrel with some man."

"Some man? But we have established it was Timothy."

"But Miss Harriet also informed the man that she pitied him because he did not belong to the Grays — and ordered him to get back to America. Timothy fits that description — but so does your father."

"Will?" cried Jess. "My mother would never have quarreled with Will! It's impossible!"

Cissy said, "She's right. Miss Harriet did not say *belong to the Grays*. She said she pitied him — that you all pitied him — because he was not part of *the family*. And I know for a fact that the man she was quarrelling with was not Mr. Williams — and this involves a confession, I'm afraid."

She swallowed as they all stared at her, and gathered her courage again. Steadily, she said, "A package was delivered to the hotel early yesterday morning, and I was the one who answered the door. The label had fallen off, but the boy told me it was for Mrs. Dexter."

"For me?" Megs exclaimed. "This is the first I have heard of a package!"

"That's my fault, I'm afraid. I jumped to the conclusion that it was meant for Miss Harriet, sent by someone who didn't know that she had never married Captain Dexter. So I gave it to Mrs. Williams to pass on to her mother."

"That's right," Jess said, and nodded. "I gave it to her after she got back from the tour."

"When I gave it to Mrs. Williams," Cissy went on, "she opened it, to reveal a very pretty little tin holding six little marzipan sweets."

"But who on earth would send me marzipan?" Megs said blankly.

"I have no idea. All I know is that it came from Massachusetts, because the postmark was still visible. But the story does not end there. When I found that Miss Harriet was dead, I thought that she had eaten one of the sweets, and that it was poisoned. So you can imagine how terrible I felt."

Megs cried, "*Poisoned*? But why?"

"I don't know why anyone would send you poisoned sweets, Mrs. Dexter, but I do know that marzipan smells of ground almonds, and on the tour I had learned from Mr. Daws at the Crown Mine Battery that cyanide — which is a most deadly, fast-acting poison — is not only used to extract gold from quartz, but smells like almonds, too. But then I remembered that Mrs. Williams laughed and said, *Oh well*, when she opened the tin and saw the marzipan."

"I don't see the significance," said Miss Fleet.

"That's because you are a visitor to the Thames, too," said Cissy. "But Sergeant MacDonald assures me that Miss Harriet — or anyone else who toured the Crown Mine Battery as often as she did — is most unlikely to have eaten anything that smelled like cyanide, no matter how prettily presented."

"And so, she didn't eat it," said Valentine. "And I, for one, still don't see the significance."

"What is significant is something else that Miss Harriet shouted during the quarrel we overheard — *You really want the evidence of the perfidy of your background? Have it, and welcome — and be gone with you. And have this, too! — I know it was not intended for me, unless you want my demise, as well!* It seems obvious to me that she was talking about the tin of marzipan, which was not intended for her. And Timothy must have taken it — or maybe she threw it at him — because Sergeant MacDonald found that tin in his pocket. So Timothy was definitely the man in the quarrel."

"And the marzipan was definitely poisoned," Sergeant Mac-Donald contributed. "I took it to a friend at the School of Mines, who tested it at once. Fascinating, it was to watch," he went on, his voice becoming quite gossipy. "He dissolved one of the pieces, and added sulphate of iron to the solution. Now watch, he said to me, and added acid to that; if there is any cyanide there, the solution will turn blue, he said."

"Blue?" echoed Clem.

"Aye, sir. Prussian blue. And it turned that hue in seconds. Gorgeous color, it was, or so I observed. A heavy contamination, said he."

"But who would want to poison me?" Megs cried. Her face was deathly white, except for hectic blotches of red on her cheeks. "Timothy would never do that, never!"

Cissy turned to Gladys, and said, "Had Timothy ever been on the Mystery Tour?"

Gladys laughed — not a pleasant sound. "*Him*? He never lifted a finger to help."

"So it's possible that he wouldn't know that no one here was likely to eat anything that smelled that way?"

"You're all determined to call Timothy a wife-killer," said Megs, white-faced. "Just because he took a well-earned rest when he was here, instead of escorting gawping tourists around the mines. And though the marzipan came from America, he was not the only one in that country, remember." She turned and said viciously to Will, "Your wife was drugged — and it was you who done it."

Will protested, "It was a mistake— a terrible mistake. There were two glasses of milk, and..."

Sergeant MacDonald said, "Mrs. Williams testified to me that you always brought her a glass of warm milk at night, and that has been confirmed by the cooks, who often saw you heating up milk and adding drops from a bottle of medicine. And we have found that bottle, covered with fingerprints that are undoubtedly yours, and according to the label it contains a strong solution of bromide in lime!"

Will sighed deeply. "The bromide was prescribed by Dr Springer, but for my mother-in-law, not for Jess. Harriet told me it was for the nightmares that had been troubling her. Sadly, I did not know that the nightmares were caused by her heart problems, not until the doctor told me, last night. If I had known she was so frail, I would not have allowed her to go on the tour — but Harriet had a strong will, and she insisted."

"You were always the person to administer the medicine?"

"When I was here, yes. Otherwise, Gladys did it. And the bromide was added to milk because the doctor advised it."

"And you did that last evening?"

"Yes, as I have told you many times."

"You didn't give it to your wife, instead of to Miss Harriet, to make sure that she was asleep when Timothy was murdered?"

"Absolutely not! Look." And he paused, shutting his eyes and frowning as he sorted out the right words. Then he said, "I heated enough milk for two glasses, one for Harriet, one for Jess. I added bromide to Harriet's glass, and then I put initialed napkins over both glasses, so they would not be mixed up. I carried the tray upstairs and along the corridor, and then put it on a side table, because there was an interruption."

"What interruption?'

Will winced, and said, "I can't remember — but whatever it was, the napkins must have been changed around while I was away."

"That's what you say — but I wonder why both Clem Gray and Megs Dexter lied to protect you."

Clem shouted, "I did not! I told you that Will was in the cellar when I was there, and it was true!"

"But at what time of the day?" said the sergeant in a sarcastic tone, and instead of waiting for an answer he looked at Megs.

She glared back, snapping, "I have told you time and time again that the communicating door was locked between Will's bedroom and the double room where Timothy was killed, and I did not lie."

Cissy said, "Can I ask a question?"

Everyone looked at her. The sergeant nodded.

"Mrs. Dexter, how many keys are there to the room where your husband was killed?"

Megs showed no reaction to the last words, merely saying, "There is only two keys to the communicating door. I have one, and Will Williams has the other."

"And what about the passage door?"

Megs' eyes abruptly became shuttered. She said, "There are two keys to that door, too. The one that Will Williams carries was given to Timothy when the day-room part of the double room was given to him."

"And you hold the other key?"

The housekeeper's lips shut tight, and then reluctantly opened. "I had it, until Timothy made me give it to him."

The sergeant said swiftly, "When was that?"

"About ten minutes after I settled him in the room."

"So he held two keys to the passage door," the sergeant said thoughtfully.

Silence, as everyone took in the implications of this, and then Cissy said, "Sergeant MacDonald, a ring of keys was found on the corpse..."

He nodded. "But there was only one door key to his room."

Everyone stared at Megs, and she flushed and said angrily, "I swear he had both keys."

The sergeant paused, and then observed, "You say you loved your husband, Mrs. Dexter."

"I do — I did!"

"But it seems that only you and Will Williams had access to that room. Are you are sure you are not the person who shot Timothy?"

She shouted, "Don't be a fool, man!"

It was like a dam bursting. Her voice shook with bitter scorn. "Why would I kill Timothy, tell me that? If he had lived, and contested Jake's will, he would have won, and the hotel would be mine — mine! I've worked hard enough, haven't I? Don't I deserve it, after slaving for this family all these years? But now that he is dead, I don't have a case. The hotel will never be mine. So don't look to me, Sergeant MacDonald, if you want a murderer, and don't accuse me of telling lies, either!"

Jess said, "Oh, God." There was shocked realization on the faces of all the family.

Then Cissy said, "Excuse me."

They all looked at her. Sergeant MacDonald said, "Yes, Miss Miller?"

"I think we have established that Timothy did *not* come to the Thames to contest Captain Dexter's will. When he boarded the *Royal George* he did not even know that Captain Dexter was dead. So the question remains — why *was* he coming back, if not to claim the hotel?"

Silence. Then Jasmine said musingly, "When you repeated what my grandmother shouted during her quarrel with Timothy, it included the words, *You really want the evidence of the perfidy of your background?*"

"Yes," said Cissy. "And I do wonder if by *perfidy* she meant evidence that he had been born more than nine months after Captain Dexter had sailed away — that he was, in fact, the son of the ship's owner, the man who had seduced Captain Dexter's wife?"

"Yes," said Jasmine. "You mean the Bath-sheba letter?"

"Exactly."

"But," Jasmine mused, "why would he want the letter? What use was it to him? After all, it revealed that he was a bastard, which is not necessarily something you want the whole world to know."

Cissy paused, still getting used to that scandalous word, and then said, "It might pay to have a look at the newspaper clipping that Miss Minnie included with her letter."

And she looked at the sergeant, who took a parchment folder out of his paper, and slid out the newspaper clipping.

He held it up so everyone could see it, and then turned it round so he could read it. "At the top there is a headline," he said. "It runs: DID THEIR CRIMES DIE WITH THEM? Then there is a stirring story about false gravestones being put up by the angry families of ne'er-do-well runaway sons. And underneath is a picture of a gravestone with the name TIMOTHY GRACE, with no kind of inscription, just the dates. He was born in 1848, and died in 1867."

Silence, frozen silence.

Sergeant MacDonald cleared his throat again, "And, under the picture, there is a gossipy piece, where the journalist reveals how he became interested in this bit of history. Apparently, someone had given him information that a local lawyer had been hired to prove that at least one of the gravestones was misleading, the person named on it being not just alive and well, but also the rightful heir to a family fortune."

Another silence, broken when Mr. Schuyler Bradford shifted. He was leaning back, his expression very thoughtful indeed.

"Grace," he said. "*Grace.* The big ship-owning family. The last of the old men died, and the inheritance is going a-begging. If that young man — Timothy Grace — was still alive, he would be very rich indeed."

"I think we can safely bet that he was not so young, but alive — up to midnight last night," Jasmine said, and laughed. "Oh God, the irony of it! Timothy faked his identity out of greed for Jake's small wealth, and his greed cost him mighty riches. Valentine, it's worthy of the stage!"

"Indeed," said Valentine. "And the dates do fit. Timothy Grace was nineteen years old in 1867 — right? And Timothy, who wanted to be called *Dexter*, told Captain Jake that he was twenty — which would make it feasible — just — that he had been conceived before Captain Jake sailed. But, if he was, in fact, only nineteen..."

"And Mr. Timothy Dexter told my mother that he loved to sail the leisurely way, under canvas," said Cissy, "but then he abruptly changed his mind in San Francisco, when my mother casually repeated some gossip she had heard from a lawyer in New York."

"Do tell," Jasmine urged.

Cissy looked at her mother, who readily complied. "The story my lawyer told me was about an old lady who had very recently died. There was a problem with her will. She left all she owned to the lady who had been her companion, but it turned out that there was no *money* was involved, as the old lady had been living on the income from the family trust, which stopped at her death. The true heir to the family fortune had died many years before, and now it looked as if the money might go to a distant cousin, though that was questionable, too."

"But was that old lady a Grace?" Mr. Bradford queried.

"It seems very likely," said Cissy. "After Miss Minnie had put the clipping in the envelope, she allowed me to take the rest of the page, to wrap up the costume she loaned me — and, quite by coincidence, that page had the local death notices. They meant nothing to me at first, but then, when I heard my mother's little story, one of them became very significant indeed."

And she produced the death notice of Miss Hetty Grace, of Salem, Massachusetts, who had expired of a sudden and violent gastric convulsion.

Jess Williams said, "Oh my God."

They all looked at her. She had gone whiter than ever. "There was another box of marzipan."

Megs said swiftly, "*Where?*"

"When I opened the package I was told that an identical tin had been sent to an elderly cousin. Oh my God, was that poisoned, too? Did it come from the same person?"

"And Miss Hetty Grace, of Salem, Massachusetts, expired of a sudden and violent gastric convulsion," said the sergeant in his deliberate voice. He pulled out his notebook and wrote a sentence, then underlined it. Cissy could almost hear him composing a wire to the Boston Police Department in his head.

Jasmine said, "So who was it who told you about the elderly cousin, Mama?"

Jess paused, shutting her eyes briefly as she brought back the memory. Then she opened them again, and said, "Miss Fleet."

They all looked at the American woman, who simply spread her hands and shook her head.

"It was an idle comment, and merely a coincidence," she said. "There must be thousands of boxes like that."

"It must have been Timothy," said Valentine. "He posted two boxes of poisoned marzipan before he left Boston, one to this Miss Hetty Grace, so that the fortune would be put in question, and the other to Megs, his wife here in the Thames — a wife who would be very inconvenient if he managed to claim his inheritance."

"But why?" Megs cried.

"Well, I think we have established that Timothy was Timothy Grace, who was supposed to have died in 1867, but instead had scarpered to New Zealand, leaving a father so furious that he put up a misleading gravestone."

"My Timothy — a *killer*? I don't believe it, I can't believe it, I can't, I can't!"

Poor Megs, thought Cissy, forced to face the truth about the man she'd loved so much that she had stayed in a place she hated, doing work she loathed, and living with a family she despised, while she waited for him to return.

Clem said thoughtfully, "Minnie was positive that Timothy engineered Robert's death."

"Possibly so," mused Valentine. "And it is possible, too, that the accident that half-crippled Aunt Gladys and ruined her theatrical career was not, in fact, an accident. Which means that he probably well deserved his nasty fate — but we still don't know who did the world that favor."

"I'm afraid I do," said Cissy, and blushed.

Everyone stared at her. "Do tell us," urged Jasmine.

"Miss Fleet. Elspeth Grace Fleet."

"*Grace*," said Mr. Schuyler Bradford, and stared at Miss Fleet, his expression speculative. "So this is the distant cousin?"

"*She* shot him?" Megs Dexter demanded.

Instead of answering either question, Sergeant MacDonald reached out, grasped Miss Fleet's reticule, and tipped the contents onto a table.

Miss Fleet shouted, "You have no right to do that! It's private property!"

Sergeant MacDonald didn't bother to answer that, either. Instead, he held up a key, then gave to Megs, and said, "Do you recognize this?"

"I do," she said, thin-lipped as she turned it over in her hands. "It's my key — the key Timothy forced me to give to him. It's the key to the room where he was sleeping."

"Which is the reason she was able to let herself in, and then lock the door again, after she had shot him dead."

And creep into his room the night we arrived, thought Cissy.

"Lies!" shouted Miss Fleet. "Officer, give me back my property, or I will be consulting a lawyer!"

"My, my," said Jasmine, sounding impressed. "You'd really sue the Hauraki Police Force?"

Megs ignored both, shouting, "She must have stolen it! Why would Timothy give it to her!"

Cissy said, "There is something else in that reticule that explains their ... relationship. When Miss Fleet came into the room, I gave her a handkerchief, telling her that she had dropped it."

"That proves nothing! I drop handkerchiefs all the time!"

"But you did not drop that handkerchief here, Miss Fleet. It's the handkerchief you dropped on the deck outside Timothy's cabin door, the night of the masquerade ball, just before you joined him. And it is embroidered with the letter H — H for Hetty Grace, whose clothes you inherited."

"His *cabin*?" Megs wailed. "She joined him in his *cabin*?"

Cissy winced remembering the sounds she had overheard. "I'm afraid so," she said. "And that night she told him that she had broken that newspaper story, thinking it would help prove his identity as the heir to the Grace fortune ... and I believe the reason she helped him was that she expected to marry him, once he had inherited."

"*Marry* him?"

"Yes — and that is why she killed him. She had found out that marriage to Timothy was impossible, because he was married to another woman, and so she made sure of her own inheritance, instead."

Megs was on her feet, striding across the room towards Miss Fleet like an avenging angel, and her voice was a strident shriek. "You slept with my husband, and then you murdered him? You adulterous *bitch!*" She sprang forward, her hands like twisted talons, and it took both Clem and the sergeant to pull her away. Forcibly dropped into an easy chair, she covered her face with her hands and wept, shaking with fury and misery.

Miss Fleet said calmly, "Prove that I shot him. I defy you to prove it."

"But it is perfectly logical," Sergeant MacDonald pointed out. "The victim and yourself were the only people who had a key to the passage door to his room. Miss Miller is my witness that I had to break it down, when I responded to the shot. You shot him, snatched the letter, pulled the wardrobe away from the connecting door to place suspicion on Will Williams, and then left the room by the passage door, locking it behind you."

"You have no evidence at all that I intended to marry Timothy Dexter!"

"Timothy *Grace*," Valentine corrected.

"And you have no evidence that Timothy Dexter was a man called Timothy Grace — Timothy Grace, who has been dead for thirty-eight years!"

"Because you burned the evidence, by setting fire to the hotel?" the policeman enquired.

"So you are accusing me of arson, too?"

"I am," said Sergeant MacDonald, and nodded at the constable, who, with remarkable timing, had just come back into the room.

The constable was holding a bundle of black cloth. He handed this to Sergeant MacDonald, who shook it out, revealing a voluminous black skirt. "I think most people here can identify this skirt as the one you were wearing at the masquerade party, Miss Fleet — a skirt that is stained with ash, and smells of smoke and paraffin," he said. "And so, I charge you with a second crime, that of attempting to burn down the hotel."

"Just the painted parlor, I think," said Cissy. "She wanted to remove all traces of Timothy's connection to the Grace family, so that she had a better case for inheriting the fortune herself — and, as Mr. Bradford will confirm, the ships painted on the walls were all Grace Brothers ships."

"He painted them to taunt Captain Jake?" said Valentine.

"Well, it does sound in character," said Cissy.

32

The Sabbath afternoon was sunny again, most surprisingly warm for the time of the year in this part of the world, perfect weather for a stroll. Cissy encountered Jasmine on Pollen Street, promenading with her hand tucked into the arm of an elegant gentleman Cissy had never seen before. Cissy nodded, smiling but too shy to speak, but the beautiful blonde woman stopped her.

"Harlequin, were you? Arlecchino?" she enquired, without bothering to introduce her companion.

Cissy blushed. "Yes."

"And Aunt Minnie loaned you the costume?"

"Yes."

"H'm. Along with a mysterious letter and newspaper clipping, and a bundle of enigmatic instructions. How like our dear little Minnie! But you carried out her errand very well indeed."

"You think so?"

"Indeed I do." And the elegant parasol that Jasmine carried was pointed upwards at the romantic balcony of the Golden Goose.

For a confused moment Cissy did not understand, but then she saw Will and Jess Williams leaning close together. He had his arm around her shoulders, and they were deep in conversation.

"I doubt that Papa will be gallivanting off about the world so much."

"Oh!" Had that been part of Miss Minnie's plan? Cissy doubted it, but merely smiled.

Then she ventured, "Miss Williams? Is that your name, or are you...?" Then she silenced, thinking that Jasmine was so like her grandmother, that she, too, might prefer to remain unmarried.

Harriet's granddaughter smiled, and said, "Call me Jasmine."

"Oh. Thank you. Can I ask a difficult question?"

"Of course."

"What is going to happen to Megs Dexter?"

"That is indeed a hard one," Jasmine agreed. "We can't make her stay, poor creature, because I am sure she doesn't want that. We'll pension her off, I think, give her a monthly income to keep her in reasonable comfort, and let her go wherever she wants."

"I'm glad," said Cissy, and then said, "Who chose the scenario for the Murder Play?"

"Where the scheming nephew and his mistress plot to kill the old woman, so he can inherit the family fortune? My grandmother did, of course. But that's interesting! Do you think she chose it because she divined that Timothy had brought a mistress with him? It would have been entirely in character for my darling grandmother to make sure she had the last laugh."

"That's what I hoped," said Cissy.

When she went back into the lounge, Sergeant MacDonald was filling out his report. "Aha, Miss Miller," he said when he looked up and saw her. "That went rather well, don't you think?"

"As good as a play," Cissy agreed.

"We produced a witness — the man who was out in the street, and gave the alarm when the painted parlor caught fire. When he identified Miss Fleet as the woman he had seen silhouetted in the flames, she caved in and confessed. Once she got talking, she was very righteous about her motives for the murder. She reckoned she was fully entitled to at least half the fortune, as she had put up with the old aunt for so many years, and that marrying Timothy was the most efficient way of making sure of it. Then, as you pointed out, she found out that Timothy was already married, which spelled his doom."

"I wonder what will happen to the fortune?"

"The lawyers will have a fine time of it — particularly if they open Timothy Grace's grave, and find it empty. Megs Dexter might even inherit, though Timothy married her under an alias, not his legal name. But who knows the circumlocutions of American law, huh? We'll leave all that to the legal beaks."

"Of course," said Cissy, remembering her mother observing that lawyers had a most *interesting* time, despite popular expectations to the contrary.

"But you were most helpful, Miss Miller, a proper little sleuth, you were. Though I must admit that if I had realized you were quite so young, I might not have paid as much attention. It was that costume that fooled me."

"I think that was what was intended," said Cissy, thinking of Miss Minnie.

"And your name is Cissy? Short for Clarissa?"

"No, no," said Cissy. "My *proper* name is Agatha."

Old Salt Press is an independent press catering to those who love good books about ships and the sea. We are an association of writers working together to produce the very best of nautical and maritime fiction and non-fiction. We invite you to join us as we go down to the sea in books.

From other Old Salt Press authors

Alaric Bond

Honour Bound
—In this, the tenth book of the Fighting Sail series, Commander King is seized by the enemy. In an atmosphere of mounting tension, he is forced to survive in hostile territory.

The Blackstrap Station
— Christmas 1803, and there is nothing to celebrate, as the shipwrecked crew of HMS *Prometheus* are forced to pit their wits against the enemy force sent out to hunt them down.

HMS *Prometheus*
— In the eighth book of the Fighting Sail series, HMS *Prometheus* sets sail from the shipyard at Gibraltar, to face the greatest challenge yet.

The Scent of Corruption
— Sir Richard Banks is appointed to HMS *Prometheus*, a seventy-four gun line-of-battleship which an eager Admiralty loses no time in ordering to sea — a non-stop nautical thriller in the best traditions of the genre.

The Torrid Zone
— She's a tired ship with a worn out crew, but *HMS Scylla* has one more trip to make before her much postponed re-fit — a trip fraught with unexpected dangers.

The Guinea Boat

— Set in Hastings, Sussex during the early part of 1803, *Guinea Boat* tells the story of two young lads, and the diverse paths they take to make a living on the water.

Turn a Blind Eye

— Autumn, 1801. Newly appointed to the local revenue cutter, Commander Griffin is determined to make his mark, and defeat a major gang of smugglers.

Linda Collison

Rhode Island Rendezvous

— Adventure on the high seas in New England and the West Indies during the early days of Revolution. The third book in the popular Patricia MacPherson series.

Water Ghosts

— *"I see things other people don't see I hear things other people don't hear"* — a paranormal thriller set on board a junk peopled by troubled teens.

Rick Spilman

Evening Gray Morning Red
— A young American sailor must escape his past
and the clutches of the Royal Navy, in the turbulent
years just before the American Revolutionary War.

The Shantyman
— A gripping tale of survival against all odds at sea
and ashore. A Kirkus Best Indie Book pick.

Bloody Rain
— A novella of blood and madness on the Hooghly
River.

Hell Around the Horn
— The ordeal of a captain, his crew and his family in
an epic doubling of Cape Horn.

Antoine Vanner

Britannia's Gamble
— It's 1884. A fanatical Islamist revolt is sweeping
the Sudan and General Charles Gordon's hold on
Khartoum is tenuous. There is only one way for
Dawlish to come to the rescue — by an antique steamer,
on a hostile river.

Britannia's Amazon

— A Victorian melodrama in which Florence
Dawlish, left behind in England, risks her life to save
the lives of others.

Britannia's Spartan

— A gripping yarn of convoluted diplomacy and
bloody conflict in the Sea of Japan.

Britannia's Shark

— A maritime thriller set in the time of America's
Gilded Age.

Britannia's Reach

—The action-packed second volume of the Dawlish
Chronicles naval fiction series, in which Dawlish is
forced to face his own conscience in a conflict of
morality, in the midst of South American chaos.

Britannia's Wolf

—**An exciting debut that** introduces a naval hero
who is more familiar with steam, breech-loaders and
torpedoes than with sails, carronades and broadsides.

Joan Druett

Joan Druett is an independent maritime historian and writer, married to Ron Druett, a highly regarded maritime artist.

In 1984, while exploring the tropical island of Rarotonga, she slipped into the hole left by the roots of a large uprooted tree, and at the bottom discovered the grave of a young American whaling wife, who had died in January 1850 at the age of twenty-four. It was a life-changing experience. Her immediate interest in whaling captains' wives at sea was encouraged by a Fulbright fellowship, which led to five months of research in New Bedford and Edgartown, in Massachusetts, Mystic, Connecticut, and San Francisco, California, and resulted in her study of whaling captains' wives under sail, *Petticoat Whalers*.

The success of this book, and a companion volume, *She Was a Sister Sailor*, was followed by *Hen Frigates, Wives of Merchant Captains Under Sail*, which was given a New York Public Library Best to Remember Award, while *She Was a Sister Sailor* won the John Lyman Award for Best Book of American Maritime History. Joan Druett's ground-breaking work in the field of seafaring women was also recognized by a L. Byrne Waterman Award. Her non-fiction account of a double castaway experience in the sub-Antarctic, *Island of the Lost*, has become a classic in the genre. Then her strong interest in the stories of the Pacific Islanders who sailed on Euro-American ships led to a biography of an extraordinary Polynesian star navigator, *Tupaia*, which won the general nonfiction prize in the 2012 New Zealand Post Book Awards.

Joan Druett is also the author of the popular Wiki Coffin mysteries, which have a half-Maori, half-Yankee hero. Her publications, which include three romantic sagas, have been translated into Chinese, French, Italian and German.

www.ingramcontent.com/pod-product-compliance
Lightning Source LLC
Chambersburg PA
CBHW070909180626
46817CB00003B/977